ALL IN THE MIND

To John

Judith Cranswick

Best wishes

Judith Cranswick

This book has been printed digitally and produced in a standard specification in order to ensure its continuing availability

Published by Antony Rowe Publishing Services in 2005
2 Whittle Drive
Highfield Industrial Estate
Eastbourne
East Sussex
BN23 6QT
England

ISBN 1-905200-07-2

Printed and bound by Antony Rowe Ltd, Eastbourne

Like her main character, Judith Cranswick was born and brought up in Norwich and now lives in Swindon. After many years as a deputy and a headteacher in various Secondary schools, she spent two years in an FE college before ending fulltime employment as the manager of an Education Business Partnership. She gave up her full time career to devote more time to writing though still teaches Creative Writing and is a part time Tai Chi and Yoga instructor.

For more information, see

www.judithcranswick.co.uk

For Mum

I am grateful to the many people have helped in the writing of this book, but my special thanks go to the agent, Kate Hordern, whose suggestions have made this a much better story; my brother, Jamie, a police inspector, for his advice on police procedures and my husband, Alex, for sorting out the multitude of computer problems that beset me and for copyediting the manuscript.

Chapter 1

The hollow clack of her high heels echoed in the confined space and was strangely disconcerting. Perhaps it hadn't been such a good idea to come through the underpass at this time of night. Not that it was late – a little after eight o'clock – but it was getting dark. Vandals had smashed the overhead lights. In daylight, it had never bothered Sarah that she couldn't see through the passageway to the exit although that fact had never registered on the few occasions she'd used it before. Now in the gloom, the whole place, with its low ceiling and grim graffiti-daubed walls, seemed to close in on her and took on a distinctly menacing feel.

Sarah slowed her pace. Tiredness was making her oversensitive. It had been a long and gruelling day; interminable meetings, a difficult governor, frustratingly recalcitrant colleagues and not a moment to herself. Logic told her that there could be nothing lying in wait beyond the bend. There was nothing forcing her onward. She could always turn back and take her chances crossing the busy dual carriageway but why face the long diversion to get round the central barrier?

Instinct made her glance back over her shoulder. A dark shape silhouetted against the light from the entrance was rapidly getting closer. She moved nearer the wall. Embarrassed by her sudden cowardice, she strode on, fighting the urge to run. She sensed rather than heard the figure come alongside. As she glanced across, a hand darted out to grab the handbag slung over her shoulder.

She swerved violently sideways, all apprehension lost in indignant fury. He tried to yank it from her but she dropped her briefcase and seized the strap with both hands, twisting it around her wrist, and threw her weight backwards to counter his superior strength. Taken off guard, he stumbled knocking them both sideways. His hot breath hissed on Sarah's cheek.

A fist came towards her. The crack on the jaw sent her head slamming against the roughcast wall.

The next thing she remembered was the stench. That and the itch of the slow trickle of blood running down from her raw grazed cheek. Her jaw was screaming to the point that she dared not touch it in case it had been shattered. First she needed to get up and away from the overpowering acrid stink assaulting her nostrils. She clambered to a sitting position trying to ignore the discarded crisp packets and dirty scraps of assorted rubbish beneath her. Her assailant was long gone; she could rest for a moment. The cold was seeping into her bones. She must force herself to move. Someone else was approaching. Crawling painfully to her knees, she turned for help.

A late night shopper. Even in the gloom, she could make out the look of startled horror on the pale face. The middle-aged woman sidled past her, keeping her distance, using assorted, well stuffed carrier bags as a barrier between them. Sarah watched dumbfounded as the woman scurried away to the far end of the underpass.

That abandonment was more painful than her tortured face. Sarah wanted to call out, to tell her that she wasn't some down-and-out drunk or one of the rising number of homeless aggressively begging from every passer-by. There was no point. She was too weak to explain. She slumped back and was as near to tears as she'd been in a long time. Waves of self pity washed over as her state of absolute helplessness hit her.

The sound of talking and laughter broke the lonely silence. She looked up to see a young couple.

'Please help me. I've been attacked.' All pride had gone.

They came running. The man helped her up, hoisted her arm around his shoulder and slowly led her to the end of the dismal tunnel, up the steep slope and back into the open. There were no seats in the immediate vicinity so they settled on the low wall of one of the raised flowerbeds outside the old Post Office.

'My briefcase!'

'It's okay; Carole's got it. She'll stay with you while I ring for the police.' He brought out his mobile and moved off a few paces.

'Sorry to be so much trouble,' Sarah lisped painfully through clenched teeth.

'Ben will soon have it sorted.' The girl fished in her pockets for a clean tissue and began dabbing at the blood oozing down Sarah's cheek. 'There, that's better. Are you hurt anywhere else?'

Sarah tentatively put a hand to her jaw. It still hurt like hell but at least it wasn't broken and it gave her something other than her pounding head to focus on. 'I'm fine,' she answered and foolishly attempted a smile. To hide her grimace she turned away to look at the large clock over towards the bus station.

'Were you supposed to be meeting someone? Will they be wondering where you are?'

Sarah shook her head. Another mistake. Things began to swim before her eyes and it was a while before she could mumble, 'I was on my way home.'

'Is there anyone we can contact for you?' She glanced at the ring on Sarah's left hand. 'Your husband?'

'I live alone.' She hoped she didn't sound as sorry for herself as she felt.

Ben returned and Sarah was saved from further explanation.

'They'll be here soon and there's an ambulance on its way,' he said.

'I'm not badly hurt. Just a bit shaken,' she protested, momentarily jerked from her dazed state.

'You were knocked unconscious. It's best they take a look at you at the hospital, just to be on the safe side,' he said firmly. 'They won't be long. We'll stay until they come.'

'It's very good of you,' she murmured meaning every word.

Even though it was a warm evening, Sarah began to shiver. Ben took off his jacket and swaddled it around her shoulders. Her two companions sat protectively on either side of her, perched on the wall. Sarah could hear the pleasant drone of Ben's voice, low and comforting, but the actual words washed over her.

The police were the first to arrive. As the car drew up on the far side of the square, Ben walked across to the two officers.

The constable, a stern faced man in his late twenties, barely paused to listen. He strode up to Sarah, took out his notebook and started firing questions. He frowned as Ben and Carole chipped in with the details she'd given them earlier about the mugger and the stolen handbag.

'Let the young lady speak for herself, please if you wouldn't mind,' he cut in sharply. Sarah noted the patronizing adjective – he was at least five years her junior – but she couldn't summon up the energy to take offence let alone object. 'Right now, shall we start at the beginning? Name and address.'

The WPC standing behind her dour colleague gave Sarah an encouraging smile as she answered, but Sarah saw the girl sneak a look at her watch. Presumably it wasn't long till the end of their shift and having to sort out all the paper work would prolong their duty. This minor incident was all they needed.

'Can you give a description of the man?'

'It all happened so quickly...' Sarah felt flustered and upset at her incompetence. 'He came from behind; I didn't really see him.'

'You must have noticed something. What about his clothes?'

She closed her eyes and forced herself to think back. 'It was too dark to see much. Possibly a tracksuit with the hood pulled up. And he must have been wearing trainers because I didn't hear him until he was almost on top of me.' Her slurred speech became a little stronger. 'I'm sure there was something else but...' Had there been something familiar about him or was she imagining it?

'Yes?'

Sarah shook her head. 'No. It's gone.'

'He only took your bag?' asked the WPC. 'He didn't pull at your clothing or... try anything else?'

Carole gave a faint gasp. A shudder went through Sarah. The thought of rape hadn't entered her mind before. Carole's hand closed over Sarah's in a reassuring squeeze. Trying to assert herself, Sarah explained briefly how she'd come by her bruises and deliberately made light of his single blow.

'Can we have a description of the bag, please?' The disgruntled policeman was keen to get back to the main issue. This talk of violence would only complicate matters.

'Black leather with lots of pockets. And my initials, SH, in gold on the catch.'

'Contents?'

'I never carry much money so I don't suppose there was more than a five pound note and some small change in my purse... My credit cards... A couple of computer disks... Oh, and my keys.'

They were interrupted by the arrival of the paramedics. At least the man who knelt down in front of her was more sympathetic. He asked Sarah to follow the finger he waved in front of her face and wanted to know if she was feeling nauseous. In the state she was in, she wouldn't have been surprised if he'd started lecturing her for wasting his time calling them out.

She was vaguely aware that some kind of argument going on. She could hear Ben stridently insisting that she should be allowed to go to the hospital without delay. She was too groggy to concentrate on what the policeman was saying. All she wanted was to curl up in her own bed. It crossed her mind that she ought to cancel her credit cards as soon as possible. She pushed the thought away; too weary to bother. Then it struck her, how was she going to get into her flat without her key? The Ericksons, who lived in the flat below, had a spare but they were away on holiday somewhere on the south coast with their eldest daughter and her family. She swallowed the rising panic. There was always Elizabeth.

Ben's jacket was removed and replaced with a blanket. Strong, reassuring arms gently lifted Sarah to her feet.

The frowning policeman positioned himself in front of her.

'We will need to take a further statement, Mrs Harcourt. Perhaps you'll be good enough to call into the Princes Street Station tomorrow so we can have the rest of the details.'

She could hear Ben and Carole muttering away behind her, something about who was supposed to be the culprit.

The policeman stuck out his chin and, before the paramedic could elbow him aside, demanded, 'Was there anything else in your bag?'

She started to shake her head and then she remembered. 'My diary!' All her appointments plus the accumulation of addresses and telephone numbers! Meetings dominated her working life. How on earth would she know where she was supposed to be or when? She couldn't take any more.

Suddenly, to her intense chagrin, she was aware of hot tears coursing down her cheeks.

Chapter 2

'How could anyone have just walked past and left you?' The ring of the mug as it was slammed down on the table echoed around the kitchen.

'Perhaps she thought I was some prostitute beaten up by one of my clients and didn't want to get involved.'

Elizabeth scowled, far too indignant on Sarah's behalf to be mollified by the feeble attempt at light heartedness.

'What I don't understand is what you were doing in that part of town in the first place.' Sarah had been wondering when Elizabeth would get round to the inevitable question.

'My car was in for a service and by the time I'd remembered about collecting it, the garage had closed. I should have told them to leave it on the forecourt but there was a long queue when I dropped it off.'

Elizabeth stared across at her waiting for more. 'So?'

Any hope that all her prattle would deflect her friend faded. Elizabeth had always been persistent. 'I was on my way to the bus station,' she mumbled. Elizabeth's eyebrows shot up in disbelief. 'I know,' Sarah cut in crossly before the predictable lecture, 'I should have phoned for a taxi, but I didn't think of it at the time. Put it down to my frugal upbringing.'

No one on the Capstick Estate of her childhood would ever have dreamed of taking a taxi. Sarah wasn't ashamed of her working class background but, for all her current affluence and success, every now and again her roots had a habit of catching up with her.

The sound of the television in the adjacent room filled the silence.

'This isn't fair on Graham. He must be wondering what we're up to. It's one thing to drag you out to bring me back from the hospital and give me a bed for the night but quite another to keep you out here all evening.'

'Don't be silly. He's fine on his own. Drink your tea.'

'I do appreciate all this, you know,' Sarah muttered. An inadequate word to express the depth of her feeling.

'You'd do the same for me.'

Slowly sipping the strong, sweet tea Elizabeth had insisted that was good for shock, Sarah looked across the table into the warm, hazel eyes. Their friendship had stood the test of time. They'd shared a room at university; two naïve, young people who'd discussed innermost fears and ambitions until two in the morning on far too many occasions. They'd remained close despite going their separate ways. Even after they were both married, they'd never diluted the intimacy by getting together as a foursome. Naturally Sarah had met Graham frequently at various social gatherings, as Elizabeth had Nathan, but their girls' get-togethers, if less frequent, were sacrosanct.

Elizabeth, one of life's practical people, had already phoned First Direct and ensured that Sarah's credit cards were cancelled. She'd even been through the local telephone directory and sorted out a locksmith for Sarah to ring first thing in the morning. It was a relief to be able to pass responsibility to someone else for awhile. Even if she had been able to get into the flat, the last thing Sarah wanted was to be alone with her fears. That nasty little incident had robbed her of more than her handbag. She had always thought of herself as strong and independent but now she was finding it difficult to keep out the dread of nightmares and the self-doubt that now threatened to overwhelm her.

'I'm not sure I can cope any more.' It was out before she'd realized.

'That doesn't sound like superwoman.'

'I'm hardly that,' Sarah snapped.

Elizabeth snorted and raised her eyes to the ceiling. 'Come on! You're at the top of your profession in a man's world.'

Sarah sighed. True there were only a handful of women Principals in Further Education in the whole country, and it had been necessary for her to fight her way up against all the odds. There was no denying she was good at her job but she wasn't so naïve that she didn't appreciate that she'd been used as a pawn in someone else's greater plan. Alan Sheringham had great vision for Silbury College, already one the largest FE complexes in the south, and appointing a woman principal, especially one so young, would make everyone sit up and take notice. Though, had he survived that unexpected heart attack, Sarah wondered if the Chairman of the Board of Governors would have found her quite as malleable as he'd anticipated.

'Successful at work maybe, but not much else. My personal life is an utter mess. I don't seem to be able to relate to my family any more and I couldn't even make a go of my marriage,' she finished bitterly.

'Oh come on!' Elizabeth was exasperated. 'You can't take the blame for that. The man was a rat. He cheated on you.'

'It takes two. If I hadn't been so wrapped up in my work and had more time for him, it might never have happened.'

'Nobody forced him into bed with the tantalising Tanya.'

'Perhaps not but I didn't give him much thought when I insisted on hightailing it up to Manchester for that month's management course. I should have realized I was pushing him too far.'

'He knew you weren't going to be the house-proud, coffee-morning, little wife when he married you, so stop making excuses for the creep.'

'You never did like him, did you?' Despite her mood, Sarah found herself smiling.

'My mother taught me to be suspicious of all excessively handsome men.' Elizabeth scowled as she stirred her coffee vigorously.

'If you don't put that spoon down, you'll wear the pattern off the inside of that mug.' It was difficult to hold back the laughter that was threatening to erupt.

Elizabeth had the grace to see the funny side. 'I wouldn't be much of a friend if I didn't take your side, would I?'

She was one of the few who had, but then that was only to be expected. Though none of the others had openly blamed Sarah, there'd been a distinct cooling off from the majority of their joint acquaintances after the break-up with Nathan two years previously. One or two still made an effort to keep in touch, determined to be impartial, but inevitably the invitations came less frequently.

'You need to get to bed.' Elizabeth roused Sarah from her reverie.

She couldn't argue. It was easier to let herself be gently bullied. Elizabeth insisted on leaving a message on Sarah's office answerphone to explain to her secretary what had happened and that she wouldn't be in next day.

Sarah spent a fitful night. It wasn't just the strange bed. Every time she closed her eyes, pictures of pale, grimacing faces came at her from out of the darkness. However much she tried to think pleasant, restful thoughts, the terror soon crept up on her. It wasn't helped by the discomfort of her grazed left cheek, the side on which she normally went to sleep. Thankfully, the pain in her jaw had subsided to a dull ache. She dropped off eventually in the small hours only to wake up late feeling distinctly groggy and unrefreshed.

Elizabeth insisted on staying home from work until Sarah had managed to get hold of a locksmith who promised to come out within the hour. It took some persuading to stop Elizabeth staying with her once she'd run her over to the flat in one of the villages perched on the edge of The Downs just outside Swindon.

Once the locksmith had gone, Sarah made herself a coffee and collapsed into a chair. There was still a lot to be sorted but she didn't have the energy. She curled up and closed her eyes. The telephone roused her from a doze.

'I haven't got you out of bed have I?' Sarah must have sounded as groggy as she felt. 'How are you?'

'No Lucy. I'm up and feeling fine. You got the message then?'

It took all Sarah's powers of persuasion to convince her secretary that she hadn't been badly beaten up and that the trip to the hospital had been a matter of routine.

'Did they manage to catch the culprit?'

'He was long gone by the time the police arrived. I couldn't give them a description either so I doubt they'll ever make an arrest. Anyway, I should be back tomorrow. I'd be there now,' she lied, 'but my keys were taken and I've only just got back into the flat. The police want a detailed statement as soon as possible and there are a few more things I need to do.'

Full of sympathy, Lucy promised to rearrange Sarah's appointments for the day and let her know if anything urgent cropped up.

It still took Sarah the rest of the morning to summon up the energy to tackle the trip to the station. She'd grown up with an irrational dislike of getting involved with the police. At fourteen, she and a friend had been stopped when they were out on their bikes one afternoon and taken for questioning. There had been an unpleasant incident nearby involving an old man injured by teenagers throwing bricks through his window. It had taken a long time to get their parents down to the station before the girls could be interviewed. Even Sarah's parents had quailed under the bellicose sergeant's accusations. Had it not been for her friend's father insisting on bringing in his solicitor, Sarah was convinced they would have been charged and locked in the cells. The unpleasant exchange of the previous evening hadn't altered her reticence to face yet more police officers but she knew it was something that she would have to tackle sooner or later.

It was only when she went to get her keys that she remembered about the car. It was enough to make her want to curl up and go back to bed. Firmly telling herself not to be such a wimp, she reached for the phone and called for a taxi to run her to the garage. She wouldn't make the same mistake again.

Chapter 3

Sarah mounted the steps to the police station, pushed open the door and walked briskly over to front desk wearing her best schoolmarm expression.

'My name is Sarah Harcourt. I was asked to come in to give a statement about the theft of my handbag,' she said crisply.

To her surprise the sergeant smiled warmly and, before she could give any further explanation, he summoned one of the constables from the small office area behind. 'If you would like to go with this officer, madam, she will show you where you can wait. Inspector Grant will be with you directly.'

Sarah was shown into a pleasant room just large enough for the four easy chairs arranged around a circular coffee table. It was a far cry from the austere, clinical interview room she remembered from her teenage encounter.

'May I get you a cup of tea or coffee, madam?'

She hardly had time to sit down and take her bearings before a thickset man in his early forties hurried in, an A4 manila folder clutched under his arm.

He introduced himself, offered his hand then curled himself into the chair opposite.

'Thank you for coming in so promptly, Mrs Harcourt. I do hope you've recovered from your unpleasant experience.' He laid the folder on the table and opened it out. 'I'm afraid we haven't found your handbag. Sometimes these young tearaways take out the money and credit cards as soon as they get round the corner and lob the bag over the nearest hedge. Unfortunately, if we don't find it in the first couple of hours it isn't likely to turn up at all.'

'There wasn't anything of real value in it.' She'd not expected to see it again so was quite resigned to its loss.

He shuffled through the sheets of paper in front of him. The pleasantries completed, he evidently wanted to get on with the job in hand.

'Before I forget,' Sarah interrupted, 'I wonder if you could help me.' He smiled encouragingly. 'There was a young couple who helped me yesterday. Ben was the one who contacted the police. It's been on my conscience that, in the confusion, I didn't thank them for all they did. I seem to remember they gave statements and I wondered if you had their addresses?' His face took on a guarded expression. 'I quite understand,' she went on hastily, 'that you can't give out such information but if I wrote the letters would it be possible for you to forward them? I appreciate I'm asking a lot.'

'No problem. I'll see Mr Coltishall gets it.'

'You know him?'

'We have met,' he said tersely.

'He doesn't have a record does he? He seemed so ...'

'Oh no.' He gave her a rueful smile, 'but I've had the benefit of his strongly held views on police intimidation and lack of consideration. Highhanded officiousness, I believe was one expression he used.' She looked at him in surprise. 'He came in first thing this morning to make a complaint about the way the officer at the scene dealt with the incident. He claimed you were very badly treated. More like the perpetrator than the victim according to our Mr Coltishall.'

'I don't think it was quite that bad.'

'I have spoken to both officers involved and, although it may not warrant further disciplinary action, I do think that an apology is called for.'

She couldn't resist a gentle jibe. 'Is that why I'm getting the special treatment?' She waved a hand to encompass the room. 'I did wonder why a senior officer was dealing with such a minor incident.'

A knock at the door interrupted their conversation. At the inspector's bark, the WPC brought in a tray with two cups, a milk jug and a non-matching sugar bowl.

'Including proper china cups with saucers!' he said with mock gravity. 'Though it probably doesn't taste any better than the stuff we get in the polystyrene variety.'

She couldn't help smiling and warmed to the self-effacing man and his easy manner. If she was to be given the red-carpet treatment in order to persuade her not to make an official complaint, she wasn't going to let on that she'd never had any intention of doing so in the first place.

Thanks to the urbane good humour of Inspector Grant, Sarah came out of the station into the mid-afternoon sunshine feeling much more like her old self. As she walked back to her car, she made a sudden decision to go to the college. Not that she intended to do any work but the loss of her diary had left her feeling bereft at not being able to check on her appointments. It would take some time to put together all the addresses and snippets of essential information that made that little book such a life-line but, with the help of Lucy's desk diary, at least she would be able to sort out the priorities for the next few days.

Millie, who was showing the ropes to the new girl in reception, looked up the moment she walked through the main door.

'Mrs Harcourt, how are you? We thought you were still in hospital,' she called across the wide expanse with a total lack of her usual decorum. Gone was the usual deference. Suddenly Sarah was no longer the remote figurehead but a fellow human being in need of succour.

'Oh your poor face.'

'Have the police caught him yet?'

'Have they got your stuff back?'

Questions came tumbling one after another giving her little time to answer. They seemed genuinely concerned for her welfare although she suspected that they were both enjoying the vicarious thrill of being close to someone who'd been through an experience that would be a talking point amongst their friends for some time to come. Though they'd enough savoir-faire not to ask outright if she'd been raped, from the veiled comments, it was clear that the stories circulating around the building had grown out of all proportion. She needed to stop and scotch the worst of the excesses.

The telephonist, who'd seen her through the glass screen behind the reception area, also abandoned her post to join them. Within minutes the caretakers were out of their little office and, before long, Sarah was surrounded by a small crowd.

Despite her protestations of being perfectly fit and well, all the attention made her weak at the knees and she felt an overwhelming need to sit down. Pleading that she'd to speak to a colleague before he left for a meeting, and with promises to talk to them all later, Sarah hurried away down the corridor.

The Principal's office was on the fourth floor and Sarah invariably used the stairs. She disliked being hemmed in and tried to avoid even the garishly-lit lift when she knew it would be crowded. Today was an exception. She pressed the green up arrow button and watched the numbers light up in descending order. As she was whisked up to the heights, she lent back against the cool, steel wall feeling mentally as well physically exhausted.

She peered suspiciously round the softly hissing doors as they opened but the place was deserted. For once there no one at the photocopier which sat in front of the full-length windows looking down onto the central grassed square. Passing into the Administration Wing, she walked, if not exactly stealthily, trying not to attract attention from those working in the offices beyond the patterned glass windows that lined the corridor.

When she reached her office, she was relieved to find that Lucy wasn't at her desk; presumably she was taking the day's correspondence down to the post room. Sarah would be able to slip into her inner sanctum and have a quiet sit down and get herself together before Lucy returned and the questions began again.

The door to her inner office was ajar. She pushed it open and stopped in mid stride. Sitting in her chair, busily tapping away at her computer, completely oblivious of her presence, sat George Fitzgibbon, her Vice-Principal.

'Good afternoon, George,' she said icily. 'Perhaps I ought to tell you that I am not yet ready to relinquish my position in this college even if you do appear to be all set to jump into my chair.'

The look of horrified stupefaction on his face as he stared up at her might have made her laugh if she hadn't been so angry.

'Sarah,' he spluttered. 'It's not how it looks.'

'Really? So what are you doing in my room going through my private files? And, even more to the point, where the hell did you get my password?'

They probably heard her down in reception.

Chapter 4

'We weren't sure when you'd be fit enough to come back to work.'
He got to his feet, recovering rapidly.

'Evidently.'

'I was checking your appointments so we could deal with anything that was urgent.'

'Lucy has my diary. You could have spoken with her.'

'That's what I was going to do but she wasn't in the office when I arrived.'

'So you thought it would be a good opportunity to come in here and rifle through my files.' As Sarah marched round her desk, he backed away trying to squeeze through the narrow gap between the table and the wall.

'No,' he protested, losing some of the righteous air he'd tried to adopt. 'As you're addressing the Chamber of Commerce next week, I thought I'd see if you'd had time to finish the presentation slides while I was waiting for Lucy.'

'Really?' It was amazing how much scepticism she was able to inject into the single word. 'And just what is that to you?'

'Be reasonable, Sarah. We need sponsorship for the new Business Centre and we can't miss out on this opportunity. If I was going to have to give the presentation, I needed to see all the information.' His Adam's apple quivered in the skinny, stretched neck and the thin strand of hair pasted across his balding pate flopped forward.

She sat down leaving him standing like a naughty schoolboy in front of her.

'As you can now appreciate, your services will not be required. And, if by any remote chance, I do decide to pass on the responsibility for any of my presentations to someone else, let me assure you, I will fully acquaint that person with all the material that he might need.'

Sarah glanced down at the computer screen and she could see that George hadn't managed to get past her log-on.

Looking up, she saw Lucy framed in the open doorway behind him. The noise had brought several others who stood peering over her shoulder trying to see what all the fuss was about. A snort of ill suppressed laughter from the outer office caused George to spin round. His face went from red to a violent shade of puce.

He turned back to face Sarah and, summoning up as much dignity as he could muster, went on. 'As you will appreciate, I was unable to get into any of your files as I didn't have the password. I think that highlights a very real problem. Should any member of staff suddenly be taken seriously ill or, heaven forbid, be involved in a major accident, the rest of us could find ourselves unable to get at essential information. I appreciate the need to maintain confidentiality but shouldn't passwords be available to senior members of staff in such circumstances?'

Sarah sat quietly for a moment. 'You may well have a point, George. I will put your suggestion forward at the next Board Meeting. In the meantime perhaps you might like to write yours on a piece of paper and put it a sealed envelope and hand it over into my safe keeping.'

George's eyes widened with indignation.

A snigger from the outer office broke the silence.

His whole body stiffened then he turned and swept through the doorway forcing the small crowd apart to let him through.

As the door slammed, Sarah slumped back and closed her eyes. What had got into her? Why had she exploded? And then to tear him to pieces like that; it just wasn't like her. She must be a great deal more overwrought than she'd realized.

What did it matter if he did get into her files? There was nothing there that he shouldn't see. All the confidential references were on a zip disk which she kept in her bag. Shit! That was lost now as well. And it was over a week since she'd backed it up. She'd meant to do it yesterday but hadn't made the time. That little problem could be sorted out later. Now she had enough to worry about making her peace with George.

It had taken months to establish a good working relationship between the two of them and now she would have to start all over again. Everyone had expected George to get the principal's post when Eric Cathcart retired. He'd had a lot of support, both on the Board of Governors and amongst senior staff in the college. It must have been a great blow to him when Sarah, a relative newcomer, over fifteen years his junior and a woman to boot, had been appointed over him. Had it not been for Alan Sheringham, the then chairman, she doubted she would have got the job. Establishing herself in the first eighteen months in the teeth of opposition hadn't been easy and, though George had never openly opposed her plans and decisions, disappointment had made him waspish and more insular. He'd always been dependable rather than dynamic and now what little spark he had left, had gone.

Although he could have gone about it more diplomatically, the poor chap had been perfectly justified in trying to ensure that things ran smoothly in her absence. The Business Centre was a costly venture and the college desperately needed to persuade local companies of the value of using its training facilities. There were times when pedantic, humourless George drove everyone to distraction but she had no right to humiliate him in front of everyone.

There was a tentative knock at the door and Lucy came in looking shamefaced.

'I'm so sorry. I'd never have let Mr Fizgibbon in here like that. He must have come in when I popped out.'

'It's all right,' Sarah interrupted. 'I know it's not your fault.' Feeling more weary than she cared to admit, she pulled herself to her feet. 'Be an angel and make me a coffee. I'll be back in a minute.'

The door to George's office was open. She looked in but he wasn't there. Perhaps he'd gone to the Administration Office. Oh well, as she'd sounded off at him in everyone's hearing, it was only justice for her to have to make her peace in public. Several heads looked up when she went in. George was standing in the far corner by the fax machine. All eyes followed Sarah as she walked across the vast expanse of the open plan office that occupied the whole of one side of the top wing of the building. Although each work section was screened off, everyone could see where she was going and the usual hubbub slowly subsided in anticipation.

As she approached, he looked up, his hooded eyes wary. She stood before him and took a deep breath. 'George, I had no right to speak to you like that and I've come to apologize.'

Even the clack of computer keys stilled as every ear strained to hear what she was saying.

The look of surprise on the gaunt features gradually turned to one of injured dignity. He took off his spectacles and began to clean the lenses vigorously with his handkerchief. Behind her, no one stirred.

She'd never found eating-humble-pie easy. As George stood silently intent on his task, she had to bite back the inclination to snap that he was the one in the wrong going into her office and switching on her machine. She tried to remind herself that he was good at his job. He was a superb administrator with a meticulous eye for detail. No report left his desk with a mistake or a single grammatical error. In many ways they were a good team – she came up with the ideas and he provided the detailed follow-up work.

His task completed, he looked up at her and said quietly, 'Apology accepted.' He turned and continued feeding paper into the fax machine.

As she made her way back across the room, heads suddenly became buried in newfound tasks and the bustle resumed.

Returning to her own office, she found Barry Waterhouse perched on the edge of Lucy's desk waiting for her.

'You look awful. Should you be here?' The over familiarity grated, but it was probably his way of trying to show sympathy.

'I'm fine,' she snapped. 'Was there something you wanted?'

'Just to tell you I had a letter from that college in Cheshire.'

'Does that mean you got the job?'

''Fraid not.'

Sarah made all the right noises. She was sorry for him, of course she was, he'd been so confident, especially after he'd been called back for a second interview, but she really wasn't in a state to worry about anyone else's problems at the moment.

'Your coffee's on your desk,' interrupted Lucy.

Lucy ushered Sarah into her room and fussed around until she was sitting comfortably in her chair.

'You really do look exhausted.'

'It was my dignity that was hurt more than anything,' she assured them. 'In fact, it got severely dented. When it was all over and everyone was fussing round me, I ended up howling like a baby. Made a right fool of myself,' she finished with a laugh.

They both looked at her incredulously.

'You!' Barry could hardly hold back the loud guffaws. Even Lucy began to giggle.

'I'm sorry,' she spluttered. 'I know we shouldn't laugh but the thought of you of all people reduced to tears.'

'The Steel Queen herself.'

Though she feigned surprise, Sarah was well aware of her nickname amongst the staff. She also knew, despite his laugh, that it wasn't a term of affection. She would've been a fool not to appreciate that she was bitterly resented in many quarters, not least because of the large number of staff redundancies since her appointment. It was true that she didn't suffer fools gladly and that she had no compunction in getting rid of much of the dead wood that had been mouldering around for far too long but it didn't give her any satisfaction to be thought of as cold and remote.

'So that's what they call me behind my back, is it?' she said with a mock frown.

'Only when you're in one of your good moods. Most days it's unrepeatable,' Barry answered in the same flippant tone.

'Yes, it probably is after that little contretemps just now,' she said, injecting a note of seriousness into the mood.

'Don't let George get to you. You know what an old woman he is.'

'The cheek of the man!' It would be some time before Lucy forgave him. 'I'll swear he waited until he knew I'd be downstairs.'

'No harm done,' Sarah said trying to calm her down. 'It's all over and done with now. And it's high time we all got back to work.'

Lucy looked at her sternly. 'You look washed out. You should be at home taking it easy.'

'She's right,' agreed Barry. 'If you carry on now it will take twice as long before you're back on form and you'll end up having to take even more time off. This place won't fall apart without you for a couple of days. Put your feet up; watch television, read a book. Spoil yourself and, for once in your life, forget about work.'

The way she felt, she knew they were right. In the end, it was easier to give in and return to her flat.

The first of the phone calls came that evening.

Chapter 5

Sarah stared up at the flickering screen and tried to concentrate once more. The predictable plot was so trite it had failed to hold Sarah's attention sufficiently to wipe out thoughts of those strange phone calls. At first, when no one had answered, she'd assumed that it was some call centre using an automated dialler, but not half a dozen times the same evening. And then last night had come the heavy breathing. Was it just some idiot trying random numbers or was she being targeted deliberately and if so, who by? Her number was ex-directory so it was unlikely to be a student. It was easy enough to tell herself to ignore them, stupid to let them unsettle her, but she was finding that increasingly difficult to do.

When the credits began to roll and people started moving, she turned to Elizabeth. 'I enjoyed that,' she lied. 'Haven't been to a decent weepy in ages.'

'Me neither.' Elizabeth slipped her arm through Sarah's to stop them being swept apart by the crowd as they made their way up the gentle ramp to the exit. 'Graham wouldn't be seen dead at a chick flick.'

'Shall we go for a drink or do you fancy coming back to my place for coffee?'

'To tell you the truth, all that emotional drama has made me peckish.'

They settled on the pizza place a few hundred yards from the multiplex. At least in a public place there would be plenty of distraction.

'Sorry I was such a misery when you brought me home the other day.'

'Think nothing of it. Being attacked by a yob in broad daylight in the middle of town does tend to take the sparkle out of one's persona.'

'Perhaps,' Sarah laughed. 'But that's no excuse for wallowing in self pity.'

Once they'd ordered, Elizabeth took a small package from her handbag.

'This is for you.' She put it in front of Sarah. 'It's something I know you'll never get for yourself but I'd feel a lot better knowing you had one.'

Sarah opened the paper bag and pulled out a cardboard box.

'I appreciate you've always said mobile phones are an invasion of privacy but you don't have to give anyone your number. Keep it just for emergencies. With all the driving you do it's only sensible to have one in case that fabulous car of yours breaks down, save you wandering about trying to find a phone box. And before you say anything about the cost of rental, it's one of these pay-as-you-go things.' She eventually drew breath and stared at Sarah defiantly.

Sarah leant across the table and put her hand on Elizabeth's. 'I don't deserve a friend like you.'

'I was expecting an argument.'

They were both saved further embarrassment by the arrival of the food.

Sarah jumped as the phone rang beside her. Despite all her resolutions, her hand went out automatically to cut off the jarring intrusion into her peace and quiet. As she put the receiver to her ear, she held her breath and waited.

'Sarah, are you there? It's me.'

A wave of relief swept over her. 'Hi, Liz. How's you?'

'Is everything all right?'

'Of course. Why shouldn't it be?' Even to Sarah, her voice sounded strained.

'Then why didn't you speak when you picked up the phone?'

Elizabeth wasn't one to be fobbed off. She would go on and on until she'd ferreted out the problem. Sarah explained about the calls.

'Have you tried 1471?'

'All I get is, "The caller withheld the number".'

'What about reporting it to the police?'

'It's hardly the crime of the century,' Sarah protested with a laugh.

'I'm not trying to worry you, but could it be connected to when you were mugged?'

'I did wonder about that. The calls began the day after it happened. If he'd search my bag, he might've discovered my address and, as he also has my keys, he could be ringing to see if I was in before planning an easy burglary. He wouldn't know the lock had been changed. But that's just me being silly. He wouldn't be able to get hold my number.'

'Umm.' Elizabeth sounded doubtful.

'I did think about having the number changed but, apart from the inconvenience of having to let friends and family know, it smacks too much of giving in to the bastard.'

'All the more reason to report it.'

'The police will think I'm neurotic! They'll probably try and persuade me to go and see my doctor.'

There was a long pause. 'All the same, it would do no harm to have a chat with that nice inspector chappie you were telling me about.'

'I don't think inspectors deal with nuisance phone calls,' Sarah teased. 'Anyway, were you calling about anything special?'

'I was wondering if we could have lunch some time next week.'

'Love to. Thursday suit you? Meet at the wine bar?'

'Let's go mad and indulge ourselves. Gianni's? One o'clock?'

'Super. See you then.'

During the day, things were so hectic that Sarah had little time to think about her problems. As she had difficulty explaining to friends and family with no experience of Further Education, even with no students, the end of the so-called summer holiday was a busy time. Come the GCSE results in late August, there were many last minute changes of plan for students who didn't get the grades they'd been predicted and the College was still recruiting people onto courses days before term was due to start.

It wasn't only Eunice Robinson's Student Services team conducting the Admissions Interviews who were run ragged. Trying to discover if there would be sufficient numbers to make a course viable or enough to justify an extra group plus all the staffing and rooming implications provided headaches for all the faculty managers.

It was well after nine o'clock when she got back home. Sarah couldn't be bothered to cook herself a proper meal and decided to make do with fruit and a bowl of cereal. She was half expecting a call that evening. Her nephew, Todd, who'd been unwell for some time, was due to see a specialist and her mother had promised to get in touch if there was any news. The moment the jarring note sounded, she stabbed at the mute button on the television remote and snatched up the receiver.

She reeled off her number and waited. The silence went on for several seconds. Another of those stupid calls! She was about to replace the phone when a low, hollow laugh, full of menace, sounded in her ear. Taken aback, it was several seconds before she banged down the receiver.

Sarah was angry rather than upset. Angry with herself for letting the sick-minded creep, who was trying to taunt her, succeed. A week ago, she would have dismissed the whole thing without another thought. This pathetic reaction was simply delayed shock from the events of the mugging on top of overwork, she told herself firmly. In a few days she'd be back to normal. Not knowing the reason that lay behind these childish games was more unsettling than she cared to admit.

She slumped back in her chair and returned to the programme she'd been staring at. It was impossible to find anything even remotely amusing in the pathetic sitcom which she'd hoped would lighten her spirits. She was about to switch off the television and have an early night when the phone rang again.

She stared at it, deciding whether to pick it up. It could well be her mother. Slowly she lifted the receiver and waited.

The silence went on. Getting her to lose her temper was probably exactly what he wanted so instead she laid the receiver down on the table as quietly as possible. She sat staring at it, her hands clenched, determined he should be the first to have to ring off. It would be a small victory; an attempt to show him that she wasn't bothered by his silly games.

She began to think that she'd won when she heard the whispering.

'Ssaaaraaah.' It was a hoarse, breathy, unreal noise that chilled her spine. He must have heard her stifled sob because, as she re-coiled into the depths of the chair, she could hear the peal of maniacal laughter. Too late, she seized up the receiver ready to let loose a stream of invective but he'd already rung off.

She couldn't get to sleep that night. Her brain wouldn't relax. She kept thinking of all the things she should have said. When she even-tually managed to close her eyes and begin to doze, that dreadful, sibilant wail filled her skull. She got up and paced from room to room and made endless cups of coffee. In an effort to shut out the memory, she tried to read but she couldn't concentrate. Eventually she switched on the television only to find a late-night horror movie.

'You again! You seem to be spending as much time in here as you do in your own office.'

Barry Waterhouse looked up from where he'd nonchalantly draped himself over the desk. He gave her his usual, charming smile, completely unabashed, although Lucy's sudden preoccupation with sorting through the pile of papers in front of her wasn't lost on Sarah.

'I'm beginning to think you must have designs on my innocent secretary,' Sarah went on, eyebrows raised in mock-horror. 'And you a married man with three small children!' She didn't want to play the heavy-handed boss or sour the good relationship she had with her secretary by giving Lucy a lecture on avoiding the flattery of a middle-aged Lothario. She had to trust to Lucy's good sense and hope that she would take the hint.

'I was waiting for you actually. I wondered if you've got a minute to look through the applications for the Media Studies post.' He tried to follow Sarah through into her room.

'Not now I'm afraid,' she replied glancing pointedly at her watch. She wasn't so busy that she couldn't make time for him but she was still too keyed up to have to cope with his constant attempts to impress. Besides, there was no reason why he should need to bother her with such details at that stage. As Director of the Social Studies Faculty, he was able to draw up the shortlist far better than she was. 'Why, is there a problem?'

'Thought you might be interested.' He shrugged with just a tinge of criticism.

'Of course I am,' she said mustering a smile. 'When you've had a chance to narrow down the field, we can look at the selection together. Have a word with Lucy and she'll put it in my diary.'

She was about to shut her door when Lucy called her back.

'Your messages are on your desk. Michael Wyatt from the Chamber of Commerce would like you to ring back before the end of today and Eunice Robinson came up while you were out.' Sarah groaned. 'She asked if I'd let her know the moment you got in. She seemed a bit uptight about something,' Lucy added apologetically.

'Our dear Eunice is always on the rampage about something. I wonder who's rattled her cage now. Time for a quick exit. Best of luck, Sarah.' Barry, now all smiles, gave a wave and disappeared.

Sarah sank into her chair. The pile in her in-tray stared at her accusingly though she knew she wouldn't be able to concentrate on anything else until she'd dealt with whatever was upsetting Eunice. The Head of Student Services wasn't the most popular lady in the college. Sarah lifted the receiver.

Eunice arrived minutes later, eyes blazing, lips narrowed.

'What's the problem?' Sarah waved her to the chair but Eunice stood glaring down at her.

'The printers are waiting for the proofs of the Community Education booklet.'

'So, what's the hold-up?'

Because of staff changes and a string of minor delays, distribution of details of the adult evening courses was already weeks behind schedule.

'You still have all the paperwork,' Eunice accused.

'But I haven't seen it!'

'I brought it all up here personally last Tuesday just after five. Lucy had already gone so I put them on your desk in here in a white and green folder,' she insisted with all the resigned patience of someone speaking to a difficult child.

Though they needed her final approval, passing them to Sarah was little more than a matter of courtesy. Such was the urgency, everything should have been returned immediately.

Sarah checked all the filing trays without success then buzzed through to Lucy who proved to be as mystified as she was. Eunice stood bristling with ill concealed irritation as she watched Sarah hurry over to the collection of folders propped on the shelves.

'That could be it,' Eunice snapped pointing to one covered with bright emerald lettering as Sarah flicked through the assortment.

Sarah pulled it out and breathed a sigh of relief when she saw the printer's logo stamped on the front. She carried back to her desk and opened it. Her heart sank when she saw that it was empty.

'It will all have to be done again if they're not found. That's weeks of work and the printers will want paying for their extra time!'

'I appreciate that,' Sarah replied through gritted teeth. 'They must be here somewhere. Lucy and I will to have to go through every pile of papers until we find them.'

Sarah managed to get rid of Eunice with an assurance that she'd send them down immediately they turned up. The last thing she needed was Eunice standing over them, huffing her disapproval. She and Lucy began a systematic search. Wherever they were, the proofs were certainly not obvious. Sarah went through the drawers in her desk while Lucy tried the cupboards. Twenty minutes later, having eliminated every other alternative, they started on the filing cabinets painstakingly inspecting every folder. Sarah found them in the end, tucked away at the back of the Student Admissions file that she hadn't touched for weeks.

'How on earth can they have got in here?' Sarah caught the look on Lucy's face. 'I didn't put them there,' she protested.

'Of course not.' Lucy's answer came quickly though whether she believed Sarah was another matter.

Sarah checked that the proofs were all there then sent Lucy to put them straight in Eunice's hands. Once the door was closed, she slumped at her desk. All this could've had serious repercussions. Finding the documents may have solved one problem but how on earth had the things got there in the first place? It was just possible that one of the cleaners might have tidied the folder away by putting it on a shelf although it was hard to imagine why anyone should want to take out the contents and file them in the recesses of her cabinet. Had all the recent upsets made her so distracted that she'd done it whilst her mind was on something else entirely?

Such a major lapse just wasn't like her. Even after all the trauma of throwing Nathan out, and God knows that broke her heart in little pieces, she'd been able to function efficiently. It didn't make sense that a few phone calls should reduce her to a zombie. There had to be another explanation. Try as she might, she could not think of one.

Chapter 6

Had it not been for Elizabeth, Sarah would probably have done nothing. She knew that Elizabeth wouldn't let the matter rest. Unless she reported it to the police, Elizabeth would offer to go with her to the station which was as good as a threat to drag Sarah there personally. Even so, it took a couple of days to pluck up the courage to call in at the Swindon Divisional Police Headquarters in Princes Street.

There was a sergeant on the front desk though not one Sarah had met before. When she asked if it was possible to speak to Inspector Grant, he merely asked for her name in a bored voice. He phoned through the message then, waving her to the padded bench along-side the wall, said the inspector would be with her in a couple of minutes.

Sarah sat for quite a while although, as she'd expected to be fobbed off or at least to have to provide a long explanation of why she wished to see the Inspector, for once she was prepared to wait. Given her frenetic lifestyle, patience had never been one of her virtues.

The Inspector's broad smile seemed genuine as he held open the door and signalled her through. As he ushered her ahead of him down the long corridor, she hoped he'd be as pleased when he heard the reason for her visit.

'I'm afraid someone's already in the room where we were last time and the other interview rooms are a bit stark, would you mind coming into my office?'

They settled themselves in his small, cluttered room and it came as no surprise to Sarah to see his desk was a shambles, with piles of papers and assorted folders covering every square inch.

He apologized for the mess and got straight down to business. 'Now, what can I do for you?'

Sarah told him about the phone calls. 'I appreciate that there's nothing that the police can do but, because it might just be the same person who took my bag, I thought I ought to report it.'

To Sarah's immense relief, he didn't seem to think that she was wasting his time. With the precision of the very untidy, who nonetheless know the exact location of every slip of paper; he extracted her file from the heap and prepared to take notes.

'Can you remember when they began?'

'The evening after the attack, which is why I wondered about a connection.'

'There's no regular pattern to the calls?' She shook her head.

'Sometimes there's nothing for two or three days and I think it's stopped and then he starts up again. At first I got angry demanding to know who it was and telling him to stop it and slamming down the phone. When I realized that was what he wanted – to get me upset – I stopped saying anything, not even giving my number. That was when the heavy breathing started.' Despite her resolve, the degree to which the calls were disturbing her was beginning to show. Her voice faltered a little as she told him about the laugh and the breathy voice calling her name.

'Could it be a student prank?'

Sarah shook her head. 'I doubt it. I'm ex-directory to prevent anything like that.'

He frowned and obvious concern showed in his face. 'To be honest, it doesn't sound the sort of thing a petty thief or an opportunist burglar would do.'

She had to agree. She told him how she'd tried the ring back the number but the caller must have been using a payphone.

'Then getting one of these new phones with a display unit won't be much help. Do you have an answering machine?' She shook her head. 'It might not work, however if all he got was a pre-recorded message he wouldn't have the satisfaction of knowing how much he was upsetting you. If you leave it on all the time, you need only pick up the receiver if it's a genuine call that you want to answer.'

Relief swept through her. It seemed such an obvious solution. He walked back with her along the corridor to the reception area and, as they stood shaking hands, Sarah apologized again for taking up so much of his time.

'It's no trouble at all, Mrs Harcourt. Please let me know if it works. Though do remember, a lot of people are put off by answering machines or they won't want to leave a message, so not all your silent calls will be malicious.'

Sarah hurried along the pavement weaving her way through the mêlée of lunchtime shoppers crowding the High Street. As she turned the corner, she glanced up at the old-fashioned clock hanging outside the jewellers. Seven minutes past! An elderly woman

27

with a dog on a lead came between her and the pedestrian crossing just as the green light began flashing. She swore silently as she stabbed the button and glared at the traffic trundling past.

She could see Elizabeth seated at one of their favourite window tables. The service in Gianni's was always leisurely and customers were expected to take time savouring each course. The concept of fast food was more than an anathema; it was a sacrilege to all that the restaurant held dear. As a consequence, the place was rarely busy at lunchtime which made it something of a haven of calm in the town's usual midday bustle.

'I'm so sorry. One of my reports went missing. I had it yesterday and I thought I'd left it on my desk but I couldn't find it anywhere this morning. In the end I had to print out another copy. Luckily, I had it on disk though a seventy page document takes for ever.'

Elizabeth waved away Sarah's gabbling protest. 'You know you don't have to worry about keeping me waiting.'

'I knew you'd understand but that's all the more reason not to abuse our friendship. Thanks for the drink.' Sarah picked up the glass of orange juice and lemonade Elizabeth already had waiting and took a long, refreshing gulp. 'Have you ordered?'

'Not yet though I think I'll have my usual.'

Sarah turned and waved to attract the waiter. Even though there were no more than a handful of customers in the place, he was maintaining his distance. 'I won't bother with a starter; just the smoked ham tortellini. I can't afford to be away too long.'

They had almost finished their meal when Elizabeth said, 'I'm glad to see you're looking a bit more like your old self than when you arrived.'

'Meaning?' Sarah looked up sharply.

Elizabeth ignored her question and responded with one of her own, 'Are you still getting the strange phone calls?' Sarah pulled a face. 'Then I hope you got in touch with your dishy policeman?'

'He's hardly that!' Sarah laughed. 'He's short, bordering on chubby and going grey. But he is very easy to talk to.'

'It goes with the job.'

'Not necessarily, as I know to my cost. Not all policemen are sympathetic.'

'So, did you see him?'

'I always take your advice. Problem solved.'

'So, if it's not that, are you going to tell me what the problem is?' Elizabeth persisted.

'I haven't been my usual efficient self just lately. I went to finish off a document yesterday and it wasn't on the computer. I must have pressed the wrong button last time I saved it and then the backup was corrupted so I'd to start the whole thing again. Everyone is being very understanding and making excuses for me which, to be honest, I'm finding more disconcerting than the usual knives in the back. It makes me feel that I'm not coping any more. Perhaps the job's getting too much.'

'Fiddlesticks,' Elizabeth snorted. Sarah knew she could rely on her friend not to come out with sympathetic platitudes. 'You're a fighter, Sarah. You always have been and always will be. You're the best principal that place has ever had so go and prove it.'

Sarah gave a low chuckle. 'You're good for me; you know that?'

Elizabeth was right; she was a fighter. Something was happening and it was up to her to get to the bottom of it.

Chapter 7

Sarah tapped out the final corrections and hit the print button. As the machine clicked into action, she sat back and listened to the gentle purr. Another job completed. She picked up a pen, pulled her pad across and ran a satisfying black line through one of the items on her list of tasks. Her eye ran down the page to sort out the next priority. Nothing quick and easy. She glanced at the clock. It was only a quarter past ten but it seemed pointless to start something else only to stop for coffee as she was getting into the flow of it.

'I know it's a bit early but fancy a drink?' she asked Lucy as she wandered through.

'Shall I go and make it?'

'No. You carry on. I've come to a natural break and I need to stretch my legs.'

In the little kitchen at the end of the corridor, she found George hovering by the sink. Sarah hadn't seen much of him in the two weeks since their little fracas over her computer and she suspected he'd been avoiding her. He'd been decidedly terse at their regular weekly sessions and she suspected it would be sometime before the incident would be forgotten.

'Good morning, George. How's life with you?' she asked doing her best to show that she for one bore no grudges.

He gave a muttered, noncommittal response and continued to stare at the kettle as though willing it to boil more quickly.

'I wanted to have a word with you about the proposals for the Faculty Review in advance of the governors' meeting.'

'Not all the figures are in yet,' he put in quickly. 'I can't produce the statistics you need until all the faculty directors hand in their reports.' He gave her a wary look.

'And no prizes for guessing the culprit,' she said giving him a broad smile.

'I have reminded Tom every day for a week now.' A deep frown furrowed his forehead.

It didn't take much to imagine the offhand way Tom Appleby had responded to George's request for him to provide details of the number of students turning up for the courses on which they'd been enrolled. The office had the registration figures, but there was often a considerable discrepancy. Many students, even those on two year courses, failed to put in an appearance and chasing them up was a lengthy business at a time when lecturers felt they had better things to do. Tom had never been one for paper work at the best of times and did little to nag his heads of department to come up with the information.

'I'll have a word with him,' Sarah promised. He wouldn't give her the run-around that he enjoyed occasionally inflicting on George.

The trouble with Tom was that he'd lost interest in the job. In his mid-fifties and, with the coming reorganization of senior positions in the college, he thought he stood a good chance of getting early retirement with a nice enhancement to his pension. There were times when his slipshod methods bordered on negligence although he knew, if he wanted Sarah's support when the subject came up with the governors, he'd have to toe the line with her.

George looked unsure whether to be pleased with her offer or annoyed at her interference.

'Actually, it wasn't the figures I wanted to talk about. I'd like to pick your brains about the working party.'

'Oh yes?' George looked a fraction happier.

'I've been giving it a lot of thought and I've come to the conclusion that it's best if I'm not actually a member of the group, however I will need someone there who can keep everyone on track. Obviously the people we select are going to have their own agendas so it's vital that there's at least one person I can trust to keep the needs of the whole college in mind. I know you've a lot on at the moment, nevertheless I really would appreciate it if you'd consider taking charge.'

'You want me on the working party?' He sounded surprised.

'Umm,' she nodded earnestly.

There were times when George needed his ego stroking but she wasn't sure if she'd gone over the top.

'I'd have thought you'd have preferred someone like Barry.' Now she was getting to the real problem!

'Good heavens no. Why should I want him?'

'It's not gone unnoticed that he seems to have your ear at the moment. He's always in your office these days.'

Sarah wondered if that was the general opinion or George taking the opportunity for a dig.

'Not at my invitation,' she said firmly.

'He's also very thick with Sir Richard these days and he has his pals on the governing body.'

'Really? That's news to me,' she said truthfully. Sarah had always appreciated that Barry Waterhouse was ambitious though she'd not realized that he'd been campaigning quite so actively in high places. 'As far as I'm concerned, you're the right person for the job. I need someone I can trust.'

'I see your point although, as you said earlier, it is a busy time for me at the moment.'

No more than for the rest of us she thought but then it would have been foolish to expect George to respond in any other way. He felt he needed to be seen to be doing her a favour. Perhaps she could push just a little more. 'It does concern me that the group will have to work under the full glare of all the college and I can't afford to have the whole thing hijacked by members using it as an opportunity to pursue their own interests. And of course, I need someone at the highest level who will be able to report back not only to me but to the governors.' It wouldn't hurt to point out the high profile opportunity it would be for him.

'I suppose there really isn't anyone else who can be seen to have no axe to grind.'

'Exactly.'

'If you put it like that, I'd be happy for you to put my name forward.' He seemed to grow an inch as he straightened his thin shoulders and smiled down at her benignly.

'Great. Will you have a think about who else it might be good to have on the working party? Obviously each faculty must have the chance to nominate a representative but I think we could drop a few hints in the right places. Let's get together sometime tomorrow?'

'Certainly and I'll see what I can find out on the grapevine. We might need to do a bit of damage limitation in case things don't go quite as we'd wish.'

'There're bound to be some difficult characters elected. That's why I need someone who can handle them,' she warned. Surely he appreciated that it wasn't going to be an easy ride?

'Oh quite,' he smiled almost slyly. 'However I think, between us, we can rise to the challenge.' With that he made an exit.

At least something was going right at last. She was back in George's good books, at least temporarily, and it looked as if some of his old sparkle was coming back. Perhaps all he needed was something to shake him out of his rut.

'Get a move on, sunshine.'

The driver of the Royal Mail van was oblivious of her scowl and continued to pull out across her path at a speed that a crippled hedgehog could have bettered. Knowing that she would have to battle her way through the morning rush hour traffic to reach the sorting office on the far side of town, Sarah had given herself plenty of time but the stop start journey hadn't improved her temper. The only consolation was that the complex provided a visitors' car park even if it was as far from the reception as it was possible to get.

Clutching the card she'd discovered pushed through her letterbox on her return the previous evening; she hurried through the glass doors and followed the clearly marked signs. Apart from the natural curiosity of finding out what was in the parcel that the postman had been unable to deliver, she thought she stood a better chance of finding the place less busy than at the end of the day. She turned the corridor and saw an elderly man already standing at the collection point desk. After a minute or so, having lost the little patience she had left, she gave an involuntary sigh which prompted him to turn and give her a rueful grimace.

'Have you rung the bell?' She could hear the implied criticism in her voice so trying to sound more friendly, she added. 'I'll be late for work at this rate.'

'They can't seem to find my package. I think I know what it is. I've been expecting some photographs from my daughter. Our first great-grandchild is nearly a month old.'

'How nice.' He must have taken her comment as interest and after a lengthy account of the new baby's progress, proceeded to tell her how difficult it was to get out to this part of town by public transport. Sarah looked at her watch although she could see the clock on the wall behind him quite clearly. She knew she was going to feel a heel for the rest of the day for not volunteering to run the old boy back into town but, after all her recent inefficiencies at work, she didn't want to add lateness to her rapidly tarnishing reputation.

A face appeared as the counter window.

'I'm sorry the postman doesn't appear to have brought it back yet.'

'It's a pity he couldn't have left it next door.' The previously languid voice became fractious. 'It would have saved me the bus fare...' Sarah forced herself not to start tapping her foot as the pensioner repeated the account of his problems.

'Don't worry,' interrupted the receptionist catching Sarah's scowl and ill concealed sighs, 'I'll make sure we get it sorted for you. You won't have to come back. And if it ever happens again just tick the box on the back of the card here saying when you'll be in and we'll deliver it.'

Sarah pushed over her card as soon as the man moved away from the window, resisting the temptation to snap. No doubt the woman had to take the brunt of everybody's complaints about the inconvenience of undelivered mail on a daily basis so adding her two pennyworth would get Sarah nowhere.

She was back almost immediately. With a quick, 'Thank you,' Sarah took her parcel and hurried back to the car.

As she tore off the wrapper, three books, "A Chinese Odyssey", "Treasures of Beijing" and "A History of Imperial China", slipped onto her lap together with a glossy brochure advertising The New History Book Club. She remembered looking through the same literature several times – a copy fell out of the colour supplement almost every Saturday. She'd even toyed with the idea of sending for some of the books but she couldn't work out why she'd been selected to be sent books on spec. She scrabbled for the accompanying paper work.

'Please find enclosed the three books you selected on our introductory offer. If you are happy with your choice please forward the sum of...'

Her eyes went no further. She reread the first sentence. A brief moment of panic took hold of her. Although the books were ones she might well have selected, Sarah had no recollection of filling in any form. Reason returned. She hadn't yet been reduced to a state where she didn't know what she was doing. Her anger was mixed with a tinge of unease. This was more than some silly prank at her expense. Someone was intent on making her life a misery. Perhaps they were trying to make her think she was loosing it. And if you don't pull yourself together they'll damned well succeed, she told herself. But who? That someone appeared to know all about her fascination with ancient Chinese culture.

Chapter 8

Sarah sighed. Saturday afternoon wasn't the best time to visit the main library. Half the population of Swindon seemed to want to change their books after the weekend shop. Though the mobile library that served the village had the advantage of being less crowded, it carried only a small selection of books and was always the last in line for the latest acquisitions.

After a dismally chilly week, the unexpected late summer sun appeared to have attracted the emergence of an army of elderly folk to add to the general tumult. Sarah tried to peer through the crowd gathered around the just-returned shelves only to find herself skilfully elbowed to one side by an old dear armed with a lethal assortment of carrier bags. As Sarah reached over the knitted woollen hat for the latest P D James, a deft swing with the woman's package-laden armoury caught Sarah on the shins causing her swift retreat. When she turned back to her prize, she saw her assailant already had it firmly tucked under her arm.

Feeling more than a little aggrieved, Sarah decided to abandon her quest and hobbled to the exit. Manoeuvring her way round the corner of the travel section, she came upon a familiar face.

'Hello, how are you?' His voice was full of surprised delight.

'Apart from just being assaulted by a geriatric mugger, fine,' she replied rubbing her complaining leg.

'As I'm out of uniform, I'm not in a position to make an arrest, I'm afraid,' he responded with an easy smile.

They waited together for the queue of people to file through the detector gates of the security system by the door.

'You off to do your shopping?' he enquired.

'I'm on my way home. I only came in to replace the library card that disappeared with my handbag and, because it's all computerized, they couldn't issue me with new one on the library van. Such is progress!'

'If you're not in a rush, do you fancy a coffee?' The invitation came as a surprise. 'Why not?' Sarah replied after only a second's hesitation.

The nearest reasonable café was in Theatre Square only a couple of minutes walk. As they crossed the pedestrianized area at the top of Regent Street, he asked, 'I'm glad I bumped into you, I've been meaning to get in touch. Are you still getting those calls? Did you know BT has special nuisance call advisors?'

'Actually, your suggestion about the answerphone seems to have done the trick. I've heard nothing for a week now. I was thinking only this morning that I should write and thank you.' So that was the reason for the invitation. Sarah felt vaguely disappointed. Perhaps she should mention the incident with the mail order books. She decided to wait. Best not to seem completely helpless. She could always drop it into the conversation later.

'That's good. I've been looking into it and, if they do start up again, ring the phone company straight away and they can put a block on that number so they can't ring your phone any more.'

Should she feel flattered that he'd bothered to chase it up on her behalf? She hadn't requested police action.

When he straightened up, which he did only rarely, Sarah realized he was taller than she'd remembered him. Out of uniform, the slightly dishevelled air was even more marked. His tie was askew with the knot loosened a fraction from the collar. As they sat down at one of the outside tables, he leaned back in the chair opposite and she could see the badly-ironed shirt, though clean, gaped a little as it stretched over the stomach bulging slightly over his low slung, faded brown chords.

The sheltered corner of the square formed a pleasant suntrap and, as they sat sipping tea and munching on toasted teacakes, the conversation flowed easily about all manner of inconsequential things. They were soon on first name terms and Sarah could not help being flattered by the way the smiling eyes never left her face and seemed to hang on every word she uttered even though she kept telling herself it was all part of the natural technique of his job.

As she sat looking into the warm, sympathetic face, she wondered, not for the first time, why it was that eyes held such fascination for her. While other girls had swooned at his rugged good looks, it'd been the unusual light golden brown of Nathan's eyes fringed with long ginger lashes that had first attracted her to him. Matt's were a greeny-blue and changed colour as he moved his head.

He didn't probe, no intrusive questions, if fact he said very little. Soon Sarah found herself telling him about Nathan and how they'd met at Bath University. She'd gone back to complete her PhD and he was in his final year of a Science degree. Although the mature students on post graduate courses didn't go in for a great deal of socializing, the Student Union wanted to put on a summer production to raise money for charity and Sarah was talked into taking part in one of the choral pieces.

'Bit of a whirlwind romance really. We were married six months later. A rather bleak November day, as I recall. Perhaps I should have taken that as an omen! Anyway, we both loved the West Country and had friends in the area so we decided to find jobs locally, which is how I come to be here.' The warm eyes never left her face. 'I can see why you're so good at your job,' she said with a laugh as she poured out another cup of tea. 'Ve have vays of making you talk! I bet it takes you no time at all to get people to part with all their secrets.' Sarah was embarrassed at revealing so much of herself to this comparative stranger. 'Now it's your turn. Tell me something about you.'

'Not much to tell,' he shrugged. 'I'm a real local. Born and brought up in Swindon, never lived anywhere else. Been in the force for over twenty years now. A widower. I live with my son, Paul in the next street to my mother who helps bring him up. That's about all there is.'

'How old is your son?'

'Thirteen, with a birthday coming up in a couple of months. He's a good kid.'

'It must be difficult for you bringing him up on your own.'

It was on the tip of her tongue to ask how long his wife had been dead but decided that if he'd have wanted to talk about her he would have said. Sarah struggled to think of something to fill the sudden uncomfortable hiatus in the conversation.

Sarah stared across the square at the prominent poster on the wall of the theatre advertising the coming production of "The Way of the World".

'I wouldn't mind seeing that,' Matt said following the line of her gaze. 'I quite enjoy restoration comedy.'

'It should be good. The company are doing a pre-London run. I think we saw something by the same director three or four years ago although I can't remember which play.'

'You like the theatre?' he asked casually.

'We used to go regularly but I haven't been in ages.'

It was one of the things she missed most after the break up with Nathan. Though the Wyvern Theatre didn't have a lot of drama on offer, with several cities within an hour's drive, such trips had been a regular treat, what Nathan laughingly called their one extravagance. It never seemed the same going on her own. She'd tried once but felt so out-of-place standing about staring at the paintings on the wall while sipping the poor quality, white wine during the interval that she'd never repeated the experience. And it took away much of the enjoyment not being able to discuss the play with anyone afterwards.

Sarah sat lost in her thoughts for a while. When she glanced up, he was looking at her thoughtfully.

'Would you think me very forward if I suggested we see it together?'

The invitation came as a surprise, however, Sarah agreed. Apart from the regular get-togethers with Elizabeth, it had been a long time since she'd spent an evening out in pleasant, undemanding company.

'I think the box office opens around four o'clock. We could wander over now, if you like, and see if they have any seats.' He raised a questioning eyebrow.

Sarah picked up her bag and, with all the bustle of signalling the waitress and paying the bill, the slight tension disappeared.

Inevitably the seats for the next week's Friday and Saturday performances were already fully booked but the girl in the kiosk managed to find something to offer them for the Thursday.

'Could you make it?' he asked tentatively as if expecting her to find an excuse to claim she was already busy.

'That would be fine.'

He brushed aside her tentative suggestion that they should go Dutch. It was a strange situation with the two of them dancing around one another in the attempt not to make too much of spending an evening together.

'We could meet downstairs in the bar before the performance.'

'Only on condition that you let me buy the drinks,' she said, trying her best to sound suave and at ease.

Neither of them quite knew how to bring the meeting to a close and they wandered over to look at the productions stills and read the reviews displayed on the wall.

'I love all the costumes and wigs. They're certainly very colourful.' It was time to go their separate ways. 'Still,' she said, looking at her watch, 'I must be getting back. Thank you for the tea.'

'My pleasure. See you next Thursday.'

At the big glass doors, Sarah turned back and gave a wave. He returned a broad smile then continued studying the reviews. Anyone would think they were gauche teenagers rather than professionals who spent their working lives dealing with people, she thought as she walked briskly back to the car park.

Chapter 9

Having worked her way through the half dozen sections of The Sunday Telegraph, Sarah picked up the general knowledge cross-word from the previous day's paper and half-heartedly attempted to fill it in. She managed most of the history and literature questions but she couldn't be bothered to get up from her comfortable position, feet up on the settee, to check the atlas for the couple of geography teasers that lay teetering on the edge of her memory.

It was the Sunday between the Italian and Luxembourg Grand Prix. Perhaps, she thought to herself ruefully, her enthusiasm for Formula One was as much because it took up most of the endless afternoon as anything else. It certainly didn't have the appeal it used to back in the days when races where won by drivers making daring overtaking moves that had your heart in your mouth. The most exciting thing that'd happened in the last race was Ferrari's Technical Director, Ross Brawn, eating his mid-race banana while Michael Schumacher continued to lead the pack around the circuit as he'd been doing all season.

When the rest of the world was busy being a family together, there were times when Sunday afternoons stretched interminably. Was it any wonder that so many single career women became obsessed with work? She'd made a pact with herself when she moved into the flat that, baring genuine emergencies, she wouldn't allow herself to even think about anything to do with college on Sundays.

The sky was a uniform drab grey as she turned to look out of the window and the sudden gust that spattered noisy spots of rain against the pane put the final damper on any idea of braving the cold and going for a walk.

At the end of the lecture to herself on indulging in blatant self pity, a trend to which she seemed to have become pathetically prone of late, the phone rang. Her body tensed, even though the last menace call had been over a week ago. The pre-recorded message kicked in.

'It's me. Only rang to see how you are. I'll try and catch you later.'

As soon as she heard a normal voice, she put out her hand and lifted the receiver before even registering that it was Nathan. Had she realized, she might have left it and given herself more time to compose herself. Over the couple of years since the separation, mutual friends had passed on news of his welfare but it'd been a good six months since they'd last spoken to each other.

'I'm here,' she interrupted, uncertain of how to continue.

'I've only just heard about your dreadful ordeal, I'd have got in touch sooner...'

Sarah cut him off, dismissing it as a minor incident she'd almost forgotten about. He even knew about her being taken to the hospital and she'd to explain that as well.

He seemed reluctant to hang up and asked after her family. 'How's Todd? Did the specialist come up with anything?'

She gave him the latest news. Her eight-year-old nephew had been ill for several months with bouts of high temperature and stomach upsets. He'd changed from his normal happy, highly active state to mooching around complaining of feeling generally unwell. At first, the doctor had talked about some vague infection but no amount of antibiotics seemed to make any difference. Diagnosis was proving difficult and Todd's poor state of health was inevitably a cause of great concern to all the family.

'How did you hear about Todd's latest tests?' she asked suspiciously.

'Your mother told me.'

'Why did she contact you? Was it to tell you about the attack on me?' Sarah was beginning to feel betrayed on all sides.

'No.' She could hear the surprise in his voice. 'She happened to mention your mugger when I rang. She thought I'd already heard. You know we still keep in touch.'

'Of course. I'd forgotten.'

Though Sarah had never been persona grata with her in-laws, surprisingly Nathan had always got on well with her parents. His privileged, public school background had proved no barrier and there were times when she'd felt he was more eager to make the trek across to Norfolk to see them than Sarah had been. Even now, she thought ruefully, he probably found it easier to find things to chat about with her mother than she did. She loved her parents dearly, but they shared so few interests. She'd never been able to persuade them to come and stay in the new flat and her visits back home only seem to underline the growing distance between them.

'Thanks for getting in touch.' She tried to bring our conversation to a close.

'Actually, Sarah, there was something else,' he hesitated. 'I wondered if we could get together, perhaps have a meal somewhere?'

'I am very busy,' she answered apprehensively.

'You have to eat.' Trust him to think that she'd been referring to work rather than a hectic social life. 'Please. There's something I want to ask you. How about Tuesday?'

'There's a prize giving at one of the schools I can't get out of.' She felt rather smug that he'd chosen the one evening she couldn't make.

'Sounds fun.'

'It involves several of my students who are going back to get their exam certificates and I'm presenting the prizes.' She could hear the testiness in her voice and resented the way he'd managed to put her on the defensive. The picture of a crabby old spinster with no life of her own he'd made her portray was too close to home.

'How about the week after?' There was an urgency in his voice that made her feel cold.

'All right,' she agreed grudgingly.

'I'll pick you up at your place at half seven.'

He put the phone down before she could change her mind. 'Damn you,' she said to the dull ringing tone and replaced the receiver with a bang.

Nathan still had the power to upset her. The break-up had been entirely her doing. She was the one who'd thrown him out. For months afterwards Nathan would phone or turn up on the doorstep pleading with her to forgive him. She'd even had him in tears, begging her on his knees. It had taken a long time to convince him that there was no going back. Neither of them had wanted to remain in the house they'd shared so they agreed to sell the place and go their separate ways though neither of them brought up the word divorce. Her staunch Catholic views may have taken a jolt, but for her, it still wasn't an option although she could hardly expect Nathan to see things the same way. After two years, he probably wanted to make it all final.

When Nathan assured her that his betrayal had happened only the once, she believed him. And, though he never tried to put the blame on Tanya, Sarah never doubted that it been she who made all the running.

In retrospect, she found it hard to feel bitterness towards Tanya. The girl had always been besotted with Nathan. All her life, she'd been brought up by both her mother and his to assume that her place would be by his side. Even after Nathan and Sarah were married, when they met at some family get-together, Tanya would be there at his elbow with those enormous, Princess Diana eyes gazing up into his giving her shy, beguiling smile. There was no doubt that she wanted to be queen of his heart! It never occurred to Sarah, even at the time, that Nathan had deliberately planned to be unfaithful. If she was honest she could see how it all happened. She'd been preoccupied with her new job and then abandoned him for a four-week course up north leaving him feeling lonely and neglected. The whole sorry mess had probably started as a pleasant meal with an old friend, then coffee at Tanya's place when he took her home, another brandy, seductive background music and easy conversation by the warm glow of the fire.

What had added to all the pain was the way Sarah had found out. After that fateful evening, Tanya, no doubt believing that she'd at long last won the man of her dreams, confessed as much to her mother. It was a matter of hours before the good news was passed on to her dearest friend, Sarah's mother-in-law, Geraldine. Perhaps, if it hadn't been dear Geraldine who'd accidentally on purpose let it slip, Sarah would have come round to forgiving him. Perhaps not. She was a product of her upbringing.

Sarah knew in some quarters she had the reputation for being hard and without feeling but she'd never worn her heart on her sleeve. Friends and family only saw an unforgiving woman, the perfectionist, who wouldn't tolerate a single meaningless mistake. What they didn't understand, and she couldn't explain, was the depth of pain that betrayal had caused. Sarah knew that Nathan had a string of affairs before they were married. At university, women lined up for the chance of getting into his bed. It may have been her religious upbringing or perhaps her naïve, romanticized view of love and marriage, but Sarah had lost something precious that she could never have again.

Nathan was the only man, was the only real boyfriend, she'd ever had. At her all girls' school she'd been too busy studying and in the wild, heady days as an undergraduate, she'd done all her socialising within a group. Naturally there'd been the odd date, but she'd never been out with the same bloke more than two or three times – not wanting to get involved. Nathan's interest in pursuing their friend-ship came as a great surprise to her as much as to everyone else.

Sarah still found it amazing that the man who could have any girl on the campus had eyes for her. Nathan had the stature of a Greek god with broad shoulders, narrow hips, breathtaking good-looks plus great wit and what was more he was always the life and soul of any gathering. She, on the other hand, was the archetypal ordinary – average height, mid-brown hair and eyes, a reasonable figure and if not exactly plain, nothing special either and, in those days, she wore glasses. None of that would matter, of course, if she had a sparkling personality but she'd always been the serious, retiring type with no small talk whatsoever. Her only claim to fame was what the Deputy Head at her Convent school called, a first-rate brain.

Her relationship with Nathan had developed against all the odds. She could imagine his crowd asking what he saw in the pathetic mouse so much older than him. Sarah heard on the grapevine that they'd nicknamed her Anne Boleyn because she tantalized him by holding him at bay – the only woman who refused to jump straight into his bed. Later, his mother moved heaven and earth to keep them apart. It took a long time for Nathan to persuade Sarah that there was a future for them both. That single night with Tanya, which others saw as a small indiscretion, had destroyed the world that she'd stepped into so tentatively.

If only, if only! There was no point in going over it all again.

She'd expected that, when he eventually accepted that the marriage was over, he would ask for a divorce. It hadn't happened. When Tanya realized, even after the separation was final, that Nathan was never going to marry her, she decided to cut her losses. She found herself a new man and, to the best of Sarah's knowledge, was now living happily somewhere in the Midlands and was probably a proud, adoring mum.

It was foolish to think that Nathan would wait around forever in the hope she'd change her mind. She'd no idea who his latest girl friend was. Though mutual friends let her know what he was up to every now and again, they tactfully kept that little snippet of information from her.

It must have been her generally depressed state that made the prospect of taking that final irrevocable step fill her with such emptiness. What right had she to deny Nathan happiness when she'd been the one to end the marriage? And, more to the point, why should she feel so miserable at the thought that he now had some else?

God, she hated Sundays!

Chapter 10

After a typical busy Monday, Sarah arrived back at her flat in the early evening tired and hungry. It didn't improve her humour when she saw the pile of junk mail on the mat. To add to the ever growing assortment of freebees pushed through the letterbox, over the previous few days she'd had to contend with an influx of unwanted holiday brochures, plant catalogues and all manner of special offers addressed to her personally. Muttering curses on the database that had released her details, she bent down to scoop it all up and discovered a small square package hidden beneath the free local newspaper. Resisting the temptation to open it there and then, she made her way up the stairs.

The seal broke easily and she flicked back the card cover protecting the plastic box to reveal a CD of "Les Miserables". The unexpected present gave her a warm glow. She'd raved to anyone who'd listen about that trip to the Hippodrome in Bristol to see the show. It'd been one of the last outings with Nathan before the break-up, but even that painful association couldn't spoil the memory of what had proved a magical evening.

Although musicals weren't really her thing, Nathan had been keen to go. After all the hype about the production, she'd been even more sceptical although, as they made their way out of the theatre at the end of the performance, she confessed that it was the best thing she'd ever seen. For the rest of the evening they'd talked endlessly about the passion of the music, the quality of the singing and not least the sheer drama of the massive dark structures that moved across the stage to form the oppressive buildings crowding the Paris slums and then later twisted and turned to become the massive barricades. If it hadn't been so difficult to get tickets – the show was sold out within weeks of it being advertized – they would have gone a second time.

The next day, Nathan had made a special trip into town to buy a video of the Concert Performance at the Albert Hall. When the two of them split up, the video went with him. Although a CD gave no impression of the breathtaking spectacle on stage, she was delighted to have the music once again. She took the case out of its cardboard cover to find the note that went it.

Her pleasure evaporated rapidly as she scanned the paper. Not a friendly missive but an invoice. Why, after the previous book fiasco, had she been foolish enough to think that it was anything another than an attempt to cause her more inconvenience? Having opened the thing, she would now have to go to the trouble of parcelling it up with a covering note to explain that she hadn't been the one to send for it. The choice of a piece of music that would have given her such pleasure made the disappointment all the more bitter. He'd succeeded in achieving more than nuisance; her persecutor had tainted a treasured memory.

The fourth Tuesday of every month was scheduled for her meeting with Sir Richard Waveny, chairman of the Board of Governors. Immediately following her appointment, she'd been left in no doubt that she wasn't his preferred candidate. He'd been openly antagonist at governors' meetings when he'd scour every report or proposal she put forward for some unsubstantiated detail. He would question every figure and demand a detailed explanation of any point where he could find an alternative to her suggestion. Though, after he'd taken over as chairman, things were no longer so acrimonious, she still had to ensure that she could justify every decision. It meant spending a great deal of time considering every option, double checking her facts and marshalling her arguments. But at least it gave her the advantage of appreciating the pros and cons of all the possible courses of action. Not only had their boardroom battles taught her to be skilful in putting the case for her preferred pro-posal, on the occasions when the voting went against her, she could accept the alternative, aware of the merits of that particular plan.

Sir Richard arrived earlier than usual for their September meeting and she was surprised when he knocked and came straight into her office without having himself announced, as was his custom.

'How are you, Dr Harcourt?' He was the only person who habitu-ally called her by her title. Apart from the college stationery, she rarely used it.

She got up and moved to join him at the large circular table. Though the college had conference rooms, including the recently refurbished Boardroom where governors' meetings were held, they weren't conducive for only a handful of people. She preferred to use her own office for small groups, particularly as much of her life seemed to revolve around meetings.

'I do hope you're over your dreadful experience.' There was genuine concern in his voice and he looked at her shrewdly.

Sarah felt a sudden alarm. How could he possibly know about the persecution campaign being waged against her?

'You were attacked on the way home, I believe. I appreciate it was some time ago, however, as you know, I was on holiday until last week and I've only just heard about it.'

A wave of relief swept through her. She could only hope her panic hadn't shown in her face. Sir Richard was not one to miss anything. 'It was a very minor incident, Sir Richard. I had my bag stolen that was all. It's one of those stories that's been much embroidered as it's spread around.'

'Still bad enough for you to have to take time off,' he persisted. 'And to my knowledge, you've never had a day's sick leave in the seven years you have been with us so it must have had some effect.'

'I did have to wait for the locks to be changed the next morning and was asked to go to the police station to make a statement but I came in later that afternoon.' Sir Richard was the last person she wanted to think that she'd used the opportunity to neglect her work.

'Really.' He looked a little surprised. 'I'd got the impression it was much longer. Still, it must have been a very unpleasant, not to mention nerve-wracking, experience.' The pale grey eyes stared at her appraisingly. What other gossip had the old boy heard? For a fleeting moment, she got the impression that he'd expected to find her jumping at her own shadow. She'd have to work hard at keeping up the efficient image.

'Shall we take a look at the proposals for handling the faculty review?' she countered. The sooner they got off the topic of her state of health the better. 'I'll get the papers.' She went to her filing cabinet.

The review was the final stage in the major restructuring of the college and the changes in the faculty system would have a major impact. Redefining the areas of responsibility of the faculty directors was always going to be a contentious issue and seeing it through would be the greatest test of her position as principal so far. The current structure was no longer suited to needs of a modern Further Education college and, more to the point, was extremely expensive. The division into five faculties, each led by a director on a top level salary scale, supported by a multiplicity of heads of department was fast becoming ruinous to the economic viability of the college. It'd been made clear at her appointment that rationalizing the whole staffing structure would be a priority.

'If you're sure you feel up to it. If you wish, I'm quite happy to postpone our meeting.'

She stopped and turned to look at him. With a confidence she didn't feel, she said, 'Sir Richard if I wasn't on top of the job, I wouldn't be here in the office. The only reason I don't have the papers ready on the table is because you are...' she glanced up at the clock, 'twelve minutes early.'

From the look on his face, she realized she must have sounded sharper than she'd intended so she gave him a broad smile and continued, 'I'll ask Lucy to get us some coffee.'

They settled down to consider her ideas on possible ways of tackling the review. She gave him little time to comment as she pushed sheet after sheet in front of him outlining the advantages and disadvantages of each strategy. They soon settled into their normal businesslike routine and each time he demanded more background detail, she was able to extract it from the file of corroborating data. Only once did he ask for information she didn't have among the papers she'd prepared but it took only moments to go to her filing cabinet and produce it.

After three quarters of an hour, he sat back.

'I can't imagine there's anything you haven't considered.' He looked across and actually smiled at her. 'So, assuming that the Board of Governors can agree the guide lines for the cross-college committee, whom would you like to see on the working party?'

'We must have representation from each faculty and at all levels, nonetheless I will argue very strongly for the inclusion of Dev Sharma and Anna Margilewska.'

'Very politically correct,' he said sententiously.

'Possibly, but I want those two there because Mr Sharma's faculty is the one most under threat and Anna isn't only bright and ambitious, she's popular with the younger staff and can take them with her when the changes come into force.' She was annoyed that he thought she'd chosen them only because one was a member of an ethnic minority and the other a woman. 'Ultimately it's up to the staff to decide.'

'True, but as chairman, I've no doubt, you'll be able to help them see the bigger picture.'

'No,' she said firmly. 'I think it would be a mistake for me to be on the working party at all.'

'You want to distance yourself from any mistakes it might make?'

'Certainly not!' she snapped. 'The thought of letting things out of my control will no doubt keep me awake at night. However, the only way to ensure commitment to the outcome is to demonstrate that this working group is a genuinely democratic means of influencing the future of the college.'

He raised his hands in surrender. 'I do appreciate that. I was only teasing.'

She felt her cheeks going a bright scarlet. 'I'm sorry, Sir Richard...'

He waved away her protest. 'I suppose that means you are happy to let George Fitzgibbon hold the reins.'

'I'm sure he will do an excellent job in keeping everything on track.' It flashed through her mind that he must know of their earlier contretemps. Not much happened around the college that Sir Richard didn't get to hear about.

They talked over a few minor details and when he left she felt utterly drained. It was a good job he couldn't see her slumped over the table looking anything but the strong arm at the helm. At least she'd given a good performance. With luck, he had no suspicions how she'd had to battle through as though it had been a normal meeting and her mind not constantly distracted by thoughts of what dire mishaps her tormentor had laid in store for her to trip over.

Except for her occasional escapes with Elizabeth, it was rare for Sarah to take a proper lunch break. Often, she made do with little more than an apple, but after that encounter, she couldn't summon up the level of concentration required to settle back at her desk. She needed some fresh air. As she was about to move, her phone buzzed.

'Sarah, have you got a minute?'

'Can it wait, Barry? I was just about to go out for some lunch.'

'It won't take long. It's personal rather than work.'

Curiosity as much as anything prompted her to agree.

He was up in a couple of minutes. He came in and carefully shut the door.

'I don't know if I should tell you this, but,' he paused waiting for her to encourage him.

She resisted the temptation to say, 'Then don't,' and kept a blank expression on her face.

'Sir Richard came to see me first thing this morning. He said he wanted an update on how the student work experience was going but then he started pumping me about you.' If Barry expected a reaction, he didn't get one. 'He seemed to think that you were a bit under power, not quite on top of things anymore. Naturally, I said I hadn't noticed any problems but I thought you ought to know.'

'Fine,' she said nonchalantly, getting up and reaching for her jacket.

He hovered at the door. It was clear he'd expected a different response.

'Was there anything else, Barry?'

He shook his head and having no further excuse to stay, went out. She could hear him laughing with Lucy and decided to wait until he'd gone.

Lucy looked up when she came out. The secretary already had her sandwich box open and was about to bite into an enormous filled bap when she saw Sarah. 'I've got a lot to get through today so I thought I'd eat this here.'

Sarah smiled. Lucy wasn't only an excellent secretary and a hard worker, she was, more to the point in that place of intrigue and cut-throat ambition, unswervingly loyal to her boss. Though the rest of the staff appeared to regard her as the formal and remote Principal, she and Lucy had a very relaxed relationship. Although Sarah would never discuss her private life with Lucy, they'd been known to have lively discussions over their mutual interest in Formula One racing. Lucy was a Schumacher fan but Sarah refused to forgive him for the time he deprived Damon Hill of the championship way back in '94.

'I'm going to pop into town. Can I get you anything?' Sarah wasn't being helpful. It was her excuse to get Lucy chatting so she could seemingly casually drop Sir Richard's name into the conversation. 'He seemed very convivial today; did he stop to talk with you?'

'Funny you should say that, he did ask me about that stuff for the printers that went missing from your desk the other week. Heaven knows how he heard about that. He wanted to know where it turned up.'

'So what did you say?'

Lucy gave her an old fashioned look. 'I told him you found it in your room and one of the cleaners must have moved it when they were tidying up.'

Dear Lucy. She knew exactly where it'd been found. Even if she thought Sarah was going doolally she'd never let on to anyone else. 'You're an angel.'

'I also pointed out that Miss Robinson should've made sure she gave it to one of us personally if she wanted it back in a hurry.' Sarah looked at her in surprise. 'If she's sneaky enough to go telling tales to Sir Richard behind your back, it's only right that someone point out that the whole mix up was her fault in the first place.'

Sarah's mind was working overtime as she went out of the building. So many silly, little things had gone wrong in the last few weeks with files misplaced and mistakes in her documents that she couldn't explain. The really worrying thing was that Sir Richard seemed to know about all about them. He must think she was beginning to lose her grip, but she could hardly tell him that she was being subjected to a hate campaign. It sounded so ludicrous that he was bound to think she was having a nervous breakdown of some kind.

Perhaps she ought to see her doctor after all. She wasn't getting enough sleep, waking in the small hours then tossing and turning till dawn. At two o'clock in the morning the mind plays silly tricks. Even the wind outside seemed to echo that awful sibilant whisper calling her name. Several times she'd got up to check the security locks not only on the door but also the windows which, as she lived in a first floor flat, would prove a difficult mode of entry for any intruder. On a bad night, she still woke bathed in sweat, trembling at the image of the shadowy face coming closer and closer to her own and the feel of hands fondling her cringing body.

Chapter 11

The doorbell rang as she was stepping out of the shower. Swathed in a bathrobe and a towel around her wet hair, she padded down to the half landing and peered through the window. Sarah groaned inwardly as she recognized the dark blue BMW parked on the road. Nathan was invariably late. It'd been one of the little niggles that she'd found so infuriating. Trust him to break the habit of a lifetime and arrive before she was ready! For some reason she couldn't adequately explain, she'd planned to give him no excuse to come up. She'd wanted her flat to be a Nathan free zone, a place with no associations with the painful past.

Downstairs, she pulled open the door trying to keep out of sight of any possible passers-by.

'You're a quarter of an hour early,' she snapped.

'I've missed you too,' he laughed. He bent to give her a quick peck on the lips before she'd a chance to step back out of reach.

As she looked up into the familiar face, a shiver went through her. She'd forgotten just how good-looking he was. Just keep reminding yourself how much he hurt you, she told herself fiercely. He's history. You've both moved on! Don't weaken.

'I suppose you'd better come up.' Not wanting to give him the satisfaction of seeing her confusion, she turned and hurried to the stairs, angry with herself for the effect he was having on her.

'What a magnificent staircase! You could walk six abreast up here.' In a few easy strides he'd caught her up and they mounted the final flight side by side. 'I didn't realize you'd moved into a stately home.'

She listened for the note of mockery in his voice but he seemed to be genuinely impressed. He stood stroking the mahogany balustrade and surveying the broad expanse of the landing larger than the main room in the majority of modern houses. His reaction softened her antagonism. Her home meant a great deal to her. Brought up in a small, cramped terrace, sharing a bedroom with a much younger sister where the only quiet place to do homework was on the lift-down flap of the kitchen dresser, she'd learnt to appreciate space.

'It's part of the original house. Late Victorian with delusions of grandeur. Apart from dividing off the stairs from the flat below and putting in a modern kitchen and bathroom, they made very little alteration when they did the conversion.' She led him into the living room. 'You can wait in here while I get dressed.'

As she watched him taking in the room's elegant proportions, she realized how much she wanted him to approve. She stayed just long enough to catch the expression on his face. Like everyone else who came for the first time, he was drawn to the enormous picture window that looked over the Vale of the White Horse. The original house had been built on the crest of the ridge; no doubt the pride and joy of some up and coming merchant eager to demonstrate his success by having a fashionable villa built in the Queen Anne revival style. Looking down, below the narrow strip of terrace that was now the garden of the downstairs flat, one could see the road before it snaked round the slither of mid 1960s development extending from the main village on what had once been the old grounds to the side of the house. Looking north, beyond the wooded slope that marked the precipitous edge of the escarpment, one could see for miles. The view alone was worth the exorbitant cost of the place and, though the high ceilings made her heating bills a nightmare, it was a price worth paying.

Her clothes were laid out ready on the bed and she was back within five minutes.

'That was quick even for you!' It'd been a standing joke that, despite makeup and putting in her contact lenses, she was always ready long before him. 'That emerald suits you. You should wear bold colours more often.'

She could tell he was trying hard. He'd remembered that effusive compliments embarrassed her, although, despite herself, she was pleased that he approved of her choice. The dress had been a wildly extravagant purchase, not only because of its cost but because its striking colour was a major departure from her usual subdued blues or bland neutrals. It'd been a rash decision, not even bought with a special occasion in mind. She'd caught sight of it on a model as she was walking through the store and had fallen in love with it there and then. Feeling vaguely sinful, she'd tried it on and when she discovered that it still looked wonderful with her inside it, the temptation was too great.

'The table's booked for eight so we've plenty of time. I thought we'd go to that new French place out at Lechlade. Have you tried it?'

She shook her head. Trust him to choose somewhere outrageously expensive.

She had to admit that the place had a wonderful setting. Because they were early, and the evening was mild for late September, they took their drinks out onto the terrace and sat looking across the river. Sarah found herself sneaking a look at his left hand as he, no doubt, did hers. He was still wearing his wedding ring. She wondered what his current girl friend thought of that.

The menu was exotic. She glanced at it and reverted to old habits. 'You choose.'

'You look as though you could do with a decent meal. You've lost a lot of weight.' It was said lightly but he looked her up and down appraisingly. 'I bet you're not eating properly.'

She'd lost a good stone, much of it in the last six months, which was the last time their paths had crossed. Most nights she worked late and by the time she got home rarely fancied eating a proper meal. There didn't seem a lot of point going to a great deal of trouble just for one. If she bothered at all, it was chilled meals from the supermarket.

'So how's work?' he asked, tactfully changing the subject in response to her scowl.

'Fine,' she answered noncommittally.

'Which means it's bloody awful. Are the greenfly still chomping all the foliage?'

She couldn't suppress a smile. Nathan had always referred to her senior staff as tiny-minded insects intent on devouring any creative ideas she came up with. He knew better than anyone how George's pedestrian attention to the minor details, Barry's plastic charm and Eunice's constant carping at the failure of teaching staff to concern themselves with the pastoral needs of students drove her to distraction. It'd been a wonderful release to be able to vent her venom at the unreasonable behaviour of so-called-professional colleagues when she got home each evening. The ridiculous word pictures Nathan painted of their antics had always helped put the petty sniping of inter-faculty rivalry into perspective.

'That's the price of management,' she said.

When the coffee arrived, he started probing again. 'Are you sure there's nothing wrong? You sounded strained when you answered the phone.'

She must have had too much wine. Before she realized what she was doing, she was telling him about the mysterious phone calls. A voice in her head told her to stop but she could read the real concern in his eyes and he knew better than to fuss. It was enough to know that he still cared.

'I expect it's the same person who's been filling in all these requests for all sorts of brochures in my name. I've been inundated with catalogues for book and record clubs and every exotic holiday going. Mind you,' she went on with a laugh, 'I thought it was a bit much when I found the stuff about orthopaedic beds, stair lifts and walk-in baths when I got back this evening.'

'That sounds like a student with a warped sense of humour.'

'I doubt it! It's someone with a good idea of my taste in literature and music and general interests. Still, the catalogues I can put up with but the special offers are getting to be a damned nuisance. Having to write back to explain that I hadn't sent for the books, jewellery or whatever, is a real pain. Yesterday, I had to traipse all the way to the post office to send back two boxes of bedding plants. Apart from causing me hassle, heaven knows why he's doing it.'

'Probably some sad individual, jealous of your success.'

'I hadn't thought of that,' she laughed, 'but don't ask me to waste any sympathy on the creep. I'm too busy feeling sorry for myself.'

'That doesn't sound like you.'

Trust him to pick up on the undercurrent in what she'd intended as a flippant remark.

'I'm not all Steel Queen,' she said, still trying to keep the whole thing casual.

He raised an enquiring eyebrow and despising herself for it, she suddenly realized she wanted his reassurance.

At first he said all the right things but then he spoilt it all. 'You're working yourself too hard.'

'Don't patronize me,' she gave a warning growl.

The last thing she wanted was sympathy. She needed him to shake her out of her self-pity, to tell her she could cope and wasn't coming apart at the seams. He flashed one of his sorry smiles with all the old charm. 'You still go jogging at the crack of dawn?'

Although he despised weight training and dismissed those who went to the gym as trendies, Nathan played squash regularly for love of the game. He'd developed his spectacularly muscled torso as a consequence of being a keen, competitive swimmer. Neither activity interested her so she'd taken up gentle running. It helped her clear her head and she preferred to exercise alone.

'I try to manage three times a week but it's not so much fun as the mornings get darker.'

55

A frown crossed his face. 'You want to take care up there where you are now. It's not as safe along those deserted country lanes as it was where we used to live.'

'If you say so.' There was little point in getting drawn into an argument about something so trivial.

'You look tired. Are you getting enough sleep?'

She glowered at him across the table. If he dared to suggest she see her doctor, she'd get up and walk out on him there and then. This wasn't what she wanted from him of all people.

'You ought to take a break. I bet you didn't have a holiday this summer.'

She could hardly deny it. It wasn't just because she'd been busy but as Nathan, of all people, ought to have appreciated, she'd no one to go with. Most of her friends were married and the only one who wasn't couldn't afford the sort of holiday that would interest her. The thought of going alone didn't appeal.

'And where did you get to this year?' she asked, as much to steer away the conversation from her affairs rather than any genuine interest.

Nathan became uncharacteristically reticent and busied himself topping up his already half full glass of water. 'I had a couple of weeks away with Mother.'

Sarah smiled in spite of herself. 'I bet that was nice. And how is Geraldine?'

To say that she and Geraldine didn't get on was something of an understatement. When Nathan rang his parents to tell them they'd just got engaged he was immediately summoned home. Nathan never told Sarah the details of that conversation but she could imagine it. Geraldine would've been in floods of tears. It was bad enough that Sarah wasn't Tanya, the daughter-in-law she'd always planned, but Sarah was far too old for him – six years his senior – and, the ultimate crime, she was a Catholic. Geraldine's father had been a Freemason and she'd grown up with some very strange ideas. When she learnt that Sarah's father worked on the assembly line in a factory, her mother was a school dinner lady and they lived in a council house, the woman nearly had apoplexy. How on earth would she be able to hold up her head amongst friends and family at her only son's wedding when all the relations on the bride's side would have no idea which knife and fork to use and had probably never used a napkin in their lives and wouldn't know what it was for?

Sarah must have given a wry smirk at the thoughts going through her head, which Nathan promptly misinterpreted.

'It was very enjoyable,' he said rather snootily. 'We went on one of those accompanied tour things advertised in the Sunday supplements so we were with other people practically all the time.'

'Where did you go?'

'Well,' He had the grace to look abashed. 'China actually.'

'Very nice,' Sarah said with a fixed smile on her face.

She wanted to call him all the names under the sun. How could he? He knew it'd been her life-long dream to go to China. Her shelves were stuffed with books on all things Chinese and she'd made him sit through the video of "The Last Emperor" three times so that she could enjoy the shots of the Forbidden City. A China tour was to have been their next holiday together. They'd even started collecting the brochures.

For the first few years after they were married, all their hard earned cash went on doing up the old house. Luxuries had to wait until central heating had been installed and the rotten windows frames replaced. Once things became a little easier and they could contemplate a holiday of some sort, Nathan had suggested they put off fitting the new kitchen and splash out on realizing her dream. She'd been the cautious one and managed to convince him that they'd enjoy it all the more if they waited another year or so. There was no need to go without a break, she'd argued, they could go camping. Never having had a holiday in anything less than a four star hotel, Nathan drew the line at sleeping under canvas. In the end they had a pleasant week bed and breakfasting in the Lake District.

'It was Mother's idea. She was keen to see the Terracotta Warriors and the Great Wall,' he excused himself.

When his father died from a sudden heart attack not long after she and Nathan were married, it was only natural that Nathan, as an only child, should feel an even stronger obligation towards his mother. Sarah conceded that it couldn't have been easy for him with such open hostility between the two women in his life, but when Geraldine sold the Surrey house and moved to be near her beloved son; life became far from easy for any of them.

'You said on the phone there was something you wanted to ask me,' Sarah said tersely before he could start telling her about all the magnificent sights.

'Yes,' he replied tentatively, 'do you still have those books on Byzantine architecture?'

This was the last thing she'd expected. 'I expect they're around somewhere. I doubt I could lay hands on them straight away. They're probably stashed in a box at the back of a cupboard somewhere but I'll root them out for you if you want to borrow them. Since when have you taken an interest in that sort of thing?'

'Oh it's not for me,' he said airily. 'Veronica's thinking of doing an Open University degree but she wants to find out a bit more on the subject before she decides exactly which course to opt for.'

'I'll see what I can find,' Sarah said trying hard to keep the ice out of her voice.

It was a bit rich expecting her to lend her things to the woman who'd replaced her in his life though she was determined not to show that it bothered her. And there was no way that she was going to give him the satisfaction of asking about her.

Angry with herself for being jealous, the last vestiges of pleasure in what'd promised to be a pleasant evening drained away.

Chapter 12

She should never have agreed to have dinner with him. Just when she'd begun to think she was over him at long last, she'd let him walk back into her life. That night, Sarah didn't sleep well. She kept playing over the evening in her mind, going over what he'd said, those looks that would soften the resistance of a granite heart, reliving the plethora of emotions. It had been stupid to let down her guard. He'd always been a charmer. She was putty in his hands and he knew it. The trouble was that however much the head knew that, the heart didn't pay attention. He'd caused her enough pain. She'd be an idiot to go through all that again. Best not to meet up in future. Strictly phone calls from now on. Time to put the past behind her and move on.

Sleep stubbornly refused to come and, however hard she tried to think of something else, her thoughts came returning to Nathan. Who knew her vulnerable spots better than Nathan? That business over the China holiday was a case in point. He must know how much it would cut her to the quick to hear about it. Give him his due, that was probably the reason he was so reticent about mentioning where they'd gone in the first place.

She suddenly went cold. There was another explanation. Could it be he was afraid she might put two and two together? If that were the case, he could so easily have lied. But who else would know the effect those books ordered in her name would have on her? Was it his way of getting his own back for throwing him out? It must have hurt his ego. She'd witnessed the golden boy who turned every woman's head at his lowest. She'd made him beg.

The staff car park was crowded when she drove in late next morning. Although Sarah didn't have an allocated parking place, a legacy from her predecessor who wanted to show solidarity with the rest of his staff – fine for him as he lived within walking distance and used his car only rarely – most people respected the fact that she was constantly in and out of the college for various meetings and left a space in the top corner for her. An old green Citroen she didn't recognize, probably belonging to some visitor, was already occupying her slot. By the time she'd wound her way around the cars illegally double parked across the already narrow row ends, she was in a foul mood. It was hard enough trying to ignore the inner turmoil churning away inside and battle through her day as though everything was perfectly normal without things conspiring against her. Eventually she managed to secure a gap half on the churned-up grass verge by the entrance.

She'd come away from her last meeting with a large cardboard box full of booklets and, having to carry it in, didn't appreciate the extra distance she now had to walk. She struggled to find a comfortable position in which to carry box, briefcase, handbag and coat and staggered up the steps into the square at the centre of the complex.

'Can I help you with that?' David Ford appeared at her elbow.

The last thing she wanted was to have to make polite conversation, but the box was heavy. Gratefully, she passed it over.

'Good grief!' David staggered slightly under the weight.

'It's the student guides for the Careers Convention.'

'How's all that going?' She appreciated that he was only making conversation but, shaking off her desire to escape to the solitude of her own room, she forced herself to make use of the opportunity to try to get him involved.

'Very well. There's a great deal of business interest and the committee has already persuaded over sixty local and national companies to take part.' She hoped she didn't sound too over the top.

'It was good last year. My students got a lot out of it, especially those who weren't afraid to ask questions; however I still think we need to do more to promote the college on our own stand. It's all very well talking to the youngsters from schools and showing them what courses are available but, if we want to attract them, we need to do more than just hand out brochures.'

'My feelings exactly.'

'Had you thought of getting the Media department to put together a video showing the students in action? Especially things they don't do in schools like car maintenance or hairdressing. The Open Days demonstrations are fine but there you only get the pupils interested in coming to the college in the first place. The Convention would reach a much larger number.'

'It's certainly a thought,' she replied eagerly. Stupid man, anyone would think he'd hit on a totally new idea. 'We do have several videos but I was wondering if we come up with something a bit more hands on.'

'Get the visiting kids involved in practical things you mean?'

'Doing is always more fun than watching.'

'It would need some thought. The Construction Days we have with the primary school kids laying bricks and bending pipes always go down well.'

'True. That's fine here on site but they couldn't do that in the exhibition hall.'

'There's scope with things like computers. We could take the CAD CAM stuff down there.'

It was good to see David so enthusiastic. When he'd first joined the college, taking over her old position as Director of Business & Information Studies, he'd had a tough time. He'd come with impeccable references and an excellent record of achievements as a Head of Department in a Hampshire college and impressed everyone at his interview with his understanding of the issues. However, after a few weeks, it was evident that he was way out of his depth in managing both people and systems. Sarah had asked Barry to act as his unofficial mentor but it hadn't worked. In the end, she was the one who'd spent hours talking David through the procedures and trying to boost his confidence. As she'd seen him at his weakest, perhaps it was only natural that David would now try to keep his distance.

It'd taken her months to find just the right place to live after the break-up. Sarah's life had suddenly been made hollow and with a hundred-mile-an-hour job, she knew that finding a perfect retreat where she could escape from all the stresses and strains was as important for her sanity as for her material comfort. Discovering the flat had proved the one glimmer of joy in those dark days. Its perfect proportions, from where she could look out over the rolling Wiltshire landscape, had exceeded all her dreams and the enveloping calm she felt take hold of her every time she climbed the stairs each evening helped her to keep things in perspective.

Thanks to some persistent joker, all that was now in danger of being destroyed. As she turned the car round the final bend and caught sight of dark blue door, she felt the tension beginning to take hold as she prepared herself for what might lie in store.

The unwanted brochures continued to arrive at intermittent intervals. Sometimes nothing for a few days then a shower of them would be sitting on the mat waiting for her. She pushed the door open slowly spreading the collection in a great arc. As she stared down, a small brown padded envelope half hidden under the assortment of gaudy catalogues, shouted up at her. Stifling a sob, she seized them up, tucked the pile under her arm and marched up the stairs straight into the living room. She was tempted to throw the lot straight into the wastepaper bin but logic said there might be some proper mail amongst all the rubbish. She dumped it all on the chair. She would sort through it later.

She was almost at the door when she changed her mind. Why ruin her whole evening? Do it now and get it over, she told herself firmly.

At least there were no cards saying that the postman had tried to deliver a parcel. Not that she bothered to go and collect them these days. There was always a slight worry at the back of her mind that she would one day ignore something genuine but if she bothered to chase up every package, she'd be over at the Sorting Office every other week. After three abortive visits, she had a chat with the woman on the desk and came to an arrangement. When she posted back the card the goods would be returned. The woman was probably breaking all the rules but Sarah managed to convince her that she'd have an easier life having to face her boss's wrath rather than Sarah's.

Sarah picked up the padded envelope. A quick glance at the details in the top corner – A Daily Telegraph Hallmarked Silver Offer – confirmed that it was another of her tormentor's hoaxes. Presumably it was a pendant or earrings. She'd seen the advertisement in the previous Saturday's Colour Supplement. At least it wasn't the arch top mantel clock pictured on the page opposite. Sarah had counted no less than eight send-no-money-now offers ranging from a patchwork bedcover to a lightweight vacuum cleaner.

The last present Nathan had given her was earrings; real pearls set in delicate gold filigree baskets. Best not to think about it.

With a thick felt tipped pen, she crossed out her name and address and printed, "Return to sender. Goods not requested by addressee." She'd long since stopped putting herself to the bother of writing a letter of explanation to the various companies concerned.

Her positive action made her feel better and from idle curiosity she glanced at each of the clear plastic-wrapped catalogues to see if she remembered seeing them in the paper. Although she always flicked over the advertisements without interest in the past, for the last couple of weekends she'd decided to turn the whole sorry business into a game and try to guess which of many brochure request forms her joker would fill in for her.

'At least I got those two right,' she said out loud, dropping "Hardwood Conservatories Giant Sale" and "Exclusive Bedroom Furniture" into the bin. The "Luxury Bathrooms and Saunas" and

"Made-to-Measure Curtains" were also fairly predictable but she'd missed the "Roof Renovation System" and the "Up-and-over Garage Doors". Nathan had excelled himself this time. He must have wasted some time sorting out this little lot.

For all the bravado, the sense of unease in the pit of her stomach wouldn't go away. Had she got it all wrong? However good a reason Nathan might think he had for trying to get his own back, surely he couldn't be this petty? But who else had any kind of reason? That was what was so unsettling. Not knowing why.

It wasn't until she got up and went to make herself a cup of tea that she noticed the flashing light on the answerphone. That was all she needed. She walked across to the little table. The red figure seven glowed at her. There was no way that she would have that many genuine calls.

Although the majority of her callers left no message, she'd no idea how many had come from her persecutor. There was a good chance that some could be from reps wanting to talk about mundane things such as double-glazing or insurance. Only rarely did her tormentor speak, more often than not all she could hear was heavy breathing or, more frighteningly, the occasional maniacal laugh.

Taking a deep breath, she pressed the play button. The first two calls were silent but then a deep, solemn voice filled the room. 'I'm calling on behalf of James Watson & Partners Funeral Directors. You completed a form requesting details of our Funeral Repayment Plan and our private Chapel of Rest. I will call again…'

Her hand shot to the stop button and it was as though all her internal organs had sudden shrunk to half their normal size. Definitely not Nathan; not even disguising his voice. It could be someone from a genuine company but she'd no intention of trying to find out.

Determined not to be cowered, she fast-forwarded to the remaining calls. There was no message on the three that followed and a surge of relief swept over her when she eventually heard Elizabeth's cheery voice.

'Do you fancy seeing a film on Friday or shall we just have a meal and a natter? Give me a buzz. Bye.'

So how did it go last night?' Elizabeth was hardly in the door before she was demanding to know all the details.

'It was quite good,' Sarah answered nonchalantly. 'Not exactly high drama but as farce goes, it wasn't bad.'

'Don't be such a pain!' she called out puffing up the stairs behind Sarah. 'That's not what I'm asking and you know it. How did you get on with the new man?'

'I keep telling you, he's just someone I went out with as a friend. That's all,' Sarah said firmly.

'It's about time you had someone special,' Elizabeth growled as she followed Sarah into the kitchen.

'I'm very happy with my life the way it is thank you. It suits me fine and the last thing I need is to complicate it.' Sarah seized the bottle of wine being held out to her and thrust it into the fridge.

Looking at her friend's decided frosty expression, Elizabeth dropped the subject, 'Smells nice, what have we got?'

'Chicken and cashew nuts in yellow bean sauce.'

It was much later, when they were both more mellow after a good meal and three quarters of the bottle of the passable supermarket plonk Elizabeth had brought, that the subject of Matt came up again.

'So, are you planning any more trips to the theatre in the near feature?'

'There's nothing much on except a few musical evenings – seventies' and eighties' bands – and the odd third-rate comic. Not my thing. There's a film we'd both like to see but we haven't fixed anything definite. I'm planning on going over to Norwich one weekend in the near future.' Elizabeth raised a sceptical eyebrow, which Sarah ignored. She had no intention of discussing Matt until she'd had more time to consider what part she wanted him to play in her life, if any. 'It was Nathan who gave me the idea. I told you, he took me out dinner earlier in the week, didn't I?'

'You did mention it. So what was Lover Boy after?'

'Why should he want anything?' Sarah said more sharply that she'd intended. Elizabeth would always believe the worse where Nathan was concerned. Best not to mention the ridiculous suspicions she'd had. 'We had a very pleasant evening, as it happens. He'd heard about that toe-rag stealing my handbag and just wanted to know how I was. He was very sympathetic though he did say he thought I needed a break which is why I've decided to go home.'

'I have to agree with him about that but a weekend with your parents isn't quite the same as an exotic holiday in the sun.'

'True. But, at least, I'll be able to get away and forget about work for a bit.'

When she recognized his voice on the phone, a strange mixture of relief and excitement swept over her. Sarah didn't need and didn't want a man in her life; still it was flattering to know that Matt was interested in seeing her again.

He chattered away about how much he'd enjoyed their evening at the theatre the previous week. 'I was wondering if you'd like to try another. The Silbury Players are doing Alan Ayckbourn's "Round and Round the Garden" at the Arts Centre this week. I know they're only a local amateur group but they're not bad and it could be quite fun,' he finished with a rush.

'Sounds great,' she said hoping she didn't sound too gushing. She'd seen the play before though naturally didn't enlighten Matt.

'Would Friday evening be all right?'

She readily agreed. Although she'd toyed with the idea of visiting her parents, nothing had been arranged and she could just as easily go across to Norfolk the following weekend.

'Will you be able to get tickets at this stage? Friday night is very popular and don't all the family and friends of the players snap them up?'

'Actually, I've got them already. One of my constables is a member. He's got a small part and now some mates of his can't go so he was offering the spare tickets around,' he admitted sounding somewhat sheepish.

'Shall we meet in the foyer?' She still wasn't ready to have him pick her up at the flat, not wanting to have to invite him in for coffee when he brought her back at the end of the evening.

'Fine. About twenty past seven? Look forward to it.' He sounded relieved. Whether that was because she'd agreed to go at all or he appreciated the fact that their friendship was going to proceed slowly, she wasn't sure.

Chapter 13

She'd only been in the flat ten minutes when the doorbell rang.

'One Hawaiian Pizza with extra topping.'

'I beg your pardon?'

The gangly youth pushed back his "Pizza Perfection" baseball cap and repeated his statement.

'But I didn't order any pizza.'

He studied the details on the till roll stapled to the lid of the box. 'This is Flat B. Your name, Harcourt?'

'Yes,' she admitted, 'however, I can assure you it's nothing to do with me.'

He glared at her for a moment but when he saw the expression on her face decided that being truculent would get him nowhere.

'If I have to take it back they'll make me pay for it. They'll say it was my fault.'

They stared at each other until the smell of the warmed fruit and melted cheese wafted across and began to activate Sarah's taste buds. He was probably telling the truth. 'Then it's lucky for you that ham and pineapple is my favourite. You'll have to wait while I go and get some money.'

As she walked back upstairs, she told herself to look on the bright side. This little trick had misfired. It had at least saved her the bother of sorting out something for tea. Unfortunately, it wasn't so easy to shrug off her misgivings. Surely this relentless drip-feed of petty inconveniences was more than someone with a warped sense of humour; it was fast becoming a sustained campaign of persecution. Perhaps she should mention it to Matt. It wouldn't do much for her image as a capable, independent woman. She'd have to find the right moment to drop it into the conversation.

Flicking up the lid, she pulled off a chunk of pineapple. Who else other than Nathan new of her weakness for Hawaiian Pizza? Don't even go there, she told herself firmly. Stop making mountains out of molehills.

The monthly faculty meetings had never been occasions that Sarah looked forward to. Though generally without incident, they were never friendly affairs. Each of the directors tended to regard the others as possible opponents, taking more than their share of the ever-dwindling resources. The only thing that seemed to unite them was their suspicion of her. Although she got on tolerably well with each of them individually, as soon as they collected round the table, they closed ranks as if she was some sort of enemy. It was difficult enough trying to carry on at work as though nothing was happening without having to keep the petty rivalries and point scoring under control or stroking egos in order to get them to come round to her way of thinking.

Tom Appleby wandered in at one minute past ten, just late enough to make a point though not quite sufficient to be open to criticism. He took his place without comment and they all sat shuffling papers and drinking coffee waiting for Frank Wagner, by far the most cantankerous of the faculty directors. For some reason the others tended to defer to Frank, probably because he shouted loudest and went on longest. He'd been at the college for over twenty years and was opposed to any form of change. It was difficult enough working with him as a co-director but, since her appointment as principal, he never ceased to denigrate any proposal that she made. He and George had been great buddies and the ill feeling he'd stirred up against her amongst the staff had taken some time to settle. At least, since she'd taken him on one side and threatened to haul him before the governors for unprofessional conduct, he'd stopped the caustic remarks about how much better things would have been if George had been appointed. She supposed she should be grateful that the sneering asides that used to punctuate their early faculty meetings were also now a rarity.

Sarah glanced around the table ready to give everyone her best rallying-the-troops smile but they all appeared lost in their own thoughts. Barry sat pensively stroking his moustache with his little finger, David was reading through his papers intent on making sure he caught no one's eye and George took off his glasses and began polishing them. The waiting was making everyone irritable. At five minutes past, she decided to start the meeting without Frank.

The first item on the agenda was the faculty reports. Barry was in mid-flow when Frank waltzed in. Frank's satisfied smirk disappeared when he realized they'd begun. He was about to interrupt when she signalled him sharply to his chair and turned back to Barry, a look of rapt attention on her face. Barry, taking his cue, continued without a pause and all the others all followed her example.

The rest of the meeting proceeded smoothly and they reached the final item on the agenda sooner than she'd anticipated.

'You all know about the Careers Convention being organized by the Education Business Partnership,' she said, trying to sound enthusiastic. 'The general consensus is that our students who went last year found it very useful and we're planning to take selected groups again this time round.'

'These things are always a bloody waste of time if you ask me. Kids just wandering around picking up leaflets about jobs they couldn't care less about.' Frank was trying to inflict his own brand of cynicism to belittle the project.

'The organizing committee is keen that it doesn't degenerate into a paper collecting exercise which is why they're encouraging contributors to involve youngsters in something more interactive. Thinking about our own stand, we need to come up with something, preferably involving a few of our existing students, to attract the school pupils. Anyone got any bright ideas?'

She looked around the table hoping to get a more positive response from the others but they all carefully avoided her eye.

'David?' she persisted.

'It would need some thought,' he mumbled noncommittally.

Sarah did her best not to let her annoyance show. She'd anticipated that Frank would try to put a damper on the idea which is why she'd talked to each of the others before the meeting. David's retreat in the face of Frank's scathing comments was particularly galling. She'd never expected gratitude for all the support she'd given him in the past but the way he chose to try to align himself with Frank in recent meetings demonstrated his weakness yet again. His defection now, after showing such enthusiasm for the Careers Convention the week before, rankled. She decided not to let him get away with it.

'David, I'm sure any of the suggestions you mentioned the other day will be fine.' She turned to the others. 'David has already said that he'd be happy to co-ordinate our contributions so if the rest of you come up with anything you can pass them on to him. I know both Barry and Dev have some ideas.' She ignored David's glare and, before he could protest, she carried on firmly, 'I would like each of you to put the Careers Convention on the agenda of your next faculty staff meeting and nominate someone to liaise with David. We need to make this a success. It's an opportunity to recruit more students and that's what all our jobs depend upon. As we get nearer to the date, Eunice will be talking to all the relevant personal tutors so that we can arrange for the students to attend the Convention. In the mean time, I want all the lecturers to talk to students so that they can get the most out of their visit.'

It was rare for her to take such a dictatorial stance but she didn't have the energy to worry about diplomacy. The sooner she could get them out of her office the better. Besides, why should the students miss out on a valuable opportunity simply because Frank wanted to demonstrate his macho image at her expense and the others were too apathetic to want to raise their heads from their bunkers in case they got caught in the crossfire?

After that gruelling morning, Sarah did something she hadn't done since she was a child.

Her mother had never been one to be quick with advice so when it was given, both she and her sister, Jenny, tended to pay attention even if they didn't always take it. Her mother's words of wisdom tended to stick in the mind. In her last year at St Margaret's RC Primary, Sarah had eventually plucked up the courage to confide her fears of going up into the big school after the summer. Sarah could picture her mother now, standing at the kitchen sink, her arms up to the elbows in washing-up suds.

'I've always found,' her mother had said after a thoughtful pause, 'if you've got something bothering you, especially if you know you can't do anything to change it, the best thing is to go along to church and light a candle to Our Lady.'

It hadn't seemed a very logical solution to Sarah's intractable problem but she'd done it any way. She could remember coming back feeling as though a great burden had been lifted from her small shoulders. With the benefit of hindsight, Sarah could see that her mother had appreciated that no amount of reasoning would have reassured a worried ten-year-old. Whether it was the act of doing something positive, the calming effect of that silent house of prayer or Mary's intervention to her divine Son on her behalf, it had the desired effect.

St Timothy's was in the centre of town. It wasn't her parish church but it was within ten minutes walk of the college. She'd never visited it before and she wasn't sure if she'd even find the place open. It was a sign of the times that so many churches had to be locked when there were no services going on, she thought as the flint fronted building came into view. She was lucky. Perhaps the priest had opened it up in anticipation of a few sorry souls looking for spiritual sustenance in their lunch hour.

Unlike her own Sacred Heart church, a modern square box with a central altar and pews arranged on three sides, St Timothy's had the traditional nave and transept which reminded her even more of those far off days. Her footsteps echoed in the empty building as she made her way down the long aisle dimly lit by high stained-glass windows. She genuflected before the sanctuary and turned into the side Chapel.

She wasn't the first to offer up a prayer that day. The last remnants of a candle flickered in the stand in front of the crude, plaster statue. Sarah knelt at the altar rails and rattled off the customary Our Father, Hail Mary and Glory Be as she'd been taught from infancy and then let her mind go still. There was no need to try to put into words her concerns or plead for the strength to meet her current challenges. Peace came easily in the secure, hallowed place where all the petty troubles of the outside world shrank into proportion. It was that rare kind of communion that comes from the knowledge that your innermost fears are known and that that is enough.

As on that occasion nearly thirty years ago, she left the church with a light heart, confident in her belief that, whatever her present frustrations, her salvation lay in her own hands and nothing and no one had the power to intimidate her.

She picked up the receiver on the first ring. '815470.'

Silence. It'd been over three weeks since the last menace call. The phone company were supposed to be blocking her calls. The system didn't help to identify where the call had been made from but, in theory, that number could not get through to her again. He could always ring from somewhere else of course.

As she'd already spoken, it would have been a sign of defeat on her part to put the phone down. The calls had long ceased to have any effect on her and she'd no intention of letting him think he still had the power to upset her.

'Hello?' she tried to inject an air of boredom. Impossible in a single word!

Still no answer.

'Is anyone there?' A hint of irritation as though she'd forgotten completely about the earlier calls.

'Saa-rah.' There was a momentary shudder down her spine. She needed to seize the initiative.

'Oh, it's my old friend with the asthma problem is it? You know you really ought to see a doctor. I hear they have some splendid ventolin inhalers these days that ease the breathing straight away.'

There was a click at the other end.

She should be feeling pleased with herself. For once she'd got the better of him. So why was she shaking? Why was her stomach churning? Why was she still thinking about him at all?

Chapter 14

For an amateur group, the Silbury Players' production of "Round and Round the Garden" was well up to standard. As they made their way out, Matt suggested they went for a drink in the pub next door. Pubs weren't really Sarah's scene but she readily agreed.

'Apart from the fact that he's too old for the part, the chap who played Norman was good enough to be a professional.' The advantage of going to a play or a film before the socializing bit was that it provided something to talk about.

'He's the group's leading light apparently. Works in one of the Building Societies in the High Street,' Matt informed her. 'I didn't see either of them, though apparently he played Norman in the other two plays in the series. The last was a couple of years ago and he's lost a bit more hair since then.'

As they chattered on, she wondered whether to tell him about the phone call she'd received the previous evening but decided against it. She didn't want him to feel sorry or protective towards her.

Somehow the conversation got round to Nathan. At the mention of his name all the tension came back. All her resolutions about pushing all thoughts of her tormentor out of her mind and enjoying a pleasant social evening crumbled away. All these suspicions about him were based on very flimsy evidence. Nathan may have hurt her in the past but he wasn't a monster.

Before she could change the subject, Matt asked, 'When did things start to go wrong?' This was far too dangerous ground.

'The moment I first met my prospective mother-in-law,' she laughed trying to dismiss the topic.

The flippant remark wasn't so far from the truth in some respects. Her first meeting with Nathan's parents was indelibly imprinted on her mind. She'd known Nathan for some months and, when it became evident that their relationship was likely to become more permanent, she'd been invited down to Surrey for the weekend. Sarah was apprehensive long before the car pulled into the horseshoe drive in front of the imposing mock-Tudor house. Naturally, she knew a little of Nathan's background; he had been educated at a minor public school, his father was something quite high up in the City and his parents were well to-do but, up till then, she'd not given it much thought. Nathan had fitted into her family so readily it'd never occurred to her that she might not find it so easy to slip into his.

From the very beginning, Geraldine had been cool and distant, her cut-glass accent accentuating the gulf that lay between them. It didn't need words for her to make it very clear that Sarah should be under no illusion that her friendship with Nathan was nothing more than passing fancy on his part – an interlude to see how the other half lived. His future was already mapped out.

Sarah didn't meet the wonderful Tanya on that first visit but Geraldine spent the greater part of that weekend telling her how beautiful she was – 'With her looks and figure she could have been a top model,' – how talented – 'She plays the flute as well as the piano and sings like an angel,' – and how close she and Nathan had been since they were small children. She even showed Sarah photographs of the two of them together from the time they were little more than toddlers.

Nathan had told her about his mother's obsession with Tanya but he'd assured her he never had, and never would, see Tanya as anything more than a friend and that living with her would drive him to distraction.

Her mother's approval of Nathan had been evident from the moment he'd walked in the door. When the two of them were alone she'd said to Sarah, 'He's the one isn't he?' At that time, Nathan and she'd only known each other a few weeks and marriage was something neither of them had even contemplated. After her visit to Nathan's parents, Sarah found herself talking over her misgivings about Geraldine's hostility towards her with her mother. In her usual way, her mother made no attempt to give her any advice. Her only comment had been a question. 'Are you sure it's really you she objects to? Wouldn't she be just the same with any woman who might take away her only son?'

It made perfect sense and from that moment, whatever the provocation, Sarah resolved never to take Geraldine's hostility personally. She convinced herself that, given time, Nathan's mother would come round and then all would be well.

Sarah was able to tell Matt the story of that first meeting in such a way that had both of them laughing uproariously, although she'd exaggerated Geraldine's behaviour only a little. What she failed to tell Matt, and the thing that pained her most about that visit, was Nathan's response to all this. Geraldine treated him like a little boy and he meekly fell into line. It was a revelation to see the lively, forceful man she'd known, so totally dominated.

She'd forgotten all about that. Weak people made to feel vulnerable might lash out in all sorts of underhanded ways. She thrust the thought from her mind. All those ideas about Nathan being her tormentor were ridiculous. She'd told herself that a hundred times in the last few days. She was getting things out of proportion. But his willingness to defer to his mother's every whim had made her think twice.

She looked at her watch. Seven minutes past. It was unusual for George to be late for a meeting. She got up and walked through to the outer office.

'Mr Fitzgibbon didn't leave any message did he?'

Lucy looked up and shook her head. Before she could ask her to ring through to see what was holding him up, the phone went. From what she could hear of Lucy's side of the conversation, it wasn't going to be a quick call so she decided to wander down to George's office and see for herself.

She knocked and went in.

'Just let me save this.'

As he sat with his back to her tapping away on his computer, she stood looking at the neat precision of everything on his desk. The pencil lay parallel to the carefully stacked pile of papers placed squarely in front of the onyx calendar and penholder stand, which obviously held pride of place.

'Sarah?'

'I wondered where you were. It's not like you to forget a meeting.' She gave him a bright smile.

'I got your message about it being postponed. It was on my desk when I came in this morning.'

'I'm sorry?' Now it was her turn to be surprised.

He bent down and rescued a piece of paper from his bin and handed it over. It was a brief printed note apologizing for having to rearrange their regular meeting to later in the day.

'But I didn't write this.'

'It has your name on the bottom.'

'Typed. It doesn't have my signature. I'm afraid this is someone's idea of a joke.'

'Who would want to do such a thing?' His frown spoke volumes.

'I have no idea but…' she'd been going to say that she intended to find out but logic told her that there was no way she would be able to trace the culprit. They all used the same computer software and printers. It could have been anyone in the college. 'I don't find it very funny,' she finished lamely. 'Let's not waste any more time. Shall we go to my office?'

She arrived in Norwich late on Friday evening and was surprised to find Greg, her brother-in-law, sitting solemn-faced with her parents in the front room.

'Is something wrong?'

'Todd's been very poorly the last few days. He's got that dreadful pain in his tummy again and he can't keep any food down,' her mother explained. 'The doctor wanted him in the hospital this afternoon and they've decided keep him in for observation for a few days. They're going do some more tests. Justin's spending the night with us so that Greg and Jenny can be with Todd.'

Despite her mother's assurances, all three of them looked strained. Greg repeated what he'd been told by the specialist and, although Todd's condition wasn't immediately life threatening, the situation was obviously serious.

'If Justin's staying here, I'll see if I can get myself a room in a hotel somewhere. Doesn't that pub round the corner take guests?'

'You'll do no such thing!' Her mother was on her feet with a speed surprising for such a large woman. 'We'll manage fine. Your room's all ready for you and Justin's on a camp bed in the dinning room. You sit there and I'll go and put the kettle on.' A nice cup of tea was her mother's solution to most of life's problems.

Sarah knew it was useless to protest. It would only make matters worse. Her mother was finding it impossible to keep still and bustled out into the kitchen.

'I'll go and say hello to Justin if he's still awake.'

The door creaked as she pushed it open. From the streetlight shining through the unlined curtains, she saw that the table and chairs had been pushed to one side. She could just make out the bundle of Justin curled up in a sleeping bag on a blown-up lilo on the floor.

'Who's that?' came a loud whisper.

'It's only me, Auntie Sarah. I didn't mean to wake you.'

He sat up straight away and held out his arms. They sat on the floor cuddling each other in the dark.

'Todd's been taken into hospital.'

'Grandma told me. But he'll be back home in a couple of days when they've had a chance to sort out exactly what's wrong.'

'He will be all right won't he?' In all their anxiety, it was evident that none of the family had thought to explain to Justin exactly what was happening. Like most brothers of that age, the two boys were constantly bickering, but that didn't loosen the tight bonds that tied them together.

Sitting beside him, arm around his shoulders, she explained, as best she could, that the doctors didn't know what was making Todd ill. He needed to stay in hospital so that they could use all their special equipment to find out.

She would like to have been able to claim that she and Justin were close but the truth was they really didn't know each other that well. She only saw him three or four times a year and always with the rest of the family. Though she'd read him the odd bedtime story, the number of long conversations between the two of them could probably be numbered on one hand.

It was a dreadful admission, she knew, but she wasn't that good with children even though, unlike many of her colleagues in Further Education, she had a teaching qualification. She was doing a PGCE the year Justin was born. Her teaching practices had all been in secondary schools and a sixth form college which was when she decided she was much better with older students. Finding the vocabulary for dealing with an eleven year old didn't come easily, particularly when he was worried and upset.

'Sorry, I've pinched the bed,' she said to take his mind off the problem.

'That's okay. I like it in here. It's like camping.' He was trying to put a brave face on things.

'There was something I wanted to ask you, young man. It's your birthday in a couple of weeks. Any ideas for a pressey?'

She had a sudden fear that he was going to say something about wanting his brother well again. He shook his head and the body sagged. Instinctively, she cuddled him closer.

'There must be something you'd like?' He gave a great sigh. 'What are mum and dad going to get you?'

That was obviously not the right thing to say. He scrubbed away a tear.

'They were going to take me and Todd to Disneyland Paris over half-term.'

'I'm sure they still will. Maybe not this holiday as it's so close, but as soon as Todd's better. They haven't forgotten all about you, you know. They still love you to bits. It's just that they're worried about Todd at the moment.'

'What's going to happen tomorrow?'

'I don't know, Justin.' She made a sudden decision. 'But when we've been to see how Todd is, you and I are going into the city. We can have a look round the shops for your present and then go and have a McDonalds. Would you like that?'

'Mum says hamburgers aren't good for you and I'm only allowed chips once a week.' He mimicked his mother's tone of reproof.

'I won't tell on you, if you don't tell on me!'

He gave a low gurgle of laughter and cuddled down. She gave him a last good night kiss. She felt quite pleased with herself for coming up with something pleasant for him to look forward to.

'Night, night poppet. Sleep well.'

Chapter 15

Sarah doubted any of them got much sleep that night. They were all up early in the morning waiting for the phone to ring. Greg had promised that he or Jenny would get in touch first thing. By eight thirty there was still no news. Her mother was making endless pots of tea and mountains of toast that no one wanted and her father kept wandering aimlessly from room to room. Justin sat curled up on the settee still in his dressing gown.

'Perhaps they're waiting until after the doctors have done their rounds,' Sarah suggested lamely. 'We could ring the hospital.'

'We mustn't do that.' Her mother became flustered. 'They'll be ever so busy at this time of day getting patients up and giving them breakfast and medicines and whatnot.' She'd always been in awe of anyone in authority and the thought of troubling important people like doctors or nurses filled her with apprehension.

'Then I'll drive down there and see what's going on.'

A worried frown creased the older woman's brow and she began to twist her wedding ring around her finger, no longer able to keep her hands still. Sarah couldn't remember seeing her mother in such a state of near panic before. She felt annoyed with Jenny for putting her parents through all this.

Sarah was about to fetch her car keys when Greg arrived with the news that Todd had spent a reasonably comfortable night. The doctors had managed to get his pain under control and had scheduled a series of tests for later in the day.

'Can we go and see him?' her mother asked. All the agitation was gone. Whatever she was feeling inside, for Greg's benefit, her mother was now trying to appear calm and matter-of-fact.

'Probably not today. They're taking him for tests at ten and he won't be back on the ward till late afternoon. They told me to get Jenny home for some rest. She's been sitting by his bed all night.'

'So when will you hear the results?'

'You know what they're like. They say it will be a few days because the labs don't work over the weekend.' He ruffled his older son's hair. 'Will you be all right here for a bit, boyo?'

'Don't worry about Justin.' Sarah smiled across at them both. 'We've got a busy day planned, Justin and I, haven't we sunshine?'

'He can stay here as long as you like. Tell Jenny not to worry.' Her mother gave Greg a reassuring pat on the arm.

Sarah was tempted to walk out with Greg to his car and give him a lecture about keeping her parents up to date with what was going on but decided against it. Greg was already under a lot of strain and her mother was sure to think that he was telling Sarah something that he'd not wanted to worry them with. The one thing she could do was to take Justin out of everyone's way.

Although visiting times were generous in the children's ward, they restricted the number of visitors at any one time. As Jenny insisted on staying by Todd's side, it was quite late on Sunday before it was Sarah's turn to go up to the hospital.

To judge by the drawn features, Todd had lost weight since she'd last seen him; nonetheless he was surprisingly cheerful and, though not quite his old bubbly self, seemed in a far better state than Jenny.

'Hi, trouble. Do I get a kiss in exchange for what's in this bag?'

Todd was delighted with his present. She and Justin had spent some time choosing something suitable. Justin wasn't impressed with her suggestion of a book and Todd was too old for cuddly toys. In the end, wandering through the arcade, they'd found a shop window devoted to marionettes. Inside was a splendid collection of glove puppets. Predictably, Justin suggested a lurid green monster with enormous plastic fangs but they eventually settled on a red squirrel with an enormous, fluffy tail. The soft, furry fabric stretched right up to the elbow. It had all the advantages of being something for Todd to cuddle when he felt all alone without any of the stigma of being a toy for babies.

After twenty minutes or so, Greg persuaded Jenny to go down to the cafeteria with Sarah while he stayed with Todd. Jenny protested that she'd no appetite. Sarah eventually talked her into having a bowl of soup. Making the excuse that she'd be driving back to Wiltshire when she left the hospital – which was true – and needed a good meal inside her before she left – untrue, her mother had cooked the usual enormous Sunday roast even though none of them could do it justice – Sarah had piled her plate high hoping that seeing her tucking in would tempt Jenny. It didn't work. Jenny crumbled the roll into small pieces and let the soup go cold after only a couple of spoonfuls.

In an effort to move the conversation away from Todd and all his troubles, Sarah told her about her day out with Justin.

'Thanks for looking after him,' Jenny muttered automatically.

'He's a smashing kid. I enjoyed it. He told me all about the birthday treat to Disneyland Paris.'

'Well that's off now,' Jenny snapped, irritated that Sarah had brought up the subject.

'But surely, it's a couple of weeks away yet. Todd will be home and you'll all be back to normal,' Sarah protested.

'I can't think about gallivanting off now, not with a sick child lying upstairs,' Jenny rounded on her sister angrily.

'Naturally, Todd comes first at the moment, but Justin has been looking forward to it so much. He is worried too you know. It wouldn't hurt to pop across and see him. He hasn't spoken to you for nearly three days and he's missing you.'

'Are you telling me how to look after my own child?' Her voice rose and several pairs of eyes swivelled in their direction.

'Of course not! All I'm saying is that Justin is your son too and...'

'Don't you tell me what to do! You think you're so bloody perfect but you don't know the first thing about relationships. You walked out on a good man because of one stupid, little mistake. Let me tell you, Miss Goodie Twoshoes, if I need advice, you're the last person I'd listen to. Go back to your ivory tower and let those who live in the real world get on with it.'

The last thing Sarah wanted was a public shouting match. She knew it was worry that had prompted the tirade but, if Jenny had intended to take out her hurt by wounding Sarah, she'd succeeded. The blazing eyes dared Sarah to contradict. Jenny had a string of accusations lined up to throw and was waiting for the excuse to let rip. Sarah could out argue Jenny any day, she could even match her temper, however making a scene in front of all these people wouldn't help either of them. Jenny needed to give vent to all her pent-up frustration and pain but this wasn't the time or the place.

Sarah picked up her bag and turned to go.

'That's right! Run away. Never face any unpleasantness.' Sarah could hear Jenny snarling through gritted teeth as she walked towards the door. She prayed fervently that her sister would stop at screaming out obscenities.

Sarah remembered little of the journey home. However illogical, she was riddled with guilt. Had the tension of the last few weeks made her insensitive to other people's problems? She should've been able to reach her sister somehow. Anyone who witnessed that painful exhibition could be forgiven for thinking that Jenny and she were always at loggerheads. It was true that they weren't exactly bosom pals, the difference in their ages made that difficult as children, but had they really grown that far apart? Jenny had just started senior school when Sarah left to go to university. After drifting into the Sixth Form, Jenny had been half way through her A' levels when she fell pregnant with Justin. Once she was married, they'd not seen so much of each other. It was easy to blame pressure of work and Norfolk was a long way away.

The phone was picked up before the second burble.

'It's only me. Just to let you know I got back safely.' Sarah always rang home as soon as she got in.

'Are you all right, Sarah?' She knew from her mother's tone that Jenny had spoken about their earlier set-to.

'Fine. The roads weren't too bad and I had a stop for a cup of tea just outside St Neots.' She wanted to tell her mother her version of events – get her to appreciate that it hadn't been her fault. She'd gone home hoping for a little TLC for herself. Todd's troubles were more than enough for all of them to cope with without her adding to the burden. Not that she'd planned to tell her parents what had been happening but to feel loved and cosseted and feel less isolated. Now it wouldn't be fair to ask her mother to take sides, especially when she was so worried about Todd. Her mother probably thought Sarah was an insensitive monster but, however much that hurt, she would have to live with it for now.

'Jenny said you two had words.'

'Sort of. I didn't mean to upset her.'

'I'm sure you didn't. She's under a lot of strain at the moment.' Her mother said all the right things, but then it wasn't in her nature to criticize or to take sides. It didn't stop Sarah wishing she knew what her mother was really thinking.

'I'm worried about her, mum. Of course she's anxious not knowing what's wrong with Todd but she really does need to get things into proportion.'

'Yes.'

'You agree with me?' Sarah was surprised.

'Of course I do. She'll have a breakdown if she goes on the way she is.'

'So why haven't you said anything to her?'

'It wouldn't do any good and anyway, both my daughters stopped taking my advice when they started going to big school.'

'Mum, that's not true!'

Sarah heard a rueful laugh at the other end.

'You two are so alike. Strong willed and stubborn, the pair of you. Where you both get it from I've no idea. It's a complete mystery to me why you two are so jealous of each other.'

Unlike most mothers, Sarah's had never been one to lecture either of her daughters. Not that they were allowed to get away with things. Their father, a quiet man who rarely expressed an opinion on anything, was frequently indulgent and they could twist him round their fingers most of the time, but not their mother. She'd taught the girls right from wrong when they were small and expected them always to know the difference. Discipline in the household, though never lax, never had to be rigorously enforced. Falling short of their mother's expectations and seeing her hurt at being let down was usually enough deterrent. Listening to the disappointment in the older woman's voice, Sarah felt all the old shame. She didn't know why because she couldn't see any truth in her mother's last comment. Neither of them had anything to be jealous about.

Sarah changed the subject. 'Look, mum, I've been thinking. Justin will be terribly upset if his trip is cancelled. I know it's still a couple of weeks away but Jenny seems to have already decided that, even if Todd is out of hospital by then, he won't be well enough to go and I understand that. But, do you think you can persuade Jenny to let me have Justin here for half term instead? I could take him to somewhere like Alton Towers or Chessington for the day. It's not the same as Disneyland I know but it would give him something to look forward to. That's if he'd like to come, naturally. And it would mean that none of you would have to worry about him when he's not in school and it might do Justin good to get away for a bit.'

'Are you sure you could cope with him?'

'I'm not that helpless and he's not a baby.' Sarah smothered her irritation. She was in charge of a college with two thousand plus full time students, double that number of part-timers and over a hundred and ninety staff, but her mother was concerned about her ability to look after one eleven-year-old for a few days. 'I've been thinking about it all the way back. I'm sure it would be fun for both of us.'

'I'll suggest it to Greg,' her mother conceded.

'Fine. I'll ring again tomorrow to see how Todd is. You've got my college number if there's any emergency haven't you?'

'Your business card is sitting here by the phone. Bye, love. God bless.'

Chapter 16

The sheer volume of work gave Sarah little opportunity to dwell on her tormentor or her family problems. Although there were no classes in the college over half term, it was rare for her not to work through the break. There may not have been any meetings but it was a good time to catch up on all the paperwork. If she was going to take time out to spend with Justin, she'd need to make some attempt at clearing her desk in advance. On Monday evening she worked right through and stopped only when the caretaker came round to lock up after the last of the evening class students had left.

Tuesday was one of those days when she seemed to be at the beck and call of everyone. She'd not had a minute to herself all morning. To get away from the frenetic atmosphere of the place, Sarah decided to take an unaccustomed lunch break despite her workload.

There was a pleasant little tearoom less than ten minutes walk from the college run in aid of a local hospice. It was rather quaint and old fashioned – chintz curtains and flower prints on the walls – although, because it was manned by volunteers, the service was somewhat variable. Though patronized mainly by middle-aged, middle-class housewives indulging in a respite during their shopping expeditions, it had the distinct advantage that it was unlikely that any of her staff or students were liable to drop in.

'Sarah! It's been ages. How are you?' The penetrating tones rang across the room. 'Do you mind if I join you?'

Sarah's heart sank as Geraldine, without waiting for a reply, came up and proceeded to arrange her assortment of packages around the chair opposite. Her mother-in-law was the last person she wanted to see. As she'd only eaten a couple of mouthfuls of the cheese and broccoli bake and not even started on her coffee, Sarah could hardly claim that she was about to leave.

'Just let me go and order myself something. What have you got, dear? They do a nice baked potato with mushroom topping.' Not waiting for a reply, she was off.

The two hadn't spoken to each other more than two or three times since the separation. Why Geraldine should greet her like a long lost friend Sarah couldn't fathom. Although she'd always been civil, at least to her face, Sarah was under no illusions that she was number one on Geraldine's hate list. She wouldn't have been surprised if the woman had completely ignored her. A brief nod of acknowledgement across the room should they happen to catch each other's eye would have been the most Sarah would've expected or wanted. Trying to work out just what that devious lady was up to, kept Sarah fully occupied until Geraldine returned.

'You're looking very smart,' Geraldine said.

Sarah was wearing a Jaegar suit, navy with a faint check. Nothing outstanding. Her working wardrobe was far from the height of fashion and consisted almost exclusively of discrete outfits designed, as Nathan always protested, for a woman a good ten years her senior. She quickly learnt that people found her less intimidating that way as they felt threatened by the image of a thrusting business woman dressed to exude power.

The reason for Geraldine's remark soon became obvious. Even though the weather wasn't particularly warm, she slipped off her jacket and hung it on the back of her chair.

Geraldine, the only person Sarah knew who habitually shopped in the West End, was sporting a simple, but extremely chic, button through, silk dress with a stand up collar in a subtle, deep mulberry. It was particularly attractive and it was clear that Sarah was expected to return the compliment.

'Oh, it's just something I picked up on holiday,' she responded to her appreciative remarks. 'Ridiculously cheap actually.'

She was waiting for Sarah to ask where, but Sarah didn't need to and, what was more, didn't feel like giving her the satisfaction. The reason for all the sudden bonhomie was now obvious. There was no way Geraldine was going to pass up the opportunity to rub Sarah's nose in the fact that she'd achieved what she knew Sarah had longed to do. Why oh why, Sarah thought, did her mother-in-law always bring out her uncharitable side with such a vengeance? Sarah dropped her gaze to her plate and resolutely held her tongue. She knew she was going to be subjected to a long eulogy on the delights of China, how fascinating a country and how wonderful the sights, however, nothing was going to force Sarah to be the woman's stooge.

'Yes, in the silk quarter in Beijing.' Geraldine paused again waiting for her response. Sarah almost flinched. Not because the location had come as the painful surprise her mother-in-law had anticipated, but because she had to stop herself from wincing at the affected nasal twang with which the woman had pronounced the word, no doubt in what she thought was a perfect imitation of her Chinese tourist guide. 'It was truly spectacular!'

'Umm. So Nathan said.'

It was Geraldine's turn to try to stifle the look of shocked indignation.

'He didn't mention he'd seen you.' Sarah could see that discovering that her precious son had been in contact and had failed to tell his own mother had severely dented the woman's composure. It struck Sarah that her erstwhile husband was in for a considerable period of quizzing. No doubt he would be made to suffer the whole gamut from tantrums of 'how could you go behind my back' to the guilt-evoking, 'have you any idea of how foolish I was made to feel?'

A little glow of triumph warmed the chill that this unexpected encounter had produced. If she wasn't careful, she'd find herself becoming as vindictive as whoever it was trying to make her life a misery. Not that it was in Nathan's nature to be spiteful, assuming it was him. That was more Geraldine's style.

Geraldine? Surely not! If she wanted to get back at Sarah for breaking her precious son's heart why had she waited till now? But that argument was true for Nathan as well. For goodness sake! It was ridiculous to consider either of them as suspects. What had she been reduced to?

For the next quarter of an hour, Sarah was subjected to the highlights of China. She had to sit through every detail from the magnificent views from Hong Kong's Victoria Peak on day one right through to the vastness of Tiananmen Square and the glories of the Forbidden City at the end of the three weeks.

'It was the most wonderful holiday I've ever had,' she simpered.

'Really?'

'And every day was so different. One day you'd be cruising along the river through this breathtaking limestone gorge and the next it would be fabulous temples or the gardens at Suzhou, not a bit like ours of course. Naturally, for me, one of the high spots was Xi'an. Words can't describe the awesome splendour of those serried ranks of Terracotta Warriors guarding the approach to the emperor's tomb.' Her voice dropped to a reverential hush. The whole exaggerated performance made Sarah squirm.

'I'm sure.'

'And one day they took us to this hospital where they use only traditional Chinese medicine. Absolutely fascinating! We went to several concerts although the Peking Opera was a real hoot.'

Sarah pushed her empty plate away hoping Geraldine would realize that she needed to be making tracks but her mother-in-law had no intention of releasing Sarah until she had recounted the saga of all her shopping exploits. She wittered on about jade jewellery, embroidered tablecloths and colossomie plus a whole wardrobe of silk blouses she had brought for friends and family until Sarah could've screamed.

'The one disappointment of the whole holiday was the weather on the day we went to see to the Great Wall. On all the photographs you see it stretching for miles, but the clouds were so low when we were there you could hardly see one from one turret to the next.'

'How frustrating.' Even to her own ears, Sarah's answers sounded mechanical, but nothing was going to stop the eulogy and she was a captive audience.

As she sat, only half listening to the grating, affected voice droning on, reason returned. The missing documents, corrupted computer files and all that had been happening at college had forced Sarah to concede that Nathan could hardly be considered the prime suspect any longer. An IT expert such as Nathan might just possibly be able to hack into the college PCs and cause havoc but there was no way Geraldine could have done. Neither was she familiar with college routines and procedures.

Looking across at the woman, Sarah was forced to admit that, for all the affectation, Geraldine's enthusiasm over the China holiday was genuine. It probably wasn't even valid to imagine that she had struck up their conversation with the intention of being able to gloat. She could simply be so desperate to find someone she could make sit attentively whilst she relived her adventures, all past antipathy was forgotten. Her neighbours and fellow bridge club members must have had their fill long ago.

She couldn't even justifiably claim that Geraldine had chosen the holiday destination out of some perverted instinct to spite her daughter-in-law. When Alan had been alive, Geraldine had always favoured cruises or lazing on some tropical beach being pampered by flunkies running around to meet her every whim. That was definitely not Nathan's scene anymore than it would have been Sarah's. If he had felt compelled to spend his holiday with his mother, then he would have insisted on something more stimulating. After all the anticipation built up before the separation, perhaps China was a natural choice for him to suggest.

Still, if the whole thing had been Nathan's idea, he was about to get his comeuppance when Geraldine let fly with the recriminations about his secret meeting with Sarah. Sarah suppressed a giggle. The wounded indignation at such treachery would linger for weeks. Dare she mention he'd been the one to call her and then compounded his crime by taking her out to dinner? Perhaps not. After all, she was a mature adult Sarah told herself and not a spiteful child trying to get its own back. Plus it would be one too many sins in one brief half hour for her poor soul's burden.

The only other consolation to this unexpected and unwished-for meeting was that Sarah wasn't obliged to contribute to the conversation. All that was required of her was the odd word of amazement, fascination or delight at appropriate intervals. She was needed only in the capacity as listener. Eventually, Sarah had to bring the flow to a halt.

'It all sounds fascinating. I'm so sorry, I really would love to hear more but I'm afraid I must to get back to work.' Sarah put her things together.

'We must arrange to meet up again. It's so long since we've seen each other.' Geraldine spoke with such warmth that Sarah could almost believe she meant it. 'And I have some fabulous photographs that you simply must see. I know you especially will really be able to appreciate them.' Her eyes were bright with enthusiasm.

Sarah said her goodbyes and hurried away.

As she climbed back up the hill to the college, Sarah found herself wondering what might have happened if she had dropped Veronica's name into the conversation. However eager she was to hear more about this new woman in Nathan's life, there was no way she would give that tiresome woman the satisfaction of knowing that she was interested in whomever her darling son was seeing. No sooner had the thought come into her head, than she felt a pang of conscience. After Alan's death and her move from Surrey, Geraldine had lost all her close circle of friends. Even the bosom pal, Penelope, Tanya's mother, had been left behind. As Sarah now knew, it wasn't easy for a woman on her own to create a social circle for herself. Geraldine must be more lonely than Sarah had realized to try to make a friend of her.

Chapter 17

'It seemed like a good idea on Sunday evening but after mum told me that Jenny had agreed and Justin couldn't wait to come, I began to get cold feet.'

Matt gave one of his boyish grins. 'What's the problem?'

'A trip around the shops for a couple of hours is fine but a whole week entertaining an eleven-year-old is quite another prospect,' Sarah said ruefully.

'There's lots you can do around here. You'll be surprised how quickly the time will go.'

'I was hoping you could give me a few ideas.'

He reeled off some suggestions.

'Great, although that's not really what's worrying me,' she said, stirring her coffee and trying to appear nonchalant. 'Mum must have told Justin that I'd mentioned taking him to Chessington. When I spoke to him that was all he could talk about.' Sarah gave Matt what she hoped was her most beguiling look.

'So?' It wasn't quite the response she'd hoped for.

'I'll let you into a secret. The thought of having to take him on all those rides terrifies me. I've no head for heights and I've never been a lover of big dippers and fair ground thrills but I can't let him down now.'

'When exactly had you planned on going?'

'We haven't fixed a particular time. Any day would do.' She knew she was being obvious, however the consequences of her rash promise were beginning to loom large and her apprehension was growing by the hour.

'As it happens, I have arranged to take a few days leave over half term to spend with Paul. I expect he'd enjoy a day out at Chessington.'

'Great,' she cut in before he'd time to change his mind. 'I'll do the driving and bring the picnic. Just tell me the day.'

'Why do I feel conned?' he laughed.

'Would I do such a thing? You made a generous offer and I accepted.'

Sarah felt much more relaxed on the drive back. She'd been so preoccupied about how she would be able to persuade Matt and his son to join them that she'd paid little attention to the film. What interpretation the rest of the family might put on Auntie Sarah's new man friend, about whom Justin would inevitably tell them all when he returned home, was a problem for the future. For some reason, she'd have preferred them not to know about Matt; at least not until she was more certain of the part he was going to play in her life.

There was none of the intense yearning to be with him that she'd known in those early days with Nathan. If she was honest, it was his friendship she valued. A convivial partner to socialize with; someone to take her out of the restricted box of work and a solitary home life in which she'd been confined too long. And there was no denying that being able to tell a policeman about the harassment, even if she had made it sound more like an inconvenient nuisance that a terror campaign, was reassuring. Someone who'd be able to do something if ever the need arose.

She still hadn't got round to telling Matt about the things that had happened at work. There was nothing to prove that they weren't mistakes that she herself had made. True it had been over a week since anything had happened but, if the opportunity did present itself when they spent a whole day together, it might be as well to admit the effect the sustained assault was having on her.

Blast! Despite her resolve to thrust all thoughts of him away, here she was letting her tormentor win again, spoiling a pleasant evening.

One evening, a little after seven, Sarah decided to call it a day and stuffed a pile of papers into her brief case. It wouldn't help matters if she tried to work when she was so tired that she made mistakes. Although she often stayed on in her office till eight or nine in the summer, as the nights drew in with the onset of winter, so her enthusiasm waned. The cold and rain she could live with, it was being in the place after dark when most of the others had gone that made it hard for her to concentrate. Despite the multitude of evening classes going on all over the campus, up on the top floor of the main building, which was given over to administration, there wasn't much activity after five thirty.

Taking the stairs as usual, she came out of the side door and was half way past the first block of unlit mobiles before she realized that she'd been too preoccupied to think where she was going. In the usual idiotic way educational establishments were designed, the car park for staff and visitors lay furthest from the main building.

Though the quickest route lay through the proliferation of wooden huts known as the temporary classrooms, that way was badly lit. Once the evenings got darker, it made sense to avoid the unseen potholes and take the path along the side of the theatre and on past the Media Arts building.

Sarah stopped and half turned, but it seemed silly to retrace her steps especially as it'd begun to drizzle. As she glanced back, a movement caught her eye. Had she imagined a figure ducking back out of sight? A flash of light raincoat? Telling herself that it was it was probably nothing more than a trick of the light, she nonetheless quickened her pace and only when she reached her car did her heart stop racing. Was her persecutor about to step up the terror or was she jumping at shadows? It could well have been someone walking through the complex on some other errand entirely. She stared at her hands tightly gripping the steering wheel. Perhaps taking a few days off at half term wasn't such a bad idea after all.

Sarah was much later getting to Norwich than she'd planned. It'd been one of those frustrating days when constant interruptions meant that all the essential last minute tasks that she'd planned to do took much longer than usual. She left late and the traffic was heavy, especially around Oxford, and, even with the new bypass to the south of Bedford, the journey was slow going. It was a long slog across country without any motorways and, although the stretches of dual carriageway were gradually increasing, it was rare for her to make the drive in less than four hours. Her parents had always been early risers so liked to get to bed soon after ten o'clock. Sarah didn't like to feel that she was keeping them up.

She was more than a little apprehensive about the reception she was going to get. Her parents weren't the problem; it was the thought of how she was going to face Jenny that preyed on her mind. On the couple of occasions when she'd rung her sister, Jenny had given a curt response to the enquiries about Todd to the effect that he was as well as could be expected before passing Sarah straight over to Justin. Though Jenny's manner was distinctly cool, at least she was speaking.

Sarah would've liked to travel down on the Friday evening, collect Justin the next morning and come straight back thus avoiding any icy silences or, heaven forbid, further outbursts from her sister over the weekend. However, her mother would've been hurt if the return journey hadn't been put off until after a family lunch on

Sunday. With all seven of them there, Sarah had to trust to luck that she wouldn't be left alone with Jenny.

Todd was now back home and, though by no means his old self, was up and about. Jenny had insisted that he stay off school claiming that, with only a few more days until the holiday, he wouldn't have been doing much work in any case. It the circumstances, it wouldn't have been politic for Sarah to mention that both academically and socially that seemed short-sighted so she kept her views to herself. From the conversation with Todd on the phone when he thanked her again for his squirrel, she got the impression that he was already feeling bored. Sarah wondered if she was doing the right thing in depriving him of his older brother's company for so long.

The test results had come through midweek but didn't prove very informative. According to her mother, they'd done some sort of 'oscopy' which none of the family understood. Although it'd apparently ruled out several serious conditions, if the doctors were any closer to finding out what was wrong with Todd, they didn't enlighten Jenny and Greg. Consultation with yet another specialist and more tests were promised in the near future.

On the Saturday, Sarah persuaded her parents to let her take them out for a meal. In the end, she had to settle for lunch in a Bernie Inn – anything more upmarket would have been deemed sheer extravagance and they wouldn't have been comfortable. When she got them back in the car, she said she fancied a trip out to Wroxham, as she hadn't been to the Broads since she was a teenager. As they didn't have a car – neither of them could drive – they relied mainly on coach trips for their outings. She knew that Greg and Jenny were very good but now that the two boys are older, there wasn't room in their old Escort for all six of them to go far. Although, squeezed into the back of Sarah's Saab Convertible, there was less legroom for her father than in her previous four door saloon. Fortunately he wasn't a big man.

As soon as she heard the boys coming down the path, her mother was at the door with open arms. Cuddles and kisses were exchanged and Sarah was relieved when she got a perfunctory peck on the cheek from Jenny.

Justin wanted to put his suitcase into the boot of her car straightaway.

'Mum's put my Wellingtons in a bin bag,' he informed her.

'I thought you were coming for a week not moving in!' she teased as Greg lifted out a suitcase, a small grip and an assortment of carrier bags.

'That's just some books and games and things mum said I ought to bring to keep me quiet when you have to do your work,' Justin protested. 'Dad said not to put them all in one big case as it would be too heavy to carry up the stairs at the other end.'

'Very sensible.'

'Don't you believe him, the little crawler,' Greg said shaking his head. 'What I actually said was that the boot on this apology for a car of yours wouldn't take a decent sized case. You do realize the only reason he wants to abandon his beloved parents is to get a drive in this flash thing, preferably with the top down?'

'Don't be so rude about the love of my life,' Sarah gave him a mock scowl. 'Flash indeed! If I'd wanted flash I'd have chosen Laser Red or Lime Yellow not a perfectly respectable Silver Grey. You're just jealous!'

Even Jenny managed a wan smile as Greg lifted in the last of the bags. 'I've packed plenty of clothes so don't bother to wash any of his things. I'll do them when he gets back.' It was the nearest thing Sarah was going to get to a peace offering from Jenny and she accepted it gratefully.

When they got into the house and she saw the two boys standing side by side, Sarah was surprised to see the enormous difference in their heights. True, Justin was at the shooting up stage but Todd didn't seem to have grown at all in the last year. She hadn't noticed when she'd seen him in hospital because he'd been lying in bed. Although she was no expert on eight-year-olds, she felt sure he was much shorter than he should be for his age. Greg must have noticed her frown.

'Don't you think Todd looks well?' he asked pointedly.

'Heaps better. How are you feeling my old soldier? Got to have you fighting fit so you can come down and spend some time with me.' She didn't want him to feel left out. It was an amazingly fine line to tread not to step on family feelings.

A little later, when she and Greg were in a quiet corner, she decided, to dip a toe into dangerous waters.

'Justin's shooting up fast. He'll be as tall as you before we know it. I expect Todd will be putting on a spurt soon.'

'He's the smallest in his class at the moment.'

'Have the doctors said anything about it?' she asked airily.

'They've mentioned it.' It was evidently a topic of some concern but it was presumably being dealt with.

'Fine,' she said and changed the subject quickly.

Lunch passed more or less smoothly and it was quite late by the time they'd finished coffee and started clearing the table.

'Thanks mum. That was super. Nothing quite like home-made apple crumble.' She kissed the rosy cheek as she sidled round the ample figure stacking the saucepans next to a pile of dirty plates by the sink.

'Just you put down that wiping up cloth. The rest of us can manage this lot. You've got a long journey ahead of you and it's gone two o'clock already. You get off so you don't have to drive in the dark.' The fact that Sarah had done the whole trip after sundown a couple of days before seemed to have eluded her mother.

Even so, with all the kisses and goodbyes it was nearly half an hour later before the car pulled away.

Chapter 18

On Tuesday evening, his face flushed with all the day's excitement, Justin sat ensconced in the big armchair chatting away on the phone to his mother.

'The Vampire Ride was really cool. You sit in these bat shaped things that hang down and you whiz along.'

Sarah couldn't hear Jenny's response.

'No. Paul was with me. Auntie Sarah chickened out and stayed with Matt down at the bottom. She wouldn't go on any of the roller coasters.'

'I went on the Runaway Mine Train,' I protested.

'That was tame! Just for wimps. You wouldn't go near the Rattle-snake.' Sarah threw a cushion at him and he burst out laughing. 'That was really wicked,' he informed his mother enthusiastically. 'Rameses Revenge wasn't bad either. I liked it better than the Pirate Ship. You go upside down when it goes right over the top. Auntie wouldn't go on any of the really good things and she even got scared in the Terror Tomb.'

'Rubbish. I love ghost trains,' she shouted out over Justin's giggles.

Jenny made some comment.

'No they weren't all scary. We went in this boat along a sort of river that kept spinning round and then at the end it went through the fountains and we all got wet.'

Sarah groaned inwardly. He was doing a good job of destroying any credibility as a careful childminder she might have had with her sister. By the time she got to speak to Jenny, Sarah would be lucky to get away without a lecture on putting Justin in jeopardy letting him go on life threatening rides and risking him catching pneumonia getting soaked.

'Auntie Sarah was ace at shooting on the rifle range in the fair ground. She did better than Matt and he's supposed to be a police-man!'

'He's not in the LAPD! I don't suppose he gets involved in that many shoot outs around here,' Sarah called out in protest.

'And then we went round the zoo but it was getting late so we only had time to see the big cats and the sea lions.'

He sat listening to Jenny, nodding and shaking his head at intervals.

'Okay, I will. I'll pass you over to Auntie.' He held out the receiver.

'He sounds as though he's having a smashing time.' Jenny sounded more relaxed than she'd been at the weekend. 'Don't let him be any trouble.'

'Don't worry. He's being a perfect guest. Good as gold.'

Once she'd asked about Todd's progress, Sarah passed the phone back for final goodbyes.

The next morning, Justin was happy to go with her to the college. Sarah didn't plan to stop but she wanted to take a look through her post and reassure herself that everything was running smoothly in her absence. She thought that Justin might enjoy looking around the place where she worked.

The Second Year Performing Arts students were due to put on a production before Christmas and Sarah wasn't surprised to find that Jim McArdle had the group in for a rehearsal. Jim was into experimental drama with a great deal of audience participation. The whole thing fascinated Justin and Sarah was able to leave him for most of the morning watching Jim put the students through their paces. Simon Ellis was also around and promised to show Justin the lighting and sound systems which, thanks to a recent grant, now had state-of-the-art computer control.

When she went over to collect him for lunch, Sarah found Justin decked in a voluminous, old shirt happily wielding a brush in the design room with the rest of the scenery painters.

Sarah liked to take visitors to the Training Restaurant during term time and show off the skills of the catering students. However, even if it had been open, the sort of menus normally on offer would not have interested Justin. The college cafeteria opened up for a couple of hours at midday even during half term because so many staff were in. It had a very limited choice of food – sandwiches, filled baked potatoes and sausage and chips – but Justin was more than content.

'It's not often we see you in here, Mrs Harcourt.'

Sarah turned to see Dev Sharma holding a tray.

'Hello, Dev. Come and join us. Let me introduce you to my nephew, Justin. Mr Sharma is in charge of the Technology Faculty.'

Dev Sharma looked somewhat apprehensive at the unexpected invitation.

On impulse, as they sat down, Sarah asked, 'We were hoping to have a look round the Technology Block this afternoon. Would that be possible?'

'Of course. I'll show you round myself if you'd like. We'll have to call by my office first to collect the keys.' He gave Justin a grin and explained, 'Because of all the expensive equipment, most of the workshops have to be kept locked so it's a good job you ran into me.'

Without students at work there was little to see in some places, however all the heavy equipment in the motor vehicle and machine shops had Justin enthralled. He was fascinated by computers and the normally reserved Dev was in his element demonstrating the CAD CAM facilities. Though Sarah hadn't planned on angling for a guided tour, she was grateful to her nephew for giving Dev the opportunity to demonstrate the strengths of his faculty to her. Sarah was convinced that Dev avoided her most of the time because he felt that his faculty was the poor relation of the college. There was a time when it had been the most thriving area in the place but things had changed. Not only did it now have the smallest number of students, it also had the highest drop out rate and the poorest examination results. Sarah didn't seem to be able to make him understand that she didn't hold him responsible and that these difficulties were only to be expected. Engineering was declining in the area in line with the national trend. His faculty also covered all the craft courses and though she saw no problem with lads not finishing their brick laying, carpentry or plumbing courses to take up a job offer, he was always on the defensive.

By the time they'd finished at the college, what Sarah had planned for a brief couple of hours had taken up the best part of the day.

They'd only been back at the flat for an hour or so when Matt rang.

'I was wondering if you two had anything planned for tomorrow?'

'I was thinking of going to the Railway Museum but the weather is so great it's a shame to waste it staying inside. I'm toying with a trip to somewhere like Stone Henge or possibly the birds at Slimbridge. I'll have a chat with Justin after we've eaten and see what he fancies.'

'The boys got on so well together when we went to Chessington, I wondered if you'd both like to come with us to the New Forest for the day. The kids love that sort of thing and I thought you might like to see the autumn colours.'

'Sounds great. Hang on a minute. I'll call him.' Justin came hurrying from his bedroom and she put Matt's suggestion to him. The beaming smile he gave was all the answer she needed.

'We're both looking forward to it,' Sarah said into the phone. 'What time do you want us?'

'Hi there, I'm back!'

Justin was obviously still engrossed in one of his games, Sarah thought, because she didn't get an answer. She staggered through to the kitchen and plonked the assortment of carrier bags on the table. How come one extra person in the house and a picnic increased her usual shop tenfold? she asked herself as she tried to rub the feeling back into her palms where the strained plastic handles had cut deep groves.

Before she could sit down with a well deserved cup of tea, she would have to put away all the perishable items. The rest could wait till later.

Though it had begun to get dark, there was no light on in living room when she pushed the door open. Justin was buried in the corner of the settee, knees to chest, curled into a ball, his face as white as chalk.

'What's wrong, sweetheart?'

Quickly she crossed the room and sat beside him, pulling him to her.

He turned huge brown eyes towards her. 'There was a phone call.'

'Not Todd!' Her heart was in her mouth.

He shook his head. 'I picked it up and before I could say anything this horrible voice said, "I'm going to get you!"' The tears he'd been holding back welled over.

She wrapped him in her arms and he clung to her burying his face in her chest.

There'd been no calls for over three weeks, why oh why now? She should have been here. She'd only left him for an hour!

Chapter 19

Much to Sarah's relief, Justin came into the kitchen, eyes shining, all ready dressed; the previous day's terror apparently forgotten in all his excited anticipation.

'You're up early! They won't be here for ages yet.'

He gave her a rueful grin and helped himself to cereal. After breakfast he volunteered to do the washing up whilst Sarah buttered rolls and made flasks of coffee and soup. Looking at the pile of fruit, crisps and biscuits lined up by the tower of sandwiches, she decided she'd prepared enough food for a small army. No doubt two growing boys and a man made ravenous by fresh air and exercise would soon demolish the lot. Her mother's first rule of catering – it's better to have too much than not enough – had been well ingrained.

Inevitably, they were both ready a good half hour before Matt and Paul were due to arrive. They checked through all the things they were to take with them for the umpteenth time and Justin insisted that they should make a start by carrying down at least the waterproofs and boots to the front door so as to be ready the moment they appeared.

To judge by their early arrival, Paul was equally excited. As the two boys began pilling things into the boot, Sarah went back up to get the food. A few minutes later, she heard Matt coming up the stairs.

'Come to help?'

He took the basket she handed him but stood looking at her with a slight frown on his face. 'I thought you said those calls had stopped.'

'Justin told you did he?'

'You told him it was one of your students playing a sick joke.'

'Damn. He didn't mention it at all this morning and I hoped he'd forgotten all about it. The last thing I want is him to be upset.'

'I think he's worried about you. He asked if I could put a trace on your phone.'

'Well that won't be necessary. I rang the phone company and they're changing my number. It'll take twenty four hours apparently and then I'll have to spend ages letting everyone know.'

Matt continued to scrutinize her expression. 'I didn't realize it had got that bad.'

'I can't pretend that the bastard wasn't getting to me but now I'm just plain angry. I could wring his bloody neck for what he did to Justin.' Sarah's vehemence brought the flicker of a smile to Matt's lips. 'We'd better get down there. The boys will wonder where we are.'

'Fine, but just you make sure you let me know if there's any problem.'

At least now she could tell him about the post and mail order parcels without worrying he'd think it was her overworked imagination but it would have to wait until there was time. There'd be plenty of opportunity at some point in the day. 'Will do. Thanks.'

If Justin was worried, he was making a good show of covering it up. For most of the journey, there was non-stop chatter from the back seat.

Justin, who'd never been to the New Forest before, was fascinated the vast numbers of ponies wandering about freely. The moment the car came to a standstill, the boys were out and moving stealthily towards a small group of mares with their foals clustered under the trees at the side of the car park. The expression on Justin's face when he found one happy to be stroked gave Sarah a warm glow. Any last vestiges of doubt that Justin was covering up some deeply traumatized state were wiped away. If Justin could manage to forget about it for awhile, so could she. Why let her tormentor ruin her day?

They eventually donned boots, stowed anoraks into the rucksacks and, armed with maps and a pair of binoculars, set off along the trail.

'What a glorious day! You'd think it was summer,' she said lifting her face to warmth of the sun. 'It's surprising how many of the trees are only just beginning to turn. After all the golds and glorious russets as we drove through Savernake Forest I hadn't expected to see it so green down here. Some have begun to change colour but there's not that many fallen leaves.'

Matt smiled at her obvious enjoyment. 'Give it one strong wind and they'll soon be down.'

'Spoil sport.'

As the boys skipped ahead, she could hear Paul pointing out the names of the various types of trees to a willing listener.

'He's very knowledgeable,' she said to Matt.

'We come here often and we've been on several of the guided walks. Paul's into the entire nature thing. At the moment he fancies being a Forest Ranger. He can tell you the difference between pendunculate and sessile oaks and you'll probably get the lecture on problems of Turkey Oak wasp before the day is out,' he said indulgently.

They had lunch in a beautiful spot by one of the huge ponds. Halfway through the afternoon, they called another halt and demolished the last of the coffee and chocolate-chip cookies.

'We haven't seen any deer,' Paul said wistfully.

'They are easier to spot when it begins to get dark. We could try stopping off on the way home at the place near Nomansland where we saw them before,' his father suggested.

'Yes, please.' Justin was so delighted at the prospect, Matt quickly stressed that he couldn't make any promises that their hunt would be successful.

It was quite a walk from where they left the car in the pull up area alongside the pub, up through the village and onto the rolling rising ground beyond. Nevertheless, once they left the road, they were soon out of sight of any sign of human habitation. After a patient wait sitting on the bank at the edge of the enclosure, their trek was eventually reward with a distant view of a fallow buck emerging from the trees. The animal stood grazing just long enough for each of them to have a turn with Matt's binoculars then, with remarkable speed, it dashed across the heath and disappeared back into the forest. It wasn't the best of sightings but at least the boys could add it to list of creatures that they'd seen that day.

As they retraced their steps, a few bullocks lifted their heads to stare at them as they passed. Neither Paul nor Justin wanted to go back when they reached the top of the gravel track that led down to the road. Despite her protests that it would soon be dark, they begged to be allowed to investigate what lay in the opposite direction. At the top of the gentle rise, a tall hedgerow with occasional breaks bordered the open land. The track appeared to continue on through a narrow stretch of woodland.

'It will probably bring us out on the far side of the village and we could walk back along the main road,' Matt suggested.

The boys thought it great fun jumping onto the bars of the cattle grid that marked the beginning of the path. A few yards further on, the two of them stopped to peer through a gap in the trees at the animals in an adjacent field.

'I'm glad there's a ditch and a fence between us and them,' said Justin.

'They won't hurt you. They're only bullocks,' Paul teased.

'Maybe, but there's a lot of them.'

As the track went deeper into the trees, it became darker. They turned the corner and came upon an enormous fallen tree trunk that barred their path. It was impossible to get round because of a muddy ditch on one side and the fence on the other.

'I think we'd better go back the way we came,' Matt decided.

Rounding the final bend, they saw the shapes of the bullocks lumbering past beyond the trees. One came to the cattle grid and stared at them along the track.

'Let's wait here until they've moved on,' Sarah said lightly. Friendly bullocks might be, but she for one had no wish to push past such a huge beast.

They'd reached the gap in the trees where they'd spotted the large herd earlier. They could see that the animals were now making their way out of their field onto the open ground through a gap in the far hedge that none of them had noticed before. It took ten minutes for them all to file through and move on up beyond the entrance of the woodland path.

'Go and join the rest of your friends,' Paul called out defiantly to the animal that had decided to station itself blocking their passage.

Reluctantly, with a toss of its head, the bullock ambled off up the slope.

Their route lay across the bottom corner of the vast stretch of open ground and was marked, at least for the first section, by a line of large, spreading oaks dotted at irregular intervals. The majority of the herd were now assembled on the rising ground well to their left and the few that remained seemed amiable enough as the small party skirted around them.

As Paul strolled ahead chattering away to Matt, Justin kept close by Sarah, his eyes darting from side to side. They'd only gone a dozen yards or so when their movement attracted the attention of the curious animals which advanced en masse to investigate. Fifty or sixty enormous animals closing in at remarkable speed wasn't a pleasant experience.

'Get behind that tree,' Matt told the boys sharply.

When they stopped, so did the bullocks. Sarah was apprehensive but gave Justin a grin as though this was all part of the adventure. After a minute or two all seemed calm.

'They're only curious. They don't mean us any harm,' Matt said encouragingly, smiling at Justin. 'When I give the word, we all walk slowly down to the next tree.'

The boys did as they were bidden trying to ignore the relentless march closing in behind them. They repeated the process from tree to tree, pausing for several minutes behind each massive trunk. Each stage brought the animals nearer. Sarah tried not to think about the final stretch which must have been a good three hundred yards long.

They were half way to the last tree when one animal, more frisky than the rest, broke into a run, which started a stampede. All four raced for sanctuary, the sound of the pounding hoofs loud in their ears.

Once they'd reached the comparative safety of the far side of the tree, Paul and Matt started laughing. For them it seemed a huge joke but Sarah was petrified. All the excitement had attracted the whole herd and now eighty or ninety beasts, ranged in a great arc, lay behind them. She accepted that they'd no evil intent, even so, the thought of those powerhouses thundering down on them wasn't one she cared to dwell upon. The pinprick lights of the house beyond the track shone in the distance. Much too far away for their cries for help to be heard.

'We'd better sit it out here until they've calmed down a bit. They'll lose interest in a while if we keep quiet and still.' Matt's voice was low and cheerful. If he felt any of the panic that was gripping Sarah, he didn't show it.

It was a very long ten minutes. Even in the open, the dusk was deepening fast. She cursed the fact that she was wearing a cream sweater and light coloured slacks. She must have stood out like a beacon. If, like Justin, they'd all been in relatively dark clothes, they might have been able to sneak away without attracting the animals' attention.

'What are they doing,' she whispered to Matt as he peered round the enormous trunk.

'They seem quiet enough now. Some have wandered off.' He turned and smiled at the boys. 'Right lads, we are going to take three or four steps away from the tree and then stop. If the bullocks don't move, we'll try a few more but if they start coming again we return to the tree. We take it very slowly. No sudden movements and don't hurry. No running. Understand?'

All three of them nodded. Sarah said a silent prayer.

With the boys in front of them, they left the protection of the tree. Her ears pricked for the slightest sound of movement behind, Sarah kept her eyes on their goal ahead in case turning back to see what was happening aroused the interest of the beasts.

At the half way stage she softly reminded the boys to keep to the slow, steady pace. They must be feeling the same temptation to make a belt for it that she was having to hold back but even at that distance, at full gallop, the bullocks would easily outrun them. Matt's hand found hers. She gripped it hard, every muscle in her body tense; her gaze still fixed on the two fence posts that marked at the end of the track.

The moment the two boys jumped over the cattle-grid, they raced ahead laughing and jumping in a great release of tension. Sarah and Matt picked their way more sedately across the rounded metal slats to safety.

'That wasn't nice,' she said meaningfully looking up into Matt's laughing eyes.

He put his arm around her and gave a comforting hug. Instinctively, she lifted her face and kissed him full on the lips. It'd been a spontaneous gesture of thanks but a wave of acute embarrassment flooded over her. It also seemed to take Matt by surprise. The two of them turned and walked side-by-side following the boys as though it hadn't happened.

'That little adventure will give those two something to talk about for a while,' he said in a perfectly normal voice a few minutes later. 'I don't suppose we were in any real danger. The bullocks were just a bit frisky and they get nervous in the dusk.' He turned and laughed. 'Goes to show what terrible townies we are. Shouldn't be let loose in the country.'

She smiled back but he must have realized how mortified she was feeling because he took her hand and gave a reassuring squeeze. He didn't let go until they reached the car park.

Both boys fell asleep in the car going home. After the fresh air and all that excitement, even Sarah found herself dozing and she didn't remember going through Salisbury. They were all tired when they got back so decided to call it a day and abandon the idea of a trip to McDonalds. Matt dropped Sarah and Justin back at her flat just before eight.

Matt helped carry the all the stuff inside while Justin stayed by the car saying his goodbyes to Paul so the adults had a few moments alone.

'I'll give you a ring tomorrow.' Matt gave her a quick peck on the cheek and hurried out to the car.

She and Justin stood side-by-side waving until the car disappeared around the corner. Sarah was the first to turn and lead the way up the stairs. She didn't want Justin to see the silly smile on her face.

Justin was happy to get to bed early. He'd already snuggled down when she took in his hot chocolate.

'Are you going to marry Matt?' Round eyes looked guilelessly up into hers from the pillow.

'No of course not,' she said with a laugh. 'You know I'm already married to Nathan.'

'But you don't live with him any more. You could get a divorce.'

'And you a good Catholic boy!' she said in mock horror, ruffling his hair. 'I'm not going to marry Matt because I don't want to. He's a friend and that's all. I do have a lot of friends and quite a few of them are men,' she finished seriously.

'You were holding hands when we crossed that field.' Justin sounded far from convinced.

'Only because I was scared out of my wits.'

The brown eyes widened and he stared at her open-mouthed. It was several moments before he spoke. 'Were you really frightened?'

'Petrified!' she answered sincerely.

'I thought I was the only one. You sounded so calm and the others were laughing.'

'Believe me they were both as terrified as we were.' She took his empty mug, sat on the bed and put her arm around him. 'You were very brave.' They cuddled closer at the memory. 'There's only one thing worse than the thought of facing a field of frisky bullocks charging about the field.'

He looked up at her, a puzzled expression on his face. 'What's that?'

'Your mum, when she finds out I took you there in the first place.'

He collapsed in a fit of giggles. 'What she doesn't hear, she won't be able to complain about.'

'Fine. Let's keep it our secret. Now snuggle down and don't forget to say your prayers. Night, night. God bless.'

He was probably asleep before she closed the door.

As she walked back to the living room, Sarah realized how much she would miss Justin when she had to take him home. He was a quiet, sensitive lad but she'd been awarded the privilege of seeing beyond the wall of reserve he'd built around himself. The past few days had been as enjoyable for her as she hoped they had for him. And, from a purely selfish point of view, she had to admit that it'd been good for her to have someone else to have to think about rather than wallow in her own fears and problems. Fluffing up the cushion on her favourite chair, she sank down with a contented sigh. Despite the rocky start, it'd been a good day.

Blast. She'd forgotten to tell Matt about the other stuff. Oh well, there was always next time.

Chapter 20

On Monday morning, Sarah could hear voices in the outer office. Anxious to get on, Sarah needed to know if there was anything urgent in the post sitting on Lucy's desk that required her attention before she started on anything else. Whilst someone stood out there gossiping, not only Lucy was being held up!

Some five minutes later, Lucy knocked on her door.

'Sorry about that. Tom was in the office and I had problems getting rid of him. I didn't want to be rude.'

'What did he want?'

'He brought up a copy of the evening class figures.'

'He could have given me those at the faculty meeting tomorrow like all the other directors.' Sarah couldn't keep the annoyance out of her voice.

'He did ask how you were,' Lucy said reproachfully as though that excused his time wasting.

'I hope you told him I was brimming with health and vigour.' It was difficult to keep the sarcasm out of her voice.

'He assumed you'd been glued to your desk all week trying to get on top of things. He seemed a bit surprised when I told him you'd been gallivanting off all over the place.'

'Why on earth should he imagine that I needed to catch up on anything?'

Lucy shrugged. 'You know what he's like. He seems to think you're under a lot of pressure these days.'

'Is that what he said?' Sarah asked more sharply than she'd intended.

'Not in so many words but he implied that's what all the other senior staff think and he keeps telling me that I need to make sure that you don't get too stressed.'

'Next time you can assure him that I am coping admirably.'

'I told him that if he wasn't careful, you'd have him up for sexual harassment.' She gave a little giggle. 'He looked a bit shocked when I told him that I thought his remarks were sexist and he wouldn't dream of repeating such stupid gossip if we had a male principal.' Sarah couldn't suppress a smile. She could picture the poor man's expression. 'He went off in a huff looking all offended. In this place, you have to stand up to these male chauvinists,' came Lucy's parting shot as she closed the door with a determined bang.

'Am I the first?' Barry put his head round the open door.

'You can come in,' Sarah responded coolly. 'Lucy's just about to bring in the coffee.'

Rather than take his usual chair he came and perched himself on the table next to her. 'I've had a few thoughts about this Working Party...'

'Can you save it for the meeting Barry,' she interrupted getting up and walking across to the door. 'I need to take a look at something before we start.' The last thing she wanted was the others coming in to find her and Barry apparently hatching plots before the rest of them had a chance to hear the latest developments.

For once, they were able to start the meeting on time. One of the issues down for discussion was the difficulties arising from the no-smoking policy. This had been introduced just before her arrival at the college and caused considerable acrimony in some quarters. There had been demands for smokers' rooms, at least for staff, which the governors had refused, but every now and again the old chestnut came up. Sarah was well aware that several of the staff continued to smoke behind the closed doors of their own offices, but the immediate problem involved the students. Although the rules were strictly adhered to within the buildings, the ever increasing number of student smokers tended to congregate in the car park.

'One of these days there is going to be an horrendous accident. It only takes a discarded butt to roll under a vehicle and the whole place could go up in flames,' David Ford argued vehemently.

'Suggestions?' Sarah looked around the table.

'How about giving them a specific area outside where they can go?' said Dev.

There were half-hearted nods of approval. 'Do you have anywhere in mind?' she asked him.

'The most logical place is at the back of the A Block; the area that looks out over the playing fields. There's a decent amount of covered space where they could stand if it's raining.'

'Sounds good to me,' Sarah replied. She'd given the matter some thought before the meeting and this had been exactly where she had in mind.

'It's a hell of a walk all the way round there,' protested Frank, the only smoker among them. 'Why not let them smoke out the front?'

The whole of that section by the steps is protected and they'd be out of the wind there as well.'

She waited for someone to point out the obvious but it seemed that none of the others wanted to take Frank on. 'It wouldn't give visitors a good impression of the place as they come up to reception,' she said mildly.

'So now we're putting the sensibilities of outsiders before the needs of our students are we?' Frank muttered just loud enough to be heard. Such a comment was typical of the way he tried to subvert the decision-making. Barry raised his eyes to ceiling, Tom smirked and the others stared ahead, faces impassive.

She wanted to scream. Here she was, desperately trying to hold it together as her world rapidly fell around her ears because of some demented maniac intent on pushing her over the edge of sanity, and her senior colleagues were behaving like a bunch of infants squabbling in the nursery to see who could get the most attention. What the hell did it all matter anyway?

'Any other ideas,' Sarah asked crisply. She let the silence go on for a few seconds. 'Then we'll take that as read. I'll put it to the governors next week but I don't anticipate any objections. I'll let you all know their decision and we'll issue the information for tutors to pass on as soon as possible. Now to the last item, the faculty review working party. As you know, the subcommittee still has to present the guidelines, however, after the next governors' meeting, it should be all go. We'll need representation from each of the faculties to join the working party and there should be one director...'

'If you're looking for a volunteer, Sarah, I'd be willing to sit along side you,' Barry cut in before she'd time to finish.

'No. I'm not actually,' she said firmly. The reason for Barry's earlier bonhomie was now clear. He'd been angling to get himself a more high profile opportunity both with the college staff and, more importantly, the governors.

As she paused to consider her words, Frank cut in. 'He can do it as far as I'm concerned. I've got enough on my plate without having to go to any more bloody meetings.' He put his hands behind his head and lent back watching her discomfort with relish.

'I have obviously discussed this with Sir Richard,' she said quickly before anyone else could pass comment. 'This place began as a Technology College. Times have changed and our courses now cover the whole range, but he feels that those traditions mustn't be overlooked and consequently the Director of Technology should be on the committee.' A few surprised looks meet her gaze. 'And incidentally, it will be George and not me on the Working Party. He's agreed to convene the first meeting and after that the group will elect their own chair.'

There was silence while they digested the news.

'I still don't see how you can have equal input from all the faculties when you've got one represented at director level and others possibly at Scale one,' muttered Frank.

'We've been all through this several times.' Her voice was icy. 'I don't propose to waste time doing it again. Every member will be there to put forward the views of their faculty not as individuals. It's up to each of you to ensure that you discuss all the relevant issues as they affect your area in your own faculty meetings so that your representative will be fully briefed. And, if I heard you correctly, Frank, not five minutes ago, you made it quite clear that you'd no wish to serve on the Working Party, so I can only assume that you're being deliberately bloody-minded.'

Frank sat up with a start. Sarah could see a few dropped jaws. Though on occasions, she'd been known to exchange heated words with individuals behind closed doors, she'd never thrown down such a challenge in public. The air was electric. Everyone sat frozen until eventually George shifted uncomfortably in his chair. Frank was still staring across the table at her but the others had all dropped their gaze.

Before Frank could explode, which he looked all set to do, she snapped, 'If that's all, good morning, gentlemen.' She pulled her papers together, stood up and moved over to her own desk. Moments later they trooped out one by one while she scribbled nonsense on a sheet of paper in an attempt to look busy. Frank, the last to leave, turned back when he reached the door. Sarah could see him from the corner of her eye and before he could say anything, she pulled the phone towards her and punched a number.

'Good morning. May I speak to Sir Richard please?'

Frank disappeared banging the door behind him, which was just as well. Thankfully she replaced the receiver. She'd dialled her own number and had been speaking to her answerphone.

Chapter 21

Getting the wrong side of Frank worried Sarah not at all. He'd been asking for his comeuppance for a long time. However, the confrontation had left her drained and more unsettled than she should have been. Try as she might, she couldn't concentrate on the work in front of her. Some half an hour later, she finally admitted defeat and decided to go and make herself a coffee.

In the corridor, she spotted Frank coming out of George's office. He didn't see her and turned and ambled off towards the lift.

It didn't make her feel any easier. Inevitably she began to wonder what the two had been plotting. No point in getting paranoid. George had seemed to distance himself from his old buddy over the last year or so but perhaps she'd been wrong in making that assumption. It wasn't the thought of the little intrigues they might be hatching that prompted her gloom. Her conviction that she'd made real progress healing the breach with George now looked hollow and all his apparent willingness for them to work together was merely a sham.

Although Justin appeared to be none the worse for the unpleasant phone call and had said nothing, at least in Sarah's presence, to his parents or grandparents about it at the weekend when she had taken him back to Norwich, Sarah was still apprehensive.

It was a relief that, whenever she phoned Jenny to enquire about Todd, if Justin was around, he would insist on talking to her. He certainly didn't sound as if he had something on his mind and surely he wouldn't be so enthusiastic to talk to her if he harboured any fears about the time he'd spent in Swindon. Sarah didn't like to ask outright if Justin had talked about it in case they suspected that the incident had been far more serious than she'd made out.

Although she'd decided to tell all the family straight away that the reason she had changed her telephone number was because she'd been receiving nuisance calls, she had tried to make light of them. Her mother had asked a couple of times if she'd had any more trouble but Sarah was able to reassure her without any difficulty. As the days past, the danger of adding to the family's worries with her problems began to fade.

Housework had never been an activity that filled Sarah with relish. She'd never got round to getting herself a cleaner. It wasn't because she was too mean to pay for one as Nathan had joked in their previous home together or, as Elizabeth suggested, that she couldn't bear the thought of someone snooping round her house when she wasn't there. The truth was that she felt a vague guilt that one person couldn't make so much mess to justify having someone else to clear up after them. Justin's visit had relieved her of the half-hearted promise she'd made to herself that she would give the flat a thorough going over during half term. Other than the routine dusting, vacuuming and basics, she tackled major jobs only on impulse. It started with getting rid of a large spider's web in the corner of the ceiling and, having got out the stepladder, she decided she might as well clean the windows. One of the problems of the flat being converted from an older house with high ceilings was that a standard cobweb brush wouldn't reach into the corners. Even dusting the curtain rails necessitated the palaver of bring up the steps from the below stairs cupboard. Once she'd got going, she soldiered on and spent a long Saturday morning giving her living room its half-yearly spring clean. The woodwork got washed down and even the heaviest furniture, including an oak sideboard – her pride and joy – edged away from the wall to allow a thorough hoovering behind.

Pleased with her efforts, she sat curled in the deep embrace of her arm chair savouring the decadence of slowly sipping the freshly ground Colombian coffee she'd allowed herself as a special totally justified treat. For a few months at least, she decided as she glanced around admiring the results of her labours, she could forget about this room – apart from the windows, she realized with a twinge of annoyance. She had a couple of goes but she could still see swirling patterns caught in the sun's rays. Over the years, she'd tried every brand of window cleaner from fine sprays, thick liquids and specially impregnated cloths to old fashioned solutions like vinegar and newspaper but somehow she'd never seemed to master the art. She made a mental note to consult her mother, the oracle on all things domestic, on her next phone call.

The front door bell rang. She took her time slopping down the stairs in her down-at-heel slippers and the shocked look on her face as she opened the door must have been all too apparent to her visitor.

'Hello, Sarah. Have I caught you at a bad moment? I tried ringing you first but all I got was number unobtainable.' She leaned forward and gave Sarah a perfunctory peck on the cheek. Geraldine was inside before Sarah had the chance to invite her in. 'I hope you're not busy. I called on the off chance. I've brought round the photographs you said you'd like to see.'

Sarah stood speechless. What was the woman doing here? Had she come to taunt her?

'I didn't realize you had my address,' Sarah said suspiciously.

'I got it ages ago. After you sent me a Christmas card, I asked Nathan so I could send you one.'

'Of course.' She really was going gaga.

She didn't want Geraldine of all people in her house though, in the circumstances, there was little she could do. Her mother-in-law had taken another couple of steps inside and stood looking at the stairs, waiting for an invitation. There was no way Sarah could ask her to leave.

'I was just about to have a bath,' Sarah said weakly still holding the door open in the vague hope that Geraldine would take the hint and leave.

'In that case I promise I won't stop long.'

'Come on up,' Sarah said with a sigh of resignation which, surely, Geraldine couldn't have missed? The woman had never been thick skinned. If anything, she'd always taken exception to any of Sarah's remarks, however innocent, that could possibly be interpreted as a slight or criticism. This new Geraldine was something of an enigma and Sarah wasn't sure how to cope.

Sarah led her into the living room where her guest looked around and made the predictable complimentary noises.

'It has so much character,' she gushed. 'And I love the minimalist look.'

It was true that the room was relatively sparsely furnished but only because Sarah was waiting to find exactly the right pieces. Even on a principal's salary, she couldn't afford antiques but spent many happy hours wandering around the local salerooms.

'I'm glad you like it,' Sarah muttered dutifully.

'It's so vast. Makes my little place seem very ordinary.'

Geraldine lived in an attractive, spacious bungalow on a select development on the east of the town overlooking a golf course. It was more than adequate for her needs although, Sarah acknowledged, she probably felt that it was a considerable come down from the near palatial six bedroom Surrey house where she'd entertained her husband's business associates to lavish dinner parties. She'd left behind much of the impressive furniture, too large and out of keeping with a modern bungalow. Losing a husband had also involved loss of a whole way of life and considerable prestige. Sarah pulled herself up with a jolt. Feeling sorry for Geraldine was getting to be a habit!

'Would you like tea or coffee?' she asked in her best hostess voice. She wasn't going to make a friend of the woman however desperate she'd become!

'Oh tea, please,' Geraldine replied as though the suggestion of coffee in the middle of the afternoon was in poor taste. 'I don't suppose you have China?'

'Pekoe, Oolong, Souchong? Or there's Jasmine if you prefer.'

For a moment Geraldine looked nonplussed. 'Oh, um Oolong would be nice.'

Sarah picked up the tray with her half-eaten cheese sandwich and disappeared towards the kitchen.

Her small sense of triumph quickly disappeared when she caught sight of herself in the hall mirror. Trust Geraldine to catch her dressed in a faded sweatshirt and baggy jogging bottoms. She plonked the tray onto the kitchen table and dashed into the bedroom. Grabbing a more presentable pair of slacks and a clean blouse from the wardrobe, she went to the bathroom. After a quick wash, she put in her contact lenses and ran a comb through her hair. No amount of persuading would make it lie in the right direction. Nothing short of a wash and blow dry would make it look presentable.

Back in the kitchen, she filled the kettle then rummaged in the back of the cupboard for the packet of mixed teas she'd bought from the specialist shop in the town centre in a fit of enthusiasm after a meal in a Chinese restaurant. Her interest had immediately waned so she'd never got round to using any of them. She dare not look at the sell by date.

'Sorry to keep you waiting. I thought I'd tidy myself up a bit whilst the kettle was boiling,' she lied.

'Oh, you shouldn't have bothered for me,' Geraldine simpered.

For the next half hour, Sarah had to sit next to Geraldine on the settee whilst the older woman talked her through two whole volumes of photographs, which Sarah was expected to admire.

'That chappie in the white shirt was our tour manager, Brian. He was an absolute gem. Nothing was too much trouble.'

Sarah suppressed a smile at the thought of the merry dance she must have led the poor man and listened dutifully to the story of the evening trip to watch the cormorant fishers.

'Of course it's all a big con really. They only do it now to amuse the tourists but it was fun watching the birds bobbing and diving from the little boats all hung with lanterns.'

'I can imagine.' Sarah battled on turning the pages.

'We weren't allowed to take photographs in the pits when we went to see the Terracotta Warriors. These snaps I took in the factory where they made the replicas. Every one of the originals is different you know. I'd no idea how many there are. The pits are vast and they've only uncovered a tiny portion of them.'

Sarah stole a glance at the clock. They still had another whole album to go.

For all her cynicism, even Sarah couldn't help being impressed with the pictures of the Temple of Heaven in the Forbidden City. Even from Geraldine's far from expert photography, the sumptuous decoration shone through.

'Did I tell you about our little sail in the dragon boat on the lake at the Summer Palace? That's the photo of it there.'

The moment they reached the last photograph, Sarah looked pointedly at her watch.

'I don't want to appear rude, Geraldine, but I really must get on.'

'Oh yes, I expect you're going out this evening. You young people lead such busy social lives.'

This little fish has no intention of biting on your line, Sarah said to herself. She gave a wan smile and stood up.

'It's the same with Nathan. I'm lucky if I get to see him for Sunday lunch these days.'

Sarah's smile remained intact. She'd no intention of asking what he got up to. His affairs were his own business. And if the name Veronica leapt to her thoughts, she wasn't about to let on.

'May I use your bathroom before I disappear?'

As Sarah waited, she imagined Geraldine checking up on her. 'Don't forget to count the toothbrushes while you're in there,' she whispered at the closed door.

When Geraldine eventually reappeared, Sarah, already on the top stair, started walking down giving her visitor no opportunity to prolong her stay.

'I have so enjoyed our little chat. We must do it again sometime. Why don't you come across to me? You must see my terracotta general, he's so splendid and I know you would appreciate all the other little knickknacks I brought back.'

'Yes, indeed. I'll give you a ring sometime,' Sarah interrupted, before Geraldine had a chance to suggest a date and time. She gave her a wave, stepped back and quickly closed the door.

As it so happened, Sarah had nothing on that evening; however the next item on her agenda was a long, hot, recuperative soak in the bath with a good book. A little of Geraldine, even when she wasn't out to get the better of her ex-daughter-in-law, went a very long way.

Chapter 22

Only after she'd locked the door and left the protection of the back of the house did Sarah realize that a fine drizzle was falling. It didn't bother her over much. Sometimes, it could be quite refreshing especially on the long slog up the hill coming back. She wasn't such a fitness fanatic that she went out when it was raining hard but this was more of a thick mist, at least for the moment. The sky looked ominously dark but the sun had only been up for ten minutes or so. Having gone to all the bother of kitting herself up, she decided to carry on.

Even at that hour in the morning, there was a fair amount of traffic as she turned from Manor Lane out onto the Ridge Top Road. As sometimes happened, the drivers already out and about seemed to think a lone jogger was fair game. They'd no compunction in speeding through the puddles beginning to accumulate in the gutters producing a shower of spray over the narrow pavement.

She passed a couple of people out with their dogs and, dancing round them plus having to shy away from every car that sped past, felt more tired than usual by the time she reached the bottom. Her normal route continued past the pub and the old village school, around by the path skirting the top fields of Wheeler's Farm then on back up the hill. The rain became more persistent and she decided to cut short her morning's exercise. She contemplated returning by way of the road but decided, although already drenched, there was no sense in subjecting herself again to the dirty spray of passing cars, so she took the path through the woodland. It could be a pleasant walk although, because of the constant hairpin bends down the escarpment, it made a poor jogging track.

She was huffing and puffing before she was even half way up and her pace slackened to a slow trot. Keeping her eyes on the ground, watching where to put her feet to avoid the rapidly developing muddy patches and slippery leaves, she sensed, rather than saw, someone watching her. She glanced back over her shoulder but the path appeared to be deserted. It was a far from pleasant sensation and she gave a spurt to get to the next bend. As she rounded the corner, she'd a good excuse to look back more carefully. If she was being followed, he or she was staying well out of sight.

It wasn't the first time she'd had this feeling. On the previous occasions she'd told herself that she was being over-sensitive. Nathan's comment about the need for her to take care in this lonely spot came to mind and she cursed him for putting the idea into her head. She sprinted along the next section but there was no way she could keep up her pace when the gradient became steeper and she soon developed a painful ache in her chest. The thought of someone coming up behind her wouldn't go away so, rather than stopping altogether, she turned and walked slowly backwards up the slope scanning the route behind.

A movement in the bushes below caught her eye. It was too high above ground to be a fox or dog and far too great a disturbance to be the odd bird. Whoever was following had abandoned the path altogether and was climbing up through the trees. Each time she came to a halt so did her pursuer, evidently listening as intensely as she was. She tried to convince herself that it was just the pattering of the rain and she was spooking herself over nothing. As she stood debating whether to go down and investigate, a sudden thunderclap made her jump. Any moment now, the steady drizzle would become a torrent. She turned and ran.

Her heart was thumping as she reached the top road and, although she felt safer in full view of the houses, she kept going and cut through the footpath onto the lane. She already had the key clutched in her hand as she rounded the corner. Slamming the front door shut and, without waiting to slide across the bolts and put on the chain, she hurried up the stairs ignoring the wet footprints and puddles of water on her beautiful, polished wood. She dashed to the living room window but, though she waited for some time, no one climbed out of the woodland. If there'd been someone there, he'd either run up behind her into cover or had gone down to the bottom road. A glance out at the back revealed nothing either. As far as she could tell, there was no one watching the house. The only consolation was knowing that if there had been a stalker in the woods, he would now be soaked to the skin.

She resolved to buy a personal alarm at lunchtime. It was something her students were advised to get if travelling out alone. Even after her unfortunate experience in the underpass, she'd never imagined that she might ever need one herself.

First thing on a Monday morning wasn't the best time for anything that took her out of college and, thinking of the pile of work mounting up on her desk, Sarah gave a deep sigh as she made her way back into the building shortly after lunch.

Had she known agreeing to act as chairman of the Education Business Partnership would involve her in radio interviews, she might well have had second thoughts. Expecting to talk about the joint projects between local business, schools and the college, she suddenly found herself forced on the defensive. Critical debate might make for interesting listening but there was no need for the adversarial stance that her interviewer had taken. Whenever she tried to outline the benefits to students, staff and business personnel of their latest projects, he insisted such activities were peripheral to the core curriculum and demanded to know how they could be justified in the current climate of poor resources in education.

'How did you get on at the studio?' Sarah's grim expression didn't go unnoticed. 'Oh dear, as bad as that?' Lucy gave her a sympathetic grimace.

'Worse.'

'Just remind yourself it's all good PR. You're the one who talks about the value of networking.' Lucy's gentle teasing became more serious, 'I'll get you a coffee. You might need it. I don't think your day is going to get any better.'

Sarah groaned. 'That sounds ominous. What's been happening?'

'There was punch up between some of the Second Year Travel and Tourism students and a group of Construction lads in the canteen this morning. Mr Fitzgibbon has been dealing with it but he asked if you'd phone him as soon as you got in.'

'Let me get my coat off,' Sarah sighed. 'And I will have that coffee.'

Five minutes later, George bustled in with Frank Wagner and a concerned looking Dev Sharma in his wake.

'So were you able to sort out the ringleaders?' she asked after George's lengthy explanation of the fracas.

'It seems Carl Evans threw the first punch and mayhem broke out as they all joined in.'

'Isn't he the lad we put on a final warning last month?'

'Exactly.' George's face was grim.

'There was a lot of stupid name calling going on between the two groups that got out of hand and one of them called Carl a thicky brickie. I call that deliberate provocation.' She'd never seen Dev so animated.

'The boy's an out-and-out thug,' said Frank casually from the corner of the low bookcase where he'd perched himself.

'According to his tutor, he's made a real effort after the last warning and he's kept out of trouble,' Dev snapped, deliberately ignoring Frank's own brand of incitement.

'That isn't the issue, Dev. The boy was on a final warning and I'm afraid that's it. He came from Kingsbury Comprehensive with a poor record; he's been in trouble on numerous occasions in the short time he's been here. He knew the consequences. It would totally undermine discipline if we let him get away with it.' She was annoyed with Dev for making her play the heavy-handed authoritarian. Though she applauded the instinct that made him support the students in his faculty, this situation wasn't negotiable and he knew it.

'We were lucky we didn't have a full-scale fight on our hands. If a group of staff hadn't come in at just the right time, it could have developed into a very nasty incident,' George put in.

'What about the others involved?' she asked.

'They've all been given a warning. They're banned from the canteen and I've told them that if they're not in lectures I don't want them hanging around on site.'

'Will you make sure that their personal tutors are aware of that?' She glared across at Frank who acknowledged her request with what in a student she would have called an insolent shrug. 'I want a list of all the lads involved and I'd like summary progress report on each of them as soon as possible.' Frank's grin quickly disappeared. A little dart of satisfaction shot through her. She'd not done it to get her own back, she would have asked for the reports in any case, but she had no compunction in putting extra work on Frank.

The three men shuffled out of her office and she could hear Frank muttering away outside. Before the door was closed, Tom Appleby put his head round the door.

'Before you get involved in anything else could I have a quick word?'

'Is it urgent, Tom? I have got a lot on today.'

'You were the one who said you wanted a chat about the Review Working Party rep from my faculty,' he said with a tinge of peevishness.

'Right,' she said hoping that her resignation didn't show. 'Come in and shut the door.' If she wanted Anna Margilewska on the team, she needed to do some sweet-talking.

It'd been a long time since she'd seen Elizabeth. Because of the accumulation of paperwork over half term, she'd to put off their usual get together. With all that'd happened in the mean time, there was a lot of catching up to do.

Soon after Elizabeth arrived, the doorbell rang. Sarah glanced out of the window as she reached the middle landing and noticed a small, white, delivery van pulled up behind Elizabeth's Renault. When she opened the door, a young man stood holding an enormous bouquet of yellow roses, looking at her expectantly.

'Mrs Harcourt?'

'Yes,' she replied somewhat tentatively, half expecting him to hand over a bill.

'These are for you, delivered by "The House of Blooms".'

Elizabeth was standing looking over the banister as she made her way back upstairs.

'They're gorgeous! Who are they from?'

'I haven't had a chance to look yet.'

She took them into the kitchen and laid them on the table. Elizabeth's impatience, as she slowly prised open the ends of the staple fixing the tiny envelope to cellophane, was readily apparent.

'So?' she demanded as Sarah read the card inside.

'It just says, "To remind you of our special day". What an odd thing to write!' Sarah said. 'There's no signature.'

'This new chap must be keen – sending you flowers.'

'It doesn't say they're from Matt.' Sarah stared at the card.

'Is it his writing?'

Sarah shook her head. 'I've no idea.'

'Who else can they be from?'

Sarah shrugged. 'I haven't actually seen him for a couple of weeks – not since we went to the New Forest. I've been so busy just lately and he was on duty over the weekend.'

'Perhaps that's why. He's worried you might forget all about him and he obviously enjoyed the trip. So what happened that you didn't tell me about?' Her eyes twinkled with mischief.

'Nothing!' Sarah could feel the colour rising to her cheeks. 'And if you'd been listening you'd remember I told you the boys were with us the whole time.'

She'd left out the bit about her holding onto Matt's hand, not to mention the impromptu kiss, when recounting the tale of their escape from the bullocks. The memory of that unguarded gesture and her petrified clinging to him still filled her with embarrassment. Surely Matt hadn't interpreted it as anything more? His peck on the cheek as they'd parted was surely only a consoling gesture. Though he'd phoned next day as promised, they'd not arranged an actual date to go out again because of his shifts. She'd been relieved by the delay rather than disappointed. After their last little encounter, she wasn't at all sure how she felt about him, she was apprehensive about what he might be thinking about her. He was great as a friend and they'd a lot in common, but she didn't want him to think that their friendship would progress to anything more. They had spoken a couple of times on the phone and he hadn't sounded any more eager to press matters than she had. Contemplating the significance of the flowers was something she would need to do alone when Elizabeth had gone. She wasn't sure if she was pleased or apprehensive. It was certainly flattering, but was she ready to let down the barriers and develop a close relationship with anyone? At least, she consoled herself, the roses were yellow rather than red.

She busied herself with the laborious process of detaching all the gold ribbons festooned around and removing the clinging layers of tough cellophane.

'It's like Fort Knox trying to break into this!' she muttered in frustration trying to release the stems from the tightly bound layers of sticky tape.

'Here let me.' Elizabeth took the scissors from the drawer, elbowed her aside and deftly clipped away the binding.

'I don't know if I've got a vase big enough for that lot. It will take me ages to arrange them all. Still, if we're going to eat tonight, I'd better stick these in a bucket for now and get on with the meal. I thought we'd have stroganoff tonight. I cut up all the beef before you got here but you can chop the onions if you like while I find something for these to stand in.'

'Only on condition you tell me all details you've missed out so far! What with trips to Chessington and walks in the country, the two of you seem to have been seeing quite a bit of each other.'

'Strictly chaperoned by Paul and Justin,' Sarah said with a laugh. 'While I think of it, did I tell you that I had a visit from Geraldine? Remind me later and I'll give you all the grizzly details. I've been seeing quite a lot of my ex-mother-in-law!'

Chapter 23

Sarah wasn't in the best of moods. It didn't take a great deal to irritate her these days but she felt she had good cause. She'd gone all the way over to the other side of town to discuss the possibilities of a joint training project with a major company only to find that the Human Resources Manager had been called away and no one had bothered to let her know. With all that she had to do, she bitterly resented the waste of time.

As she walked along the top corridor she could hear loud voices coming from her office. When she got to the doorway, she was surprised to find all the directors of faculty plus George Fitzgibbon gathered around Lucy's desk with the poor girl almost in tears.

'But I don't know anything about a meeting and Mrs Harcourt isn't even in the college. She has an appointment at Plantar Electronics.'

'What's going on?' Sarah demanded.

'Exactly. We've all been sent memos to turn up for a meeting your secretary hasn't been told about and you're nowhere to be found.' From the expressions on all their faces, Tom wasn't the only one to be annoyed.

'Memos from whom?'

'Don't tell us you've forgotten that you even sent the bloody things.' Frank's sneer made even the others wince.

She turned her head and stared at him. He didn't apologize although he looked away quickly appreciating that he'd gone too far.

'What I'm telling you,' she said in clipped tones, 'is that I know nothing about them because I didn't send them. However, the latest government directives arrived on my desk this morning. I was going to arrange a meeting to discuss them. As you're all here, we might as well do it now.' She pushed through them to the inner office door. 'Come and sit down gentlemen while I sort out the necessary bits and pieces. Lucy will get some coffee.'

She turned and gave her secretary a smile.

'Certainly, Mrs Harcourt.'

Sarah was confident that if Lucy knew that the stuff had come in the post yesterday she wouldn't let on. Though after all the mix-ups over the last few months, Lucy could be forgiven for thinking that her boss was beginning to crack under all the pressure. There was even a vague doubt at the back of Sarah's mind; she had intended to arrange a meeting as soon as possible, even though she couldn't remember sending the memos.

When Lucy had popped her head round the door to say goodnight, Sarah decided to call it a day herself. Although it was early, at least for her, even the cleaners hadn't yet put in an appearance, she clicked the save icon and closed down the computer. By the time she'd tidied her desk, checked tomorrow's programme and jotted down a list of essential tasks for the next day it was coming up to six o'clock.

As she came out into the corridor, the place already seemed deserted. The lights still filtered through from a couple of offices at the far end but all the admin staff had long since disappeared. She could hear the hum of the vacuum cleaner in one of the far rooms. Her office was at the end of the corridor next to what she laughingly called her private stairs. She seemed to be the only one, at least on the upper floor, who used the fire escape regularly. The college lift was small and claustrophobic and took an age. Waiting patiently had never been her forte.

As she contemplated what to have for her evening meal, she decided on a change and to treat herself to something exotic. After such a difficult day, she deserved to spoil herself a little. She'd plenty of time to wander through the town centre to "The Jade Garden". It was a bit of a trek but she hadn't been out for a morning jog for several days and could do with the exercise.

Even though the majority of shops had closed for the day, there was a steady throng of people criss-crossing the pedestrian precinct. She'd already passed the bank when she decided that this was a good opportunity to get out some money. The last minute decision to get a take-away would use up her ready cash.

She turned and caught sight of a figure in a pale mackintosh darting into a shop doorway. It was the sudden movement that attracted her attention. She hesitated for a moment then hurried back. He must have been watching her approach because, before she could get close, he dived out and fled in the opposite direction. After a few yards, he veered off suddenly into the arcade, coattails flapping behind him. By the time she got to the corner, he was long gone. He could have disappeared into any of the shops and several of the larger stores had exits onto adjoining streets. At least one thing was now certain – her stalker was real enough.

During those fleeting moments when she'd seen him scurrying away, the figure had seemed familiar. She told herself not to jump to conclusions. Lots of men must have beige gabardine raincoats. It was one thing to recognize a face but it could have been the back of any tall, fair-haired man, zigzagging through the crowd. She had Nathan on the brain.

Suddenly, she'd lost her appetite.

The green light was flashing on the answerphone when she got in. The illuminated number indicated that there were two messages.

The first call was from Elizabeth. Sarah felt some of her tension easing as the friendly voice filled the room. 'Sorry to pester. I seem to have mislaid my pocket book and I wondered if I'd left it round yours the other evening. Can you give me a buzz if it turns up? Speak to you soon. Bye.'

Sarah had to smile as she pressed the stop button. The thought of Elizabeth losing anything was hard to credit. Why couldn't she come straight out and say she was dying to know if Sarah had solved the mystery of the flowers? Perhaps Sarah had made her reticence to talk about Matt a little too obvious. The trouble was that Elizabeth would interpret that as an indication that he was more special than he really was. With a sigh, Sarah heaved herself to her feet. Even the simplest things in life could get ridiculously complicated at times.

She wandered through to the kitchen and pulled open the freezer door. There were a few ready meals but she didn't have the appetite for lamb paprikash, mushroom dopiaza or the cod in parsley sauce. Although she had eggs, the piece of cheese she found in the fridge was well past its prime so fleeting plans for an omelette were speedily readjusted. It wasn't until she walked back into the living room with her tray that she remembered that there was another message on the answerphone.

'It's Matt. I'm working nights again this weekend but wondering if you were doing anything next Friday. There's a concert at the Wyvern if you're interested.'

Trying to read things into a couple of short sentences on a recorded message was a futile activity; however, to her relief, it sounded much like the old Matt. As it'd been so long, she'd been concerned that her impromptu kiss may have put him off all together.

She dialled his number only to reach his answering machine. 'The concert sounds great. I'd love to come. See you in the foyer at twenty past.'

Being able to leave a message, at least got round the problem of trying to avoid any offer to collect her. Best to keep things simple.

She'd already put down the phone when her eye caught the display of roses that stood in pride of place on the coffee table. Perhaps she should have thanked him for the flowers.

As she uncurled herself from the chair, she realized that, in her haste to return Matt's call, she'd let her meal go cold. Could anything be quite as unappetising as cold scrambled egg on soggy toast?

As both of them were working the next day, she and Elizabeth decided to grab a takeaway before the film rather than eating late. To save taking two cars to the cinema, Sarah picked up Elizabeth after she left college and they called in at the Chinese place on the way back to Sarah's flat.

'The smell is driving me crazy. I didn't realize how hungry I was,' Sarah said as they drew up outside the house.

'You look as though you haven't had a decent meal in days.'

'You're turning into a right old granny!'

Elizabeth shuffled out of the car awkwardly in an effort not to tip up the two small carrier bags of food and waited for Sarah to open the front door. Sarah's heart sank when she felt the resistance as she pushed it open. There was no way she could sweep everything up before Elizabeth spotted the offending mountain of post.

'I thought you said that all that nonsense had stopped.'

'It had,' Sarah said trying to sound blasé. 'This is the first batch I've had for ages.'

'And you wonder why I fuss? Look, Sarah, you've got to do something. You can't let this keep happening to you. Don't try to kid me that it all washes over you. All this hassle is taking its toll. Just look at yourself!' Her eyes were blazing with inner fury. She was like a roller coaster nothing could stop. 'Your face is drawn, your eyes are puffy and it's obvious you're not sleeping properly. I've known you long enough to know that you're not normally ratty and irritable and if you're snapping at me then I bet you're giving them all hell at work. You're going to get on the phone this minute and inform the police.'

Sarah put up her free hand in defence. 'Hold on! I've already phoned Royal Mail and they put me onto their Mail Preferences

Service. They can't guarantee to stop it all but the woman assured me that they usually manage to cut out ninety five percent of this kind of addressed mail.'

'So what's this pile doing here?' Elizabeth said viciously kicking the couple of small packets along the hallway.

'It takes at least a couple of months before it all gets sorted. In the meantime,' she said firmly heading for the stairs, 'I promise you, Liz, I intend to forget all about it. Someone out there has a problem, I've no idea who or why he's picked on me to play his silly games but I refuse to let it get to me. Even talking about it is letting him win.'

She looked down to find Elizabeth's narrowed eyes watching her shrewdly. Even Elizabeth knew when to give up. Although Sarah had spoken with a determination that she'd not felt, she found herself convinced by her own arguments and felt considerably better.

Chapter 24

She was coming out of the door laden with empty bottles when the furniture van drew up. Assuming it was delivering something to the bottom flat, Sarah carried on to cellar to dump her burden.

'Excuse me.' She turned to see the burly driver jump down anxious to attract her attention before she could disappear around the corner. 'You Mrs Harcourt?'

She nodded suspiciously and saw a second man climb out, stroll round and start release the back flap.

'What's this all about?'

'Your display cabinet.' He was all ready to join his colleague in the depths the van.

'Just a minute, I didn't order any furniture.'

He stopped and turned back and in a pained voice as though talking to a simple-minded geriatric, he said slowly. 'Your name is Harcourt and this is Flat B Cotman House.'

'Yes,' she agreed reluctantly.

'Then this is for you.'

The younger man had already eased the cabinet to the top of the ramp and his surly expression clearly indicated that he wasn't happy at being kept waiting.

'Hang on the pair of you.'

'Look lady, stop messing me about.'

No doubt she would have been subjected to some choice language if the door to the downstairs flat hadn't opened and Mr Erickson emerged.

'Is everything all right Sarah?'

'Just a misunderstanding,' she said swallowing her anger.

The driver took the opportunity to disappear into his cab. When he emerged he was waving a clipboard which he thrust under her nose.

'See!' He pointed to the printed delivery details at the top of the form. 'Now where do you want it?'

'But,' she repeated firmly, 'I didn't order it. You'll have to take it back.'

'Can't do that. It's been paid for.' From the look on her face he must have decided that she was about to explode. He ran a hand through the lank, thinning hair, pointed to the details on the sheet and attempted a more reasonable tone. 'Look darling, telephone order 8ᵗʰ October paid with a credit card. You should have got the confirmation letter a week later. That's when you should've cancelled it if you'd changed your mind.'

Her heart sank. She was in no position to say that it'd never been sent. With so much junk mail delivered, she'd probably thrown it out without even reading it.

'As I keep telling you, I never made the order in the first place.'

They stood for some moments glaring at each other across the clipboard.

'Is that your Visa number?'

Sarah stared at the string of digits above the grubby fingernail stabbing at the flimsy pink sheet. The cold feeling in the pit of her stomach was growing. She turned in desperation to Arnold Erickson still hovering in his doorway. 'Would you mind just making sure these two don't unload that while I go and fetch my card?'

Desperately clinging on to the forlorn hope that the numbers wouldn't coincide, she raced up the stairs. By the time she returned, Arnold was stood arms folded at the base of the ramp. The deliverymen hadn't taken the offending display cabinet off the van but she noticed that it still stood at the top of the ramp.

With bad grace, she seized the proffered clipboard.

'It is my number,' she agreed reluctantly. 'Give me the details and I'll ring the supplier and sort it out straight away.'

He shook his head slowly and in a resigned voice said, 'If you want the paperwork you'll have to accept the goods.'

'Oh no!'

The impasse lasted for a good ten minutes and the sheer relief when they drove off, complete with display cabinet, sapped what little energy she had and she slumped back against the wall. She must have looked drained because Arnold invited her in for a cup of tea.

'I'm fine,' she assured him. 'I can't thank you enough. I was terrified if I went upstairs to start phoning they'd unload that thing and leave it on my doorstep.'

'They couldn't do that if you hadn't signed for it.'

'I suppose not. Still I'd better go and try and sort out this mess as soon as possible.'

'The company weren't that helpful. It was a telephone order and all the details tallied.'

'I hope you've cancelled your credit card!'

'First thing I did,' Sarah said trying to keep the annoyance out of her voice. Matt had used much the same words. Did they all think she was gaga? 'And no I haven't a clue as to how anyone got hold of my details.'

There was a long silence at the other end.

'Elizabeth? You still there? Sorry if I snapped. I've been through all this with Matt. I suppose someone must have taken them from my bag. If they put the card back straight away I wouldn't know anything had happened.'

'At least you've reported it to the police.'

'Not officially. Matt said in the circumstances he didn't think they would be able to do anything so there's really not much point.'

'Sarah!'

'You're supposed to be giving me comfort and sympathy not scolding me like a child. I know I'm lax about leaving my bag around in the office but only when Lucy's there. And no, I don't think it was Lucy for a moment and, before you make any other suggestions, Nathan doesn't have my details. Our joint cards were all cancelled when we separated.'

'Calm down. You really are in a state. You sure you don't want me to come round?'

'Sorry. I didn't mean to take it out on you.'

'That's what friends are for.'

After a few more pleasantries, Sarah put the phone down and wandered into the kitchen to make herself yet another cup of coffee. Alienating her best friend, her only friend, wasn't the most sensible thing to do. There really was no point in keep going over and over it, she thought as she banged mugs and jars about in her frustration. If only she could remember if she'd left her bag in the living room while she was getting dressed the evening Nathan took her out to dinner.

As if she didn't have enough to make her feel as though the whole world was against her. Matt had really upset her. And after all he'd said about letting him know if anything else happened! Still, that was no excuse for slamming the phone down on him. It wasn't as if she'd expected him to come rushing round full of sympathy all ready to crusade on her behalf until the problem was solved, but there was no need to be so bloody patronizing. How dare he assume she hadn't cancelled her cards after her bag was stolen? Did he think she was totally incompetent? Obviously, or he wouldn't have asked if she was sure she'd not ordered the cabinet and forgotten all about it. That had really shaken her to the core. How could he?

The next day was filled with a succession of meetings and it was a relief to get back to her desk in the late afternoon. In her usual bull-dozer fashion, Eunice Robinson arrived just after five o'clock saying that she wanted to discuss the Personal Tutor training programme with Sarah as soon as possible. Resisting the temptation to plead pressure of work, Sarah realized she'd have to face the woman sometime and might as well get the interview over with there and then. Eunice was still in Sarah's office half an hour later when Lucy tactfully knocked at her door to say she was going home.

Eunice looked none too pleased at the interruption. She was in the middle of justifying the extra resources needed for a new programme.

'I think a basic counselling course is an excellent idea,' Sarah said truthfully but nonetheless hoping to cut short Eunice's pedantic insistence on listing every point in its favour. 'And, I'm prepared to fund it from the Staff Development budget.' Anything to get rid of the woman.

Eunice visibly relaxed and very nearly permitted herself a smile. 'Even though it will require a greater time commitment, I'm sure it will be very popular.'

'Let's hope you get a lot of interest,' Sarah said pulling some papers towards her and wishing fervently that the woman would take the hint and let her get on.

'I want to make the sessions on writing applications and inter-view techniques compulsory. Several tutors haven't a clue on how to help the students with such basic things.' Eunice lips stared at her defiantly.

Sarah sighed. She couldn't let that go.

'I agree that they would all benefit but I'm not sure it would be wise to force some of the more recalcitrant ones. They didn't take kindly to having to do subject training when that was introduced.'

'Surely acting as a Personal Tutor looking after the overall needs of students is equally important?' Eunice was ready to argue the cause so dear to her heart.

'I agree,' Sarah cut in quickly. 'But we've been through the argu-ments many times before. If you force the issue, lecturers will refuse to take on the role of personal tutor at all.'

'They are the very ones who need the training most and if you give the likes of Stan Higgs and his cronies the option, they won't do it.'

'If you crack the whip and they do turn up, they'll be so set against it they'll get nothing from the session. Plus there's a real danger that they could undermine the whole programme with snide comments. They've learnt all the tricks from the boys they teach.'

'They wouldn't be so unprofessional!'

'Don't you believe it,' Sarah said ruefully. 'I've seen more childish behaviour around the boardroom table than in any classroom – all the body language, the smirk or rolling up the eyes at a crucial moment in the debate. Compulsion won't work. You need to think about ways of persuading them.'

'How can I do that when you've got morons like those Motor Vehicle lecturers who openly say that the Student Support Programme is nothing more than wet nursing?' Every muscle in the taut body quivered in indignation at the recalled slur.

'That's the sort of comment they make just to annoy you. If they really thought that, they'd never have allowed themselves to be talked into being personal tutors in the first place.' For an intelligent woman, Eunice could be so blinkered by her own zeal that she failed to see the games other people play. It was a paradox that someone who had undeniable empathy with students had an almost total lack of social skills when in came to dealing with a group of men proud of their tough, workingman image. 'If you can't appeal to their sense of professionalism try self-interest. Then they won't lose face. Rather than putting on the training at the end of the day, perhaps you could time it for the beginning of the afternoon and offer lunch as part of the deal. If needs be, I'll find the money from somewhere and it needn't all come from your budget.'

'And what happens if they have lectures at the same time.' Eunice was determined to be difficult.

'If that does happen then we could look at getting in someone to cover so they could be released. It's only an idea. I think you should to talk to Dev Sharma. It's his people you really want to get involved and he knows them better than anyone, he might have some suggestions.'

'I don't see why I should spend that amount of money from my budget, which is already overstretched, just to accommodate a handful of stubborn individuals who ought to be brought into line.'

Sarah pushed back her chair. When Eunice realized that Sarah was refusing to negotiate any further, she glared at Sarah for a moment and then took the hint. Without another word Eunice got up and swept out of the room. The door closed with a bang.

'And thank you too,' Sarah said, feeling not a little aggrieved. The woman might have shown some gratitude for the offer of extra funding even if she did reject her advice and support.

Chapter 25

That was enough. Eunice had sapped what little energy she had left. Time to call it a day and make tracks for home. Sarah glanced at the stack of filing trays perched on the far right-hand corner of her desk. In the top tier marked "urgent", a good half dozen sheets of paper and a couple of bulky folders lay accusingly. Although the middle tray had no label, it contained all the things that needed action within a day or two. The bits and pieces she'd need to create time to look at, but could get away with shelving for the moment, were stuffed into the bottom. There was no way she could face any of it now and she would take only the absolute essentials back home to tackle later. Even sorting out those would mean checking tomorrow's diary and flicking through all the stuff in the top two trays. So much for the theory that the good manager never wastes time going through papers more than twice, she thought ruefully. Nonetheless, first priority – a cup of coffee!

As she walked down the corridor towards the little kitchen, she noticed the light shining through from George's office. It was reassuring to know that she wasn't the only one still hard at it. Evenings could be the most profitable time to get on with the things that took concentrated thought because there were no interruptions. Nonetheless, it struck her how surprisingly quiet the place was. It was strange to think that on the lower floors the rooms would already be filling up with evening class students intent on trying to improve their qualifications. At seven o'clock the place would be humming with all the adult education classes.

Someone had already put away the kettle and thrown out the last of the day's milk. Oh well, black coffee would help to stimulate the old grey cells and relieve the torpor all the sooner.

As she waited for the water to boil, she stood at the window looking down at the pattern of lights shining from the occupied rooms in the adjacent buildings. She pressed her cheek against the cool pane in an effort to see if there was a light in Frank Wagner's room but it wasn't possible to see that far. Thursday was his duty night. The faculty directors each took it in turn to be on the premises until the place was locked up when the classes finish in case of any emergency. She supposed when the number of faculties was reduced, she and George would have to join the rota. As she was so often around until late in the evening, she decided it wouldn't make a great deal of difference; however it would be another chore to have to cope with.

Half an hour later, she'd pared down the pile to take home and put all the relevant papers into her brief case. As she went to switch off her desk lamp, she realized her dirty mug was still sitting there. Rather than traipse all the way down to the kitchen, she decided to leave the mug until morning and assuaged her guilt by hiding it in her drawer so that Lucy wouldn't end up having to wash it.

She picked up her briefcase and handbag, put her coat over her arm and made sure that both inner and outer doors were locked. When she pushed through the swing doors into the stairwell, her eyes had to adjust to a sudden darkness. She cursed as she fumbled around trying to get her hand, still clutching the office keys, from beneath the folds of her coat to reach the switch. She flicked it a couple of times only to turn out the weak glimmer coming up from the lights on the lower landings. The top bulb must have gone. With care, she would be able to see well enough to make her way down the upper flights by the pale moonlight coming in through the narrow ornamental glass panes running down the length of the outside wall.

At the top of the stairs, she stopped to put away the clumsy bunch of keys to leave a free hand for the banister. She put down her brief-case and felt something touching the top of her left foot. It was an odd sensation, a thin line of gentle pressure.

She looked but could see nothing in the gloom. As she bent down to feel what it was, her fingers found a taught, thin wire running across her shoe. She ran her hand along it to the point where it lay trapped beneath the briefcase. When she lifted her case, the wire sprang back up to a level just above her ankles.

She went back to the heavy swing doors and managed to wedge one open with the fire extinguisher. With the help of the extra light from the corridor, she could make out that the wire had been twisted around the metal posts supporting the handrails on either side of the stairs. If she'd not stopped at that point and inadver-tently pushed it down with her briefcase, the wire would have sent her tumbling down the concrete steps.

An icy tingling prickled down her spine. That the trap had been intended for her, she didn't doubt. Everyone else used the lifts at the other end of the corridor. She was the only person who regularly used the emergency fire escape. There was no way of telling when the wire had been put there but she was now the only one left in the Administration Block. Unpleasant phone calls and unwanted mail and packages were one thing but this was in a different league.

He'd gone too far this time. She should have confronted him after he'd scared Justin half to death. Now she had no option but to bring in the police. But what evidence did she have that Nathan was responsible? Ever since she'd seen that figure running away from her in the shopping precinct she'd been fixated on him. And who knew better than he the effect the books on China and the Les Miserables would have on her? But was that enough? Did he even know that she was virtually the only one who used these stairs? How well did he know the layout of the college? And how had he got in and out without being seen?

It was up to the police to sort all that out. Perhaps that patronizing desk sergeant would take this more seriously. When she tried to tell him about the unsolicited goods and the pizza, it was all too clear that he had her down as a neurotic woman overreacting to student games. She'd more or less been told that in her position she ought to realize that she was fair game. Perhaps if she brought up the caretaker and he could back up her story, they might pay more attention. But if it became general knowledge in the college that she'd even implied someone had deliberately tried to cause her to have a bad accident, it would fuel the rumours of her imminent mental breakdown. It was such a preposterous idea that someone would deliberately try to injure her that some people might even imagine that she'd been the one who put the wire there as part of her paranoia. Was that idea? For her to make a complete idiot of herself.

If only Matt had been more sympathetic over the display cabinet business, she could have taken it straight to him.

Trying to think about all this more rationally, it was difficult to see how Nathan could have engineered the computer clichés and memos about meetings. True he was a computer expert and might just possibly have found a way to hack into her PC but that didn't explain the misplaced files. Before you start throwing out accusations, she told herself firmly, you'd better check who else is around. She would have to concede that her tormentor was more likely to be someone who worked in the college.

Unless the books and CD were nothing more than coincidences, he must know her preferences pretty well. Not that it had to be a man. Her recent contretemps with Eunice would seem to indicate that she shouldn't rule out anyone. After all the petty sniping and running to Sir Richard behind her back, if anyone was likely to overreach the bounds of reason, she was as likely candidate as any. No, the idea was ridiculous. Surely even Eunice wasn't capable of such malevolence? For all the petty griping, it was difficult to image how any of her colleagues would go this far. And why? At least she could cobble some sort of motive for Nathan but what had she done to provoke this escalating chain of events?

There was no way she was going to sit back and let this happen. She could at least check who was still around.

The reception desk closed at five and there was no one in the entrance area when she stepped out of the lift onto the ground floor. Despite her dislike of enclosed spaces, she'd reasoned that negotiating the unlit stairs would be foolhardy. She hurried along to the Student Services section and rapped on Eunice's door and tried to turn the handle. Locked. She checked there was no light coming from under the door. Could the woman be hiding in the dark?

Both David and Tom also had offices in the main building although, as neither of them were models of dedication to the job, it was no surprise that both had long gone as she'd expected. The engineering block was in darkness as she approached and, when she walked round the side of the building, there was no light from Dev Sharma's office. Frank had to be on the premises as it was his duty night but marching into his room she found it empty although the light was on and the screen saver was flickering on his PC. The most likely hidey-hole he would disappear to was in the computer suite so she climbed up two more floors.

A couple of the part time tutors were already in setting up for their evening classes but, given the mood she was in, she didn't trust herself to ask them if they'd seen Frank. She walked through to the series of work bays towards the staff room.

She could hear Alistair Benedict's voice through the half open doorway followed by Frank's rumbling laugh.

'So this is where you're hiding.'

Frank spun round to face her.

'Sarah?' She was obviously the last person he expected to walk in.

'Surprised to see me?'

'Umm.' He nodded. 'I am actually.'

'And why, may I ask, is that.' She felt like a triumphant cat that had succeeded in cornering its prey.

He took another slurp of his coffee, presumably to give himself time to think. 'Thought I saw you driving out ages ago.'

'Nice one, Frank.'

From the corner of her eye, she saw Alistair sidle across to the window out of the firing line.

Frank gave her a puzzled look and shrugged his shoulders. 'What on earth's got into you? Am I missing something? What's going on here?'

'You tell me,' she snapped. 'I'd love to know.'

He gave a wide eyed look across at Alistair and pulled a face to indicate that he thought she'd completely lost it.

'It obviously wasn't my car you saw.'

'But yours isn't in the car park.' Alistair was looking out of the window.

'What!'

She hurried over to join him. All three of them stared down at the half dozen or so vehicles still sitting on the tarmac below. Even in the poor light, it was all too evident that her distinctive convertible was nowhere to be seen.

'I'd like to report a stolen car.'

Sarah could hear the clack of computer keys as the details were entered into the system. She was just about to mention the wire trap on the stairs when the officer broke off with a sudden, 'Would you mind holding the line a moment?'

It was a couple of minutes before he came back to her. 'Can I take it you are still at the college?' The marked change of tone from the earlier rather offhand, faintly bored voice to something much more clipped and formal, did not escape Sarah.

'Yes. I'm in my office.' A flicker of unease chilled her spine.

'Would you mind waiting there until someone comes to talk to you?' It was an instruction; not a request.

'Of course,' she said trying to keep the surprise out of her voice.

'And the person you mentioned who spotted it being driven away,' there was a pause while he checked his records, 'Mr Wagner. We'd like to talk to him too. Is he still there?'

'He's on duty until nine o'clock. Has my car been found?'

'It has.' Another long pause.

'And?' she prompted.

'DI Parson will be able to tell you more about that when he gets to you. He'll be there in fifteen minutes.' He rang off before she had a chance to ask anything further.

She called Frank and told him what to expect.

'They're sending an inspector? That sounds a bit OTT for a missing car.'

'My thoughts exactly.'

'Do you want me come down and wait with you?' Frank sounded surprisingly solicitous. No doubt the same thoughts of injured joy-riding students were flashing through his mind as they were through hers.

'I think I can cope. The old girl's not as helpless as rumour would have it.' She managed to sound light-hearted even if she was fighting off a deepening sense of foreboding.

He laughed companionably and told her to give him a bell when he was wanted.

As she put down the receiver, it occurred to her that, if nothing else, she ought to tell the duty caretaker about the broken light bulb on the stairs. At least now she'd be able to point out the wire to the police when they arrived but in the mean time she'd better make sure that no one tripped over it in the dark.

When she got down to the caretaker's office, the room was empty. Why was no one where they dammed well ought to be this evening? No point in getting bad tempered. The man had probably been called out to open some door or fetch equipment for one of the classes. That was what he was there for after all.

As she stood in the doorway irritably surveying the empty room, she noticed a large torch perched on one of the shelves. Just what she needed to inspect the wire. She turned back to the lift but changed her mind and walked resolutely along the corridor to the stairs.

Half way up she thought she heard a scuffling above. She stopped and listened but there was only an eerie silence. Treading as softly as possible, the heavy torch balanced in her hand as a weapon, she peered round each bend up the stairwell as she went. That soft swish of a door closing was probably nothing more than her imagination. She mustn't let the tension get to her. Before she mounted the final flight she switched on the torch. She didn't need to go right to the top to see that the evidence had already been removed.

She swore softly. If only she'd kept a watch instead of charging around the college, she might have caught him at it. Sitting on the top stair, she inspected the railings sliding her fingers up and down the bar at the point where she judged the wire had been, trying to find a groove. She shuffled across to the window side and repeated the procedure. Again she could feel nothing but, glinting in the light from the torch, she found small scratches in the black paint through to the bare metal.

At least that was something but she didn't relish the idea of having to persuade this Inspector Parsons to take her story seriously. She straightened up with a deep sigh. Time to get down to reception. No point in getting off to a bad start keeping them waiting.

Chapter 26

For some reason, she'd expected a middle-aged, irascible character in an Inspector Frost type mackintosh but DI Parson turned out to be a young, tall, eminently attractive man who looked more like he'd stepped out of a television commercial for some trendy new shampoo than a hard-pressed working policeman. He gave her a warm smile as he introduced himself and his colleague, DS Harper. The sergeant, a much more dour individual, with the thickset build of a nightclub bouncer with the same vacant expression, nodded but didn't shake her hand.

'Can I get you some coffee, tea?' Sarah asked as they settled themselves into the easy chairs in her office.

The inspector shook his head and got straight down to the matter in hand. 'Can you tell me the time you last saw your car?'

She wanted to ask what had happened to it but the questions, though pleasantly put, kept coming until all the details she'd given over the phone had been checked. At last she could wait no longer.

'Does the fact that you're here imply that my car has been involved in an incident of some kind?'

A silence hung in the room. She was the first to break it. 'So was it joy riders? Did you catch them or did they crash it?'

Eventually, DI Parson said slowly, 'The car isn't badly damaged.'

'But was anyone hurt?'

Another agonizing pause. 'The car was found abandoned only a few streets from here.'

Apprehension was rapidly turning to frustrated anger. She could feel her jaw tightening but the way the two of them studied her every reaction made her frame her next question politely. 'I assume that senior officers, especially detectives, aren't sent out to investigate abandoned cars, so can you tell me what this is all about?'

The inspector hesitated then asked brusquely, 'Eunice Robinson. I understand she works here at the college?'

'That's right. She's Head of Student Services. You're not telling me she took…'

'Miss Robinson has been involved in an accident.'

'How is she? I must…' Sarah was half out of her seat before he waved her back down.

'I'm sorry to have to tell you that she died before the ambulance could get there.'

'What!' She was on her feet before he could stop her. 'I don't understand. Why didn't you tell me before?' They must have stood inches from each other. Sarah, clenching and unclenching her fists – the inspector, staring impassively down while she regained her self control.

'How? What happened?' She sank back onto the chair.

'I'm afraid it was a hit-and-run.'

His steely eyes stared back into hers. It took a moment or two for realization to kick in. 'My car?' she asked incredulously.

'We can't confirm that at this stage but it looks a strong probability. A witness described a pale car with a black soft-top very similar to yours.'

'Dear God.'

'When did you last see her?'

'Earlier this evening. She came to my office. It must have been just before six when she left.'

'She was knocked down at ten past on Broad Avenue so presumably she went home immediately after.'

'She doesn't live far from there. Her house is only a few minutes walk from the college. She likes to be on hand...' It was difficult to stop thinking of Eunice in the present tense.

Before she could recover her composure, he was firing questions again. 'Can you tell me what you talked about?'

Sarah recounted as much of that last conversation as she could recall. Inevitably that led to her having to account for her movements from the time Eunice left her office to when she'd discovered that her car was missing. It wasn't quite the way she'd intended to inform the police about the wire across the stairs. When she told them all the evidence had been removed, they seemed to lose interest. In the light of the death of a close colleague, it didn't seem appropriate to insist they at least take a look or even to talk about deliberate traps set to injure her, From the sceptical look on the sergeant's face, it was all too clear that he thought she was trying to divert attention from the matter in hand with some ridiculous story. This wasn't the time to justify herself with lengthy explanations about the escalating campaign of harassment.

The subject suddenly switched back to her car and how someone had managed to drive it out of a busy car park without arousing suspicion.

'I take it you're not in the habit of leaving your keys in the ignition?'

Sarah didn't trust herself to answer civilly and by way of reply fetched her handbag, took out her car keys and laid them on the table between them.

The officers exchanged looks and, changing tack, the inspector asked her about her usual route home. She'd been aware that the sergeant had been making notes throughout the interview but it wasn't until then that she fully appreciated why. From the moment when Eunice left until Sarah had gone into computer suit an hour later, Sarah hadn't seen or spoken to any one so there was no one to confirm that she'd been in her office all that time.

She was staring at the list of telephone numbers in front of her when the phone went.

'You're still here then.'

'I've been ringing round the rest of the senior staff to let them know what's happened. I don't want them to come in unprepared tomorrow.'

'I'm coming over.'

'It's all right, Frank.' He'd already put down the receiver.

There was a knock at her door a couple of minutes later and he swept in without waiting for her to answer. 'You look dreadful.'

'Thank you kind sir. I take it our friendly neighbourhood bobbies have left?'

He nodded then slumped down onto the chair in front of her desk. 'I feel like I've been put through the wringer. All those questions! How did I know it was your car when it was dark already? I ask you, how can you miss it? It's the only bloody soft top in the place. Then, if I could recognize the car, why couldn't I see who was driving it? He made me go over my story so many times; you'd think he was trying to catch me out. Then he started grilling me about how well I'd got on with Eunice. When I told him what a bloody difficult woman she was, he wanted chapter and verse plus details of her relationship with the rest of the staff. What that's got to do with anything, God only knows. Still, it's time we both went home.' He gestured to the paper under her hand. 'Have you managed to get through to everyone?'

'Not quite. It took some time to track down Sir Richard. There was no answer from David and Tom's still out. I spoke to his wife. She's expecting him soon after ten. I couldn't just leave a message so I said I'll ring back then. Which just leaves Barry.'

'You try David again and I'll ring Barry on Lucy's line and then I'm going drive you home.'

'It's good of you Frank but it's gone half nine already. I've got to wait until Tom gets back anyway so there's no point in both of us staying here.'

'And how do you propose getting home without a car? You're not hanging around for taxis at this time of night. Do as you're told, woman. You can phone Tom from your place.'

Ten minutes later she sat head in hands, elbows propped on the desk.

'You look dead on your feet.' She hadn't heard Frank come back in.

'I'm fine. I was just wondering if I should get in touch with Eunice's sister.'

'Have you met her?'

'No. I've no idea where she even lives but no doubt Personnel will have her next-of-kin details. And I ought to give some thought to what we do as a College. Some sort of tribute.' She shook her head. 'That came out all wrong.'

'I know what you mean. It hasn't really sunk in yet.'

'She wasn't the easiest person in the world to get on with but no one deserves to be mown down and just abandoned. Perhaps if the driver had stopped and got help...'

'We can't do anything to change what's happened so there's not a great deal of point in tearing yourself to pieces over it.'

'I have this awful feeling that things are going to get a lot worse before they get better.'

Although in ways very different from those she was imagining, she'd no way of knowing then, just how prophetic her words would prove to be.

Chapter 27

By the time she'd got home and phoned Tom, Sarah decided she was too exhausted to tackle anything else sensibly. Sorting out a replacement car and all the other problems, major and minor, could wait until tomorrow. What she really fancied was a good stiff drink but, as all she could find was a miniature of some obscure liqueur of doubtful mid-European origin and the remnants of an ancient bottle of port which had never been her tipple, she decided it would have to be a cup of tea. It wasn't until she stood waiting over the kettle that she realized that all she'd eaten since breakfast was a cheese roll and an apple. The last thing she wanted was food.

'You're lucky there's no one around to nag,' she told herself out loud.

Despite her words, it had to be admitted that at times of trauma, it helped to have someone to talk to. It was the first time she and Frank had a conversation that hadn't ended with one or other of them sniping at the other although they'd probably revealed too much of their softer interiors to make their next meeting a comfortable one. It was too late to pester Elizabeth and, after, their last little fracas, she didn't want to speak to Matt. And anyway what would she say? If only Nathan were there to talk to.

'Stop it you stupid woman.'

Sometimes she managed to get through two or three days at a time without thinking about him so why start now?

She was in her office early the next morning and it was no surprise when Sir Richard arrived soon after eight thirty. There was a lot to sort out but it was evident that he felt as awkward as she did discussing what they should do about Eunice's post. It seemed disrespectful to her memory to be talking about finding her replacement only a few hours after her death but she had no deputy and there was no one in the college with the experience or expertise to step into her job, even temporarily.

They were still in the midst of discussions when there was a knock at her door. Lucy would never interrupt when she was in conference with Sir Richard so Sarah knew it had to be important.

'Detective Inspector Parson is here with his team. He would like to speak to you again and to Sir Richard as well.'

Sarah had warned Lucy that the police would be returning to interview any staff and students who might have seen anything suspicious at the time her car was taken and, for reasons that she couldn't fathom, to speak to all the senior staff. Lucy had already arranged for suitable interview rooms to be set aside and now it seemed she needed to hand over her own office while DI Parson spoke with Sir Richard.

It was as good a time as any to go over to Student Services and try to sort out with the careers advisers and student councillors what needed to be done. She and George had already arranged which of her day's commitments he would take over but that'd only increased the feeling that real life had somehow slipped into limbo. Any minute now she would wake up and reality would take over again.

That feeling stayed with her for the rest of the day. She may have appeared calm and efficient as she swept through the place, making decisions and maintaining the Steel Queen image but inside she felt totally empty. She was living on instinct and trusting that her judgements were the right ones because there was little time to work out all the ramifications. Action was needed if the whole place wasn't to fall apart. George had ensured first thing that all staff were told that no comment was to be made to reporters and Lucy was a rock when it came to fielding the constant stream of phone calls.

Sarah remembered little of the two hour interview she had with Parson and Harper except that this time it was the sergeant who did most of the talking. Anyone would think she was the chief suspect from the way he snapped out a constant stream of questions making her go over and over all the things she'd said the day before even to the exact details of the regular route she drove home from the college even though it lay in the other direction from Broad Street. More that once she'd to swallow the scathing retorts she wanted to snap at him in response to the implications in the relentless questions he kept firing at her.

There were no evening classes on Fridays and by five o'clock the college was deserted. She had every intention of getting away early herself. A long soak in the bath and an early night.

Her heart leapt to her mouth when she saw the flashing light on the answer phone. She was tempted to press the delete button without even listening to it. Pull yourself together woman!

'Hi. Sorry I've not rung before.' Matt's voice. 'I was going to ring last night but I didn't get back from Devizes until late last night. Been on this two day symposium at headquarters. Shall we meet at the theatre? Say twenty past?'

She'd forgotten all about the concert. She should have cancelled it earlier but other things had taken over. Too late now. She'd never be able to get hold of him. And he'd think she was still angry with him. An evening out was the last thing she fancied and it didn't seem right somehow. On the other hand, sitting at home with only her thoughts for company would help no one. It would be good to think about something else for a while.

As she stood under the shower, letting the stream of water massage her neck and shoulders, she made a conscious effort to relax. Best to push aside all thoughts of Eunice, the college, DI Parson and his sidekick for the rest of the day. With luck even the whole weekend!

It was not yet ten past seven when Sarah drove into the multi-storey car park next to the theatre. It took all her concentration taking the unfamiliar car up the steep ramps and tight turns especially as the courtesy car the insurance company had provided had an appalling turning circle. She sat at the wheel trying to decide whether it was better to go in and stand around like a spare part until Matt arrived or to wait in the car for a while. For some reason she suddenly felt apprehensive about their meeting. All the fault of DS Harper, she joked to herself. Enough to put anyone off the police for ever.

As she pushed through the door to the stairs, she realized that her reluctance to get out of the car was nothing to do with Matt at all. She had always hated going into that dark, enclosed stairwell and her narrow escape on the fire escape the previous evening didn't help. It wasn't a fear of being attacked, although such places were notorious late at night, it was the appalling smell, reminiscent of disgusting public toilets, that she disliked so much. Rain, presumably dripping from the coats and umbrellas of countless returning motorists, accumulated in dank, evil smelling puddles. Holding her breath she raced pell-mell down the concrete steps in her high heels in a way that wasn't only childish, it was downright reckless.

The foyer was crammed with people when she arrived. She stood on tiptoe, peering over the heads of the milling masses but it was impossible to pick out anyone from the doorway. Sidling round the various groups so engrossed in their noisy chatter that they were totally oblivious of anyone trying to get past, she eventually found a vacant space by the wall. An announcement that the performance was about to start came over the tannoy. The crowd began to thin as people went to take their places in the auditorium.

The large clock above the box office showed twenty seven minutes past seven. Only a handful of people remained and even they were making their way to the stairs. She began to wonder if Matt had decided not to come. Neither of them had mentioned the theatre visit when they had last spoken. Was this his way of getting back at her for slamming the phone down on him? Hardly. Perhaps he thought she wasn't coming and had abandoned the whole idea.

Feeling a trifle foolish she wandered back to the entrance nearest to the car park. There were two sets of doors into the foyer and she wasn't sure which way he would be coming so she didn't want to stray outside. From the open doorway, she could hear the distant town clock sounding the half hour. She was about to risk a step or two outside to take a look along the road when she heard his voice.

'Sarah!'

She turned and saw him hurrying across from the Theatre Square entrance.

'I'm so sorry,' he said breathlessly. 'What a day! I got held up. I didn't think I was going to make it.' He took her arm and propelled her down the stairs to the stalls at top speed.

The lights were beginning to go down as they squeezed their way through to the middle of the row past the line of disgruntled people, who'd been comfortably settled. She received a venomous glare from the elderly gentleman who had to remove his jacket and his wife's coat plus a long-stemmed umbrella from her seat before she could sit down.

As the curtain went up, Matt took her hand and gave it a squeeze. A wave of relief swept through her. He was the same as ever.

During the interval they went up for a drink. Because they had to follow the long lines of people slowing shuffling out of the lower auditorium, by the time they reached the bar, all the seats at the tables had been taken. Matt joined the end of the queue waiting to be served while she found a couple of perches on one of the side benches.

'That took for ever,' he said handing her a glass. 'Sorry about being late. You must have thought I wasn't coming.'

'What was the problem? Were you caught up at work?'

'Yes and no. It has been one of those days but I would have made it if my dear son had got his finger out. I promised to drop Paul at one of his friends for a birthday party and when I got home he was still mooning around trying to make up his mind what to wear.' Matt raised his eyes to the ceiling in mock exasperation.

'I thought only girls had that problem.'

'Don't you believe it. Walking the narrow line between choosing something to impress the female talent without provoking comment from the rest of the lads in the gang at the tender age of fourteen, is a major challenge.'

'Then at least age brings some compensations,' she said with a rueful grin that belied the considerable amount of time spent earlier searching through her wardrobe. Though her collection of clothes was quite extensive, it consisted mainly of smart, but dull, business suits plus matching discrete blouses or the rather disreputable casual outfits, most well past their prime, that she like to slop around in at weekends. Matt had already seen her in the few bright, little numbers she possessed that fell between the two extremes.

There was no time for any real conversation before the two minute warning bell sounded.

'We'd better drink up. Best not to repeat our performance at the start. It didn't help having seats in the very centre.'

'Let's hope the old dear sitting next to me is in a better mood when we get back. He decided to get his own back by sticking his elbow way over on to my side and the handle of his umbrella was sticking into my thigh the whole time,' she said with a mock growl.

Her only consolation for having to gulp back her wine was that she was in her seat before her irritable friend. She was able to move his umbrella into his space and firmly establish her claim to the armrest for the second half.

After the performance, Matt suggested another drink. Pubs weren't Sarah's kind of place at the best of times and "The Pear Tree" seemed to attract crowds of raucous youngsters many of whom could well turn out to be her students but she was still reticent about inviting him back to the flat as an alternative.

Matt took her arm and they made their way to the far side of the square. Perhaps it was because she was so relieved that things seemed back to normal again that she did it. Half way across she reached up and kissed him on the cheek.

'That's for the pressey,' she said.

'Pardon?' His forehead creased in a puzzled frown.

'The roses.'

'I don't understand.'

He seemed embarrassed. It was all too evident that she'd jumped to the wrong conclusion. Why did she always end up making such a fool of herself?

'Someone sent me a bunch of flowers the other day. They didn't sign the card and, for some reason, I thought they must be from you because I couldn't think of anyone else. Perhaps it's my mysterious stalker. And there was me thinking his motives were the exact opposite!' She couldn't stop the silly prattle. Her attempt at light-hearted jollity sounded false even to her own ears.

They reached the pub and she was able to cover her embarrassment as they looked around for somewhere to sit in the packed, smoky interior. She did her best to regain her composure whilst Matt battled through to the bar to get the drinks.

She managed to find a couple of seats in a corner but for the first ten minutes the place was so noisy that trying to maintain a conversation was far from easy. They shouted the predicable remarks about the concert across the table saying how much they'd enjoyed it. In fact the programme had included only a single piece by one her favourite composers and the orchestra, although passable, hadn't been outstanding. It was much easier when the other occupants of the table decided to move on elsewhere and Matt could sit on the bench seat next to her.

'So tell me about this dreadful day of yours then,' she said brightly. Anything to cover up her gaff over the flowers.

'Don't ask.' He raised his eyes to the ceiling. 'Apart from the pile of stuff that's been landing up on my desk while I've been away, I've been up to my eyes with this accident on the motorway first thing. I expect you heard about it?' Sarah shook her head. 'Luckily there were no fatalities but this chemical tanker jack-knifed and over-turned spilling its load all over the place, and then there was an enormous pileup as vehicles braked. We had to close the motorway for most of the day and reroute all the traffic through the town. As if that wasn't bad enough, I lost half a dozen men to a CID operation. It's near impossible trying to run a control room at the best of times with the number of men we've got without some DI playing at wonder boy and demanding extra manpower for a simple hit-and-run when we've got a major incident on our hands.'

'This wouldn't be DI Parson would it?'

Matt stared at her.

'The woman who died was one of my colleagues.'

'God, I'm sorry.' Poor Matt looked mortified.

'It was probably your lot I've had to put up with all day at the college then. You can have them back with pleasure,' she said trying to make light of it all. The last thing she wanted was to start discussing anything to do with it.

'So you were interviewed were you?'

'It looks like it was my car that ran her down. It was stolen from the car park.'

Matt's eyes widened. He looked at her as though she'd suddenly become a stranger. She'd rendered him speechless.

'You ready for another?' She picked up his glass and moved quickly to the bar to give him time to recover.

Neither of them referred to it again but a definite tension hung in the air and keeping the conversation going proved difficult. He seemed as relieved as she was when the bell went for last orders.

Matt insisted on walking her to her car. Although they occasionally brushed against each other, he didn't take her arm and she'd no intention of initiating any form of contact. A fine drizzle began to fall and she pulled her coat around her.

When they reached the car, she thanked him for the pleasant evening, wished him goodnight and quickly got in. He stood smiling and waving as she drove off acutely conscious that he'd made no suggestions about meeting up again.

Back in her kitchen, confused and hurt by Matt's reaction, she stood staring at the calendar on the wall in front of her as she waited for the kettle to boil. The half remembered words of a poem she'd learnt at school came back to her. "No sun, no moon....No fruits, no flowers, no leaves, no birds, November." They matched her mood. That was when it struck her. She suddenly realized who had sent the flowers. They'd arrived on November 10th – the day before her wedding anniversary. And for her bouquet, she'd chosen yellow roses. She'd almost forgotten. Trust him to remember!

'Damn you Nathan!'

Chapter 28

At least the concert provided a topic of conversation when she telephoned home. Her mother knew absolutely nothing about classical music but it gave Sarah a chance to be able to move on to something other than Eunice's death and the theft of her car. She'd toyed with not giving her parents any of the bad news but, from the way the Press had been pestering all Friday, Sarah decided they were bound to hear eventually and would then be hurt by her failure to tell them, as well as worried.

Although Sarah tried to play down the drama as much as possible, she was surprised at her mother's reaction. Apart from a few conciliatory remarks about how dreadful it must be for her, she didn't seem to take in much of what Sarah said. She was obviously preoccupied with something else. Knowing that she would get an evasive answer to a direct question as to what was wrong, Sarah struggled to find the cause of her mother's concern. Eventually, she asked after Jenny and the family.

'They're all fine. The results of Todd's latest tests should be through at the end of the week.'

'Give them all my love when you see them,' Sarah said, trying to jolly her mother along.

'Yes, of course,' came the automatic reply. 'I expect Jenny will call round in a day or two.'

Her mother's throw away remark wasn't lost on Sarah. Jenny was always in and out of her parent's house and never left without saying, 'See you tomorrow' or the day after. It was a standing joke that Justin, when he was about five, coming out of church one Sunday had turned to Jenny and asked, 'Are we going back to our house or are we going home.' For both sisters, the word home meant the house they'd grown up in. Jenny's failure to put in an appearance for several days was evidently making her mother more anxious than she cared to admit.

'Have you got anything planned for next weekend?' Sarah asked on sudden impulse.

'No, love.'

'Would it be all right if I came down?'

'Of course! You know we always love to see you.' Sarah felt a rush of warmth at the excited pleasure in her mother's voice.

Although she wanted to be there to offer what little support she could, if Sarah was honest, her motives were probably not entirely selfless. It wasn't simply a wish to distance herself from the ordeal of the last few days. After the embarrassing spectacle she'd made yesterday and his reaction to discovering that she was associated with the hit-and-run, she couldn't see Matt asking her out again. The prospect of hanging around the flat all weekend wondering if he was going to call was best avoided.

By four o'clock on Monday afternoon, the college was beginning to get back to some semblance of normality. The police had gone and she was busy trying to catch up with the paperwork. There was a knock at the door and a grim-faced George hurried in and laid a newspaper on the desk in front of her.

'I thought you ought to see this.'

The front page of the local evening edition carried a banner head-line:

POLICE IN MURDER HUNT

Beneath a photograph of the college and a much smaller grainy picture of a woman who could have Eunice, was another line in bold print running the width of the page:

College lecturer mown down by colleague's car

Sarah scanned the article quickly then reread it while George stood agitatedly twisting the signet ring on his little finger.

The first paragraph was a graphic account of how a silver convertible crawling up Broad Street, suddenly speeded up and mounted the pavement to hit a pedestrian knocking her up into the air and over the bonnet. There were statements, purportedly from an eye witness who happened to be at her window drawing her curtains, about the car driver aiming straight at the woman plus other comments from those who heard the bang of the impact and saw the car disappearing at top speed.

It wasn't until the final paragraph that there came a reference to the car believed to have been involved. It stated that it belonged to a fellow member of the college staff and went on to say, "Police are investigating the possibility that the car may have been stolen."

Sarah felt suddenly numb and cold. She heard herself say in a calm, distant voice, 'Well this isn't going to do the College reputation much good.'

'It does make it sound as though the police aren't convinced. I'm sure you've got grounds to sue the paper.'

'I doubt it. Their legal people will know exactly how far they can go. It's all innuendo. There's nothing actually libellous.'

He slumped onto the chair. He looked more angry and upset on her behalf than she felt herself. 'I'd no idea it was anything other than an accident.'

'I don't think any of us did. But, if was a deliberate attempt to run her down, it does explain all those questions on Friday.' A thought suddenly occurred to her. 'Did they ask you how well I got on with Eunice?'

He looked at her sheepishly and nodded. 'They did ask about her relationship with all of the staff but, yes, they mentioned you specifically.'

'Now we know why the national tabloids and the radio station have been pestering us for a statement though how they got wind of it, heaven only knows.'

Who would want to kill Eunice? It didn't make sense. If her death was no accident, did that mean that the wire trap had been intended for the Head of Student Services and not, as Sarah had assumed earlier, an attempt aimed at her?

But why? Did Eunice have to be silenced? What could she possibly have found out that could have been worth her life? Eunice only rarely came up to the administration block and surely it was pure chance she happened to be up there on that particular day. Had she told someone she intended to speak to Sarah? Eunice wasn't exactly the sort to gossip about her plans to anyone. As far as Sarah knew, Eunice never used the fire escape stairs. They were the wrong end of the corridor.

In any case, a trip wire was more likely to cause a broken arm or leg and that would hardly stop her talking if she had discovered some dark secret. This was the stuff of television drama. Not real life.

And why use Sarah's car? Killing someone in order to make it look as though Sarah was a murderer was totally irrational.

For the rest of the afternoon, Sarah's mind came back to those questions but she was no nearer answering them by the time it came to leave for home.

When the front doorbell jangled, Sarah was in two minds whether to answer it. As the Press had been chasing her all day, presumably tracking down where she lived was only a matter of time. She peered out of the landing window and saw Elizabeth's car parked outside.

'Thought you might like some company,' she said brandishing a bottle wrapped in tissue paper as Sarah opened the door.

They were both more than slightly merry when the phone rang. Sarah didn't get up to answer it. Having cut short two calls with a 'no comment,' not long after she got in, she'd learnt her lesson. Judging by the number of blank messages on her answerphone, there'd been a fairly constant attempt, presumably from reporters, for much of the afternoon. Just how they'd managed to get hold of her number was a mystery.

'Sarah, it's me. I've just seen the paper.' Nathan's voice boomed into the room as the machine went into action. 'I expect you're screening your calls. Don't feel obliged to call me back. I only wanted you to know that I'm here if you want a sympathetic ear.'

'Patronising git,' Elizabeth exploded. 'Does he really think you're such a weak, pathetic female that you need him to comfort you?'

'Like you did, you mean.'

Elizabeth glowered at her for a moment and then they both burst out laughing. She lifted the bottle and slopped more Bacardi into her glass. The cola had run out long ago. 'Okay. I suppose it was nice of him really. Are you going to ring him back?'

'Not till I'm sober.'

As soon as she heard her mother's voice, she knew the news was grave. She'd never phoned her at college before.

'Crohn's disease,' Sarah repeated.

'I'd never heard of it before. According to what the doctor told Greg, it's one of them things that's very difficult to diagnose but now they know what it is, they say they'll be able to sort him out.'

'That's good isn't it?

'I suppose so,' her mother said doubtfully, 'but they're going to have to put him on those horrible steroid things that have all them nasty side effects.'

'You mustn't worry about that,' Sarah said firmly trying to jog her mother out of the uncharacteristic depression she'd slipped into. 'The doctors will keep a close watch to make sure everything is under control.'

'Yes. Greg said Todd will have to keep going back until they get all the doses just right,' she went on, as much to reassure herself as Sarah.

'And is that what's stopped him growing as well as giving him all the tummy trouble?'

'Apparently. They're going to give him special hormones to deal with it. He should catch up with all the other children after a bit so at least that's one thing they won't have to worry about any more.' Despite her words, Sarah could still hear the heaviness in her mother's voice.

There was a silence as they contemplated poor Todd's future. Sarah had a feeling that yet another reason for her mother's continued troubled state lay not so much with her grandson as with her daughter whose continued overreaction didn't bode well. She wanted to ask how Jenny had taken the news but it was difficult to think how to phrase her question without sounding insensitive.

'Don't forget to give Jenny my love. I don't suppose you've seen much of her lately. She must be rushed off her feet what with spending so much time at the hospital and trying to look after Justin and Greg.'

'Umm.' Her mother's noncommittal response was all the answer Sarah needed. She was torn between sympathy and a sudden desire to shake her sister out of her self defeating wallow.

'What with all this about Todd, I forgot to ask you about your troubles. How is everything at college? I've kept that poor lady in my prayers and all the rest of you. It must be dreadful to lose a colleague like that.'

'Yes, well.' Now it was Sarah's turn to be left trying to cover up secret fears and apprehension.

'And what about your car? Did they catch those joy riders?'

'These things take time but the insurance company have given me a courtesy car so it's not a problem. It won't stop me being over with you all tomorrow anyway.' Her voice sounded unnaturally jolly but thankfully her mother didn't seem to notice.

'Yes, that'll be nice.' Her mother sounded relieved.

'Perhaps we can have a little celebration now that we know Todd will be on the mend,' Sarah went on brightly.

They said their goodbyes and, as she put down the receiver, Sarah wished fervently that she knew more about Crohn's disease.

She clicked onto the internet and spent the next three-quarters of an hour searching through the references. Not that reading up on all the details of ileocecal, small-bowel, colonic and perianal Crohn's disease was much help. Even if she could have understood all the medical jargon, she'd no idea of the specifics of Todd's condition.

Whatever they were, it didn't sound as though the family's troubles were over.

It was almost a relief when the call eventually came. She'd been expecting a summons ever since the newspaper had revealed that Eunice's death was more than a tragic hit-and-run accident. After testy encounters with Sir Richard and a few select members of the Governing Body, an encounter with the police seemed a far less daunting prospect that Inspector Parson and his morose sidekick might have hoped.

It would have come as no surprise to have DS Harper arrive at college ready to escort her off in a police car in full view of all the staff and students, but all that happened was a polite phone call requesting her to go down to the station.

As she went through the details of what she'd done in the three quarters of an hour after Eunice had left for the umpteenth time, she had the impression, from the way the inspector studied every blink of her eyelids, that he was more interested in her reactions that in her words. She'd been on enough of those body language lectures as part of Man Management courses to know what they were up to. The trouble was that trying to decide how an innocent person might react made her feel instantly guilty. The calm measured answers she was trying to give belied the turmoil she was feeling inside. She reasoned that if they'd discovered who'd taken her car, there would be no point to the interview, so presumably she was still at the top of their list of suspects.

'So remind me, what was it that you and Ms Robinson were arguing about?'

'There was no argument,' she kept her voice deliberately matter of fact. As she went over their discussion yet again, it occurred to Sarah that she ought to ask for a solicitor, not that she'd the faintest idea of how to go about getting one.

'Other members of staff seem to think that Ms Robinson felt that she'd a justifiable grievance against you.'

'Eunice was always adamant about anything she saw as a lack of attention given to the pastoral work of the college and was prepared to argue her corner accordingly. She came to discuss her plans for the next training programme. Though there's no one to confirm it now, I can assure you that, on reflection, she would have been pleased with the concessions that she gained from that meeting.'

The questions continued to dart from one subject to another. What were the exact times that Eunice left? – she'd made coffee? – had discovered her car was missing? Who saw her as she went to Eunice's room? – the engineering block? – and the computer suite? The only thing they didn't seem interested in was the wire on the stairs.

Keeping her cool under the constant bombardment of questions, and her failure to demonstrate even mild irritation at the sergeant's snide insinuations and obvious antagonism, probably labelled her as more guilty in the man's eyes than the righteous indignation that might be deemed the normal response. Nonetheless, it was a small triumph for her not to yield to such provocation.

When the questions eventually ran out, she asked pleasantly, 'Have you any idea when I can have my car back?'

There was a silence. Neither man looked at the other. It was the Inspector who eventually felt the need to explain.

'We do have a problem there, Sarah.' He must have noticed the way she bristled at the familiarity but he continued, 'Although forensics have been all over the car, the only prints they can find are yours.'

'Is that surprising?' She raised an eyebrow. 'Surely whoever did this would have worn gloves? Had the position of the seat been altered?'

She noticed the flicker of surprise in his eyes but it was something she'd given some thought to over the last few days and had wondered why no one had bothered to ask her. Perhaps they'd simply worked it out from her height but surely such things depended on leg length? Even if it had been changed, it was little help to her now. The fact that she had brought up the idea could well imply that she'd altered it herself to avert suspicion.

When he broke the silence the inspector changed tack. 'More significantly, they cannot find anybody who noticed anyone taking your car around the time it left the car park.'

'But, as I didn't drive it out, you have no witnesses to suggest that I was anywhere near it either.' Anger bubbled just below the surface but every instinct told her to keep it in check. She would gain nothing by antagonizing them.

Chapter 29

Sarah got to Norwich early for once. As usual her mother made a fuss of her and she could tell that her father was just as pleased to have her home again so soon. Naturally they asked after her troubles and, when she said the police hadn't come up with anything positive yet, were quite happy to drop the subject. They obviously hadn't had sight of the damning article that had continued to haunt her thoughts in the early hours when sleep stubbornly refused to come and she fervently hoped they never would. None of them wanted to bring up the subject of Todd's illness and it didn't seem right to chat about more trivial things so, soon after ten thirty, she pleaded tiredness and went up to her room.

Sarah had never been a particularly deep sleeper but recent events had resulted in a tendency for her to wake at the slightest noise. At first she thought it was just creaking pipes but then she realized that someone had turned on the tap in the kitchen immediately below.

Her mother was standing over the kettle when she walked in.

'I didn't wake you did I, dear?' She looked anxiously at her daughter.

'No, I couldn't sleep.' Sarah got herself a mug from the cupboard and placed it next to one stood on the work surface. 'Todd is going to be all right you know.' She put a reassuring arm around the older woman's shoulder.

'Yes, dear. I know.' Her mother patted her hand and gave her a weak smile. 'I just wish I could get Jenny to believe that. I thought things would improve once they knew what was wrong with Todd but, if anything, she's worse. She's so down and she's cutting herself off from everyone.'

'Not you surely?'

'I phone everyday of course but she hasn't been round here for weeks. Not since you brought Justin back.'

The words struck an icy chill in Sarah. Jenny and her mother had always been close and the family Sunday tea at her parent's house a tradition broken only by holiday or dire emergency. They were more than mother and daughter. They were best friends. Jenny confided in her mother about everything, from trifles such as the discovery of a new remedy for carpet stains to secret hopes and fears that she wouldn't tell to another soul. This sudden rejection had hit her mother hard. They both stared at the boiling kettle until Sarah took the teapot from her mother's hands and filled it.

'Thanks, love,' her mother said as she took hold of the steaming mug.

The two of them stood leaning against cupboards sipping their tea, both deep in thought.

'If only I could wave a magic wand and make things right for both my daughters.'

'What do you mean both your daughters?' Sarah's stomach gave a sudden lurch as for a horrible moment she thought her mother must have heard about the police suspicions. 'Why should you worry over me?'

'Did they ever catch that student?'

'Sorry?'

'The one that was making all those nasty phone calls. Justin said your policeman friend was going to arrange a phone tap.'

'No. It really wasn't necessary. Not once I had the number changed.'

'And there hasn't been any more bother?'

Bother. That was one word for it, Sarah thought bitterly. How could she add to her mother's worries by unburdening all her problems? 'Not a single unwanted call.' At least that much was true.

'But I can tell you're not happy. You've never been one to share your troubles with anyone but I know when something's wrong. You've lost weight again and your face looks drawn. I know you've got your really important job but there's more to life than work. I hope this new man of yours is treating you all right. I don't want you to get hurt again.'

'There is no new man, mum!' Time to face up to it. At least she could be honest about something.

'Justin said you were very friendly with this police inspector. I hope your coming home hasn't meant you've had to cancel anything special.'

'It's not like that, honestly. Matt is just someone I go to the theatre with occasionally. That's all. There is nothing between us so I'm not about to get my heart broken. If I've been a bit preoccupied lately, it's because things have been very busy at college but everything is under control.' Best not to get onto the subject of Eunice's death even as an excuse.

'If you say so, love.' The frown she gave belied her words.

'You can cross me off your worry list, I promise you.'

Sarah felt she was letting her mother down with all the glib assurances but she couldn't add to the burden, especially as her mother could do nothing to help.

There still had been no word from Matt. Although at first, Sarah had tried to tell herself that the ongoing police investigation put him in a difficult situation and that he was only keeping his distance until the true culprit was arrested, she knew deep down that their relationship, such as it was, was now over.

Sarah was quite resigned to the fact. She was surprised to discover that it caused her so little heartache. She had certainly shed no tears. Whether that was simply a numbing reaction to the shock of all that was happening around her, she had no way of knowing. Perhaps time would tell. Naturally it would have been a considerable boon to have his insider knowledge and his advice and support but she felt no great pangs of loss.

They could hear the boys pounding up the path long before the door was thrown open. Her mother was there ready to meet them as Todd hurtled through flinging his arms around the rotund figure and even Justin was happy to receive a hug and kisses. Sarah was relieved that Jenny didn't turn away from her welcoming peck on the cheek but she didn't miss the way that Jenny made sure she didn't have to sit next to her sister when they all went into the living room.

Todd, as well as Justin, seemed pleased to see Sarah and, for the first half hour, few of the adults got a word in as the boys prattled on. Todd looked so much better than when Sarah had last seen him and, although the diagnosis had caused alarm in the rest of the family, Todd appeared totally unconcerned about his now identified condition.

Once the boys had parted with their news, and they all sat down for lunch, the conversation became more strained. Jenny, her body tense and withdrawn, hung on to her gloom like a baby with its blanket refusing all efforts to pry it away. The rest of them tried to jolly things along but it was hard going.

When they'd cleared the table, Sarah insisted her mother should sit down and put her feet up.

'You've been on the go all morning. Jenny and I will deal with the washing up,' she said firmly.

She expected her mother to protest but for once, catching Sarah's eye, she acquiesced. Jenny glowered at her sister. Though she was always ready to help out her mother, it was evident she'd no desire to be alone with Sarah in the kitchen.

'Do you want to wash or dry?' Sarah asked brightly once she'd closed the door.

'Whatever,' Jenny shrugged noncommittally.

Sarah chattered on forcing Jenny into occasional one word replies until they'd almost finished and then she broached the subject she'd been angling to bring up.

'Mum's very worried about you, you know?'

'It's not me she should be worried about.' Jenny put the wet tea towel over the rail on the radiator and turned to face Sarah, arms folded defiantly across her chest.

'Todd's condition isn't life threatening,' Sarah tried to reason watching the jaw tighten.

'Don't you realize Crohn's disease is incurable?' Jenny snapped.

'But not untreatable. With the proper drugs they will be able to keep things under control. He'll be able to live a perfectly normal life just like any other child. It doesn't have to be a big thing,' Sarah said, reassuringly.

'But he'll be on steroids for the rest of his life!'

Sarah bit back her response about diabetics and insulin and all the other complaints that people manage to learn to cope with.

'And it will affect his growth!'

'But now they know what the problem is they can do something about that.'

'What makes you such a bloody expert all of a sudden?' Jenny fired at her.

Sarah gritted her teeth and said firmly, 'For everyone's sake, most of all Todd's, we have to be positive. Have you considered joining a support group? You don't have to go to meetings. If you don't want to discuss things face to face, there are all sorts of message boards on the WEB.'

'What gives you the right to tell me what to do?' Jenny demanded at the top of her voice, chin thrust forward, fists clenched.

'Do you want the crappy answer? Because I'm your sister and I love you. Because that's not what you're going to get.' All the pent up frustration she been nursing for the last week was released with a vengeance. 'The truth is it's high time you stopped playing the tragedy queen relishing every spot of pain you can wring from all of this. You don't give a damn about your husband or mum and dad who you are making go through every kind of hell. You've rejected Justin who you're in dire danger of losing forever if you don't show him at least a hint that you have some feeling for him. And most of all, because if you really cared about Todd, you'd think about his needs. It's time you started treating him like a human being and not some doll on whom you can play out your ridiculous fantasies.'

Jenny stood stock-still, wide-eyed and speechless; pure hatred written in every line of her face. For a long minute, there was absolute silence, neither of them moved. Suddenly Jenny turned and ran out slamming the door with a force that shook the whole house.

Why couldn't she keep her big mouth shut? She'd not planned to say any of that. Sarah doubted that she even believed it. So much for all the counselling courses she'd sat through in her time! She was the one guilty of forcing a chasm between the two of them that she might never be able to cross again. She was becoming quite the expert. First her husband and now her sister. She should write the definitive paper on "Ten Top Tips on How to Alienate Your Loved Ones." Jenny was an amateur compared with her.

Slowly, she finished putting away the saucepans and wiping down the surfaces postponing the moment when she would have go back in the living room and face everyone's hostility. When she could find nothing more to do, she opened the door and ventured into the hallway. At least they were all still in the house. It wouldn't have surprised her to discover Jenny dragging Greg and the boys down the path to their car. Though she couldn't make out the words, she could hear Jenny's voice furiously growling away at top speed. The tirade was far from over. Sarah's hand was on the doorknob but, at the last minute, her courage failed her and she crept upstairs.

She took her time brushing her hair, dabbing her shiny nose with powder and applying more lipstick. Her case was already packed so she'd no more excuses to remain upstairs. Perhaps she could plead the need to get back early to finish off some work and leave now but, even so, she would have to face them all first.

Silence greeted her entrance. It was a long walk to the only vacant seat at the far end of the settee next to Justin.

'How's school?' she asked him in as jovial a voice as she could muster.

'Fine. Did I tell you I got ten house points for my English essay?' he said with evident pride. 'I wrote about getting chased by bullocks. Mrs Hudson said I'd made it sound very exciting.'

'That's one word for it I suppose.' They both laughed at the memory.

162

The two boys seemed unaware of the atmosphere in the room or perhaps they simply refused to be cowered by it. They chattered on gradually involving the rest of them until only Jenny sat, with a face like thunder, determined to distance herself from everyone. Greg, doing his best to pretend that all was normal, asked Sarah how things were going at the college. Not surprisingly, it was evident that her mother hadn't said anything about her car being stolen or the death of a colleague and this wasn't the time to mention it. After a few glib, non-committal sentences, they talked about his job at the garage. The place where he used to work had gone bankrupt a few years previously. Things were difficult for six months or so until he'd been able to get another job as a mechanic at Mann Egerton's over in Hellesdon.

Eventually it was time for the mid-afternoon cup of tea and Sarah jumped to her feet before anyone else could volunteer to go and make it. It was a relief to reach the haven of the kitchen. She took as long as she could sorting out cups and saucers and the like. How much longer they could all keep up this polite let's-pretend-it-never-happened situation was anybody's guess but the cracks were definitely beginning to show. Only the boys seemed to be able to let it pass over their heads totally unconcerned about the adult tension.

It was a relief when five o'clock eventually came and Sarah could legitimately get up and take her leave. Greg insisted on going upstairs with her to bring down her case. Once they reached her bedroom, she tried to apologize for upsetting Jenny but he quickly cut her short.

'Don't feel bad about it. Someone needed to tell her and no one else has got the gumption.'

'She told you what I said?'

'Not exactly but your voice carries a bit. You can tell you're a teacher.' He smiled sheepishly. 'Seriously, you're one of the few people she'll listen to. She trusts you completely. I know it doesn't seem like it but she wouldn't react the way she has if you didn't mean anything to her. She's always admired you, the big successful sister. You were a hard act for her to follow.'

'I don't understand.'

'She's always wanted to be like you but she knew she'd never make it. She hasn't your brains or your drive.'

'That's silly. I never thought any the less of her because she didn't go to university.'

'She knows that deep down. It's just that at the moment, when things are tough, you're the easiest to lash out at. Every now and again she still feels jealous.'

'I don't see why,' Sarah interrupted vehemently.

'You're successful with lots of money, an important job you can be proud of and, as she sees it, you have no ties and no responsibilities,' he went on quickly.

'I'm the one who should be jealous,' she said truthfully. 'Jenny has got the perfect husband and two smashing kids. Everything any woman could want.'

He grinned ruefully. 'She'll come round. She's not really a selfish person you know. She knows she's in the wrong but she's not good at saying sorry.'

'That's something we both share I'm afraid, Greg. It's a word neither of us have ever learnt to say easily.' She let out a great sigh. 'I suppose I'd better go and eat humble pie.'

As Greg carried down her case and carried it out to put in the boot of her car, the family came out to say goodbye. All but Jenny. Sarah stood in the doorway of the living room. She called her name but Jenny continued to flick through the magazine in her lap.

'I shouldn't have let rip at you like that. I'm sorry.'

Jenny made no reply and continued reading.

Outside by the car, kisses were exchanged, both boys gave her an affectionate hung and everyone lined up to wave her off. Only Jenny stayed skulking indoors but as Sarah turned to give everyone a last wave, she caught sight of Jenny standing at the window, half hidden by the curtain, watching her go. Sarah couldn't tell if Jenny saw her blow her a kiss.

Chapter 30

'The funeral is the day after tomorrow.'

'With half the college there I presume. Are you going to have to say anything?' Elizabeth asked.

'No tributes thankfully. It's going to be a very small affair. Her sister thought that's what Eunice would have wanted so, apart from family and close friends, it will be just me and Sir Richard.'

'I don't blame her. Bad enough to lose a sister without having to worry that the whole thing might turn into a media circus after all that stuff in the papers.'

'Exactly.'

After a pause, Elizabeth asked, 'So, did you have a good weekend?'

Sarah groaned, 'Disastrous if you must know, but I'll tell you all the gory details when I see you. What time shall I pick you up on Saturday? Ten o'clock?'

'Make it nine. That will give us more time to do some Christmas shopping.'

'I thought you said this was going to be a fun weekend?' Sarah protested. 'A wander round Bath looking at the sights, a slap-up meal and then the theatre!'

'Stop being such a spoilsport. You'll love it.'

'I hate shopping at the best of times,' Sarah muttered into the mouthpiece.

'So how many more presents have you got to get?'

'All of them,' Sarah admitted.

'Just what I thought. It'll be a great opportunity. And you'll only have three weekends after that to get it all done in time for Christmas.'

'Don't remind me,' Sarah sighed.

The trip to Bath was part of their girls' weekend together. It'd been planned way back in the summer, when Graham had mentioned he'd booked a golfing trip at the end of November. They'd toyed with the idea going away to a hotel somewhere but, on the assumption that the weather might be cold and miserable, they'd settled for a day out with Elizabeth staying overnight at Sarah's place followed by a lazy Sunday.

Governors' meetings were never exciting affairs. Every now and again, they had their moments but usually they were little more than drawn-out talking shops. The real decisions were made elsewhere well in advance thrashed out in the various subcommittees. Nevertheless, as with all such groups, some members saw it as an opportunity to score points or to air his or her particular hobbyhorse. Others just liked the sound of their own voices. It wasn't unusual for a meeting, which had begun at seven, to still be going strong long after ten o'clock. When all its members were unpaid volunteers, albeit with some nominated from various interested elected bodies, and each demanded to have his say, it wasn't possible to use company boardroom disciplines to curtail the proceedings.

After a particularly lengthy and arduous meeting some twelve months earlier, with Sir Richard muttering darkly about instituting a guillotine for each item on the agenda, Sarah suggested that they changed the timing of the meeting. Although it wasn't possible for the majority of these busy people to take time off from their paid employment, if the college provided a buffet, they could have a working lunch. The necessity to get back to their various offices within a reasonable amount of time might help to keep the discussion focused. Once the idea was put to the full board, despite some predictable objectors, the decision to give it a trial run was warmly greeted by the majority. For the first time, she scored a few Brownie points with Sir Richard.

For the November meeting, Sarah was there early as usual to check that the room was in order. Sir Richard was invariably one of the first arrivals but she had little time to talk to him as the room began to fill. Inevitably, Eunice's death was the main topic of conversation and, almost without exception, the governors came over to express their condolences. Several people even made a point of asking how Sarah was as though Eunice had been a close family member rather than a colleague.

The majority of governors tended to turn up only a minute or so before meetings began and this occasion was no exception. Sarah was helping the latecomers to coffee, when Charles Shorecross, the Vice Chairman of Governors, appeared at her elbow.

'I hope you're feeling better. This latest tragedy must have made things so much more difficult for you,' he said almost solicitously. Charles, the Financial Director of Applegate Semiconductors, one of the town's biggest employers, was a pedantic little man, and rarely made himself agreeable, especially to Sarah. She tried to console herself with the thought that his dislike wasn't personal – the man was a misogynist.

Before she could reply, John Clarke, who'd overheard him, cut in, 'I didn't know you'd been ill, Sarah what's been the matter?'

An empty cup was suddenly thrust under her nose and Sarah had to turn away and give her attention to pouring coffee.

'It takes awhile to get over such an unpleasant experience and poor Dr Harcourt hasn't been herself since that nasty mugging incident before the start of term.' The two men were already moving off to take their places at the main table but, when she caught the phrase, 'having a few problems,' she decided not to let the odious little man get away with such distortions.

With an apologetic smile, she thrust the coffee jug into the hands of the next person in the queue and hurried after the two men.

'I'm afraid you've been misinformed.' She gave Charles her sweetest smile. 'It's true I had my bag snatched but it really was nothing more than an inconvenience. Now where on earth did you hear that I haven't been myself?'

'Several people mentioned what an upset you'd had,' he said warily.

'Really? And who was that?' she persisted.

'I can't remember exactly,' he blustered looking more than a little put out.

There was no opportunity to pursue their conversation as, at that moment, Sir Richard tapped on the table and asked everyone to take their places.

It wasn't the most auspicious start to the meeting and every time she glanced in his direction, she saw Charles giving her one of his tight-lipped stares that did not bode well.

After the predictable tribute to Eunice and the measures set in place to cope with her loss, the first part of the meeting passed relatively uneventfully with Sir Richard keeping things moving along in his habitual crisp style. It wasn't until item five on the agenda – the faculty review – that problems arose. This was still a highly contentious issue and not a few frowns met her gaze as she glanced around the table.

'We are all aware that, although the overall student numbers continue to grow, several courses have shown a steady decline in the last five years, the engineering courses in particular.' Several heads nodded as Sir Richard summed up the problem. 'Some areas are expanding rapidly as a result of local and national employment demands or, like the Theatre Studies, because of the good reputation those courses now enjoy. Dr Harcourt has collated the statistics for the last few years and calculated the future trends. You might all like to take a few minutes to look through them before we go any further.'

'It's a pity we weren't sent a copy last week with the all the other reports prior to the meeting,' Charles Shorecross said loudly, glaring across at Sarah.

'I apologize for not being able to include this analysis,' Sarah responded evenly. 'As you know, it takes some time to enter the data and consider possible permutations. Unfortunately, I only had the complete set of this year's figures to work on myself last thing on Friday.' She passed round the papers and there was silence as everyone studied the various sheets of tables.

'Media Studies has shown the highest percentage rise,' someone pointed out.

'True but it doesn't have the most students. The totals for quite a number of courses can fluctuate wildly from year to year,' Sarah pointed out. 'As you can see, the groupings within each of the five faculty areas are no longer sensible. Business Information Systems is now three times the size of Technology and the figures would seem to indicate that that trend will increase.'

'Mr Chairman, I'm sorry to interrupt,' Charles Shorecross paused for dramatic effect. 'These figures on the individual faculty reports and those on Dr Harcourt's statistical analysis don't seem to agree.'

Everyone started shuffling their papers to compare the sets of data.

'There do appear to be some significant discrepancies,' someone agreed in a puzzled voice.

'It's so easy to make slips when transferring figures, especially when you're working under pressure.' She knew Adam Duxbury's comment had been kindly meant but that didn't stop her wanting to snap back at him.

'Just a minute!' Sir Richard quelled the flow of chatter that had broken out. 'Every one of the figures on my copy corresponds exactly.' He'd not looked at the heavily annotated sheets in front of him. It was obvious that he must have compared them when he'd received the emailed report the day before. However much that thought rankled, his habit of checking up on her might well prove to her benefit on this occasion.

Sarah picked up a spare copy from the pile in front of her and compared the figures with the original that she had in her file. There were only one or two differences per page but they were enough to make nonsense of the whole document. 'I'm sorry gentlemen. I don't know how this has happened but this isn't what I prepared.'

'Perhaps you pressed a few wrong keys before you printed off the final copy. Easily done,' someone suggested.

'This is more than the result of a few misplaced keys,' she said sharply and turned to Sir Richard. 'We obviously can't do anything with these. I suggest I ring through to Lucy and ask her to photo-copy my original for everyone. It will take a little time but we could cover some of the other items on the agenda and come back to this.'

He nodded and called the table to order as she hurried to the phone in the corner.

When Lucy she arrived, Sarah slipped out of her place and took her into the corridor to explain what had happened. Back in her seat, she found it impossible to concentrate on the general discus-sion as the meeting continued. Try as she might, she could not account for the errors. She'd checked all the figures several times; if she had made a mistake it would be there on her original printout. There was a gentle tap on the door, she went to get up quietly without interrupting the proceedings but Sir Richard forestalled her by calling Lucy to come in.

'Would you all like to pass up the inaccurate sheets before we hand these out,' he said briskly.

During this slight hiatus, Lucy, who found Sir Richard intimi-dating at the best of times, began apologizing to him.

'No one is blaming you for the mistake, my dear,' he said.

'This was no mistake, Sir Richard.'

The whole room fell silent and all eyes turned on the small figure standing at the head of the table. Two small spots of colour glowed on Lucy's cheeks. She spoke directly at Sir Richard but her clear voice was heard by everyone. 'Mrs Harcourt gave me a disk when she came in on Monday morning. She asked me to run off sufficient copies for today's meeting and to send one to you. I sent the email immediately but I didn't get round to the printing until this morn-ing. If your copy was correct then someone must have deliberately altered the file on the disk.' She stuck out her chin defiantly.

Sarah could see the look of scepticism on several faces. One or two people actually smiled; the idea was so preposterous.

'Why should anyone want to do that?' asked John Clarke reasonably.

'I have no idea,' she responded. 'But there is no other explanation. It couldn't have happened accidentally.'

'Thank you, Lucy.' Sir Richard looked at the retreating figure thoughtfully. 'Shall we get back to the matter in hand everyone?'

Over the last few months, there'd been times when Sarah had doubted her ability to cope. It'd worried her that she couldn't account for various slip-ups, some of which, if left uncorrected, might have had serious consequences. Even when she was certain that someone was deliberately trying to manipulate situations to make her look incompetent, there had been no way she could prove it. Now she had the evidence. After the initial wave of relief knowing with certainty that she wasn't loosing her grip, came a surge of anger. Nevertheless, convincing other people that she was fully on top of the job wasn't going to be easy. She forced herself to concentrate on the discussion and to make pertinent comment. It was vital to appear capable and decisive in front of these people however much her inner feelings were in turmoil.

At the end of the meeting, as everyone was leaving, Sir Richard said quietly, 'When you come to write up the minutes of the meeting...'

'Don't worry, Sir Richard, I won't make reference to Lucy's accusation.' She was annoyed that he should think she would be so unprofessional.

'Perhaps you should.' The pale grey eyes looked steadily into hers.

'Pardon?'

'I think you should record the fact that the analysis had been tampered with.'

'Surely,' she struggled to find the words, 'minutes should record only the decisions made by the members.'

'Plus any significant conclusions. It's evident that someone tampered with the documents. We may not be able to explain why but I'm sure we both have our suspicions about what they may have being trying to achieve.'

They both knew that no such wording would ever appear in the records but Sir Richard's remarks were a clear indication of his personal support. It was his way of letting her know that he wasn't influenced by the rumours being spread to undermine her position. He stood up, gave her one of his rare smiles and left her sitting alone at the table, confused, apprehensive but feeling less isolated than she had in a long time.

Chapter 31

'I don't understand how they thought they'd get away with it!'

Sarah didn't need to ask Lucy what she was talking about. She could see Lucy had thought of nothing else while she'd been waiting for Sarah to come back up to her office. Her eyes shone with a fierce indignation. 'We can easily prove it wasn't your mistake because the original copy is on your computer.'

'But the Boardroom isn't a Court of Law. If Sir Richard hadn't had a correct copy, nothing I said would have helped. The more I protested the more paranoid I'd seem and the more my reputation would've suffered. You'll never know just how grateful I am for your explanation.'

Sarah shut the outer door. Though it usually stood open when Lucy was in the room, she didn't want anyone to overhear their conversation. Sarah led the way into her office and gestured Lucy to sit down.

'But who could have done such a thing?'

She had no more idea than Lucy? 'Let's think this through. I gave you the disk when I came in just before lunch on Monday morning.'

'And George Fitzgibbon, Frank Wagner and Dev Sharma came in while you were asking me to run off the copies for today's meeting. You didn't mention the email to Sir Richard till much later.'

'So they're the only ones who knew about it?'

She thought for a moment. 'No, I don't think so. As it wasn't urgent, I stuck the disk in an envelope and wrote "Faculty Analysis – 25 copies for Governors" on the outside and threw it on top of my in-tray. It was in huge felt tip letters, anyone coming to the office could have seen it.'

'Can you remember who did?'

'Tom Applebury was hanging around for ages that morning waiting for the others to come out of your room.'

Sarah pulled over the diary and checked to see who else had made appointments. Four more names were added to their list.

'I left for a four o'clock appointment. Can you remember if anyone else came in after that?'

Lucy screwed up her face in concentration. Eventually, looking at Sarah somewhat sheepishly, she said, 'Barry Waterhouse popped in not long after you'd gone. He was here for about five minutes. Then David dropped some stuff off for you but I don't think he stopped long enough to notice anything.'

'So, every one of the senior staff could have known about it.'

They both sat in silence.

Lucy wriggled uncomfortably in her chair. 'I've been wracking my brain but I can't understand how anyone could've got hold of that disk. No one touched it while I was here. I took the post down at about half four but I wasn't gone long enough for anyone to have altered it in that time. And I promise you, I locked the door when I left.'

'It wouldn't have been difficult to get hold of a master key. Monday was the one evening when I wasn't here till late. Whoever it was must have spotted the disk, come back for it later then slipped it in your tray again before we got here in the morning.'

Lucy's jaw tightened. 'From now on, nothing is going to be left out over night. All important documents will be kept locked in the filing cabinet. There are no spare keys for that,' she said with fierce determination.

If ever Sarah regretted the break-up of her friendship with Matt, it was that evening. It would have been good to be able to discuss the whole affair with him and ask his advice. Though Sarah had left a message on his answerphone thanking him for the concert, he still hadn't returned her call. There'd been nothing from him for over a week.

Elizabeth was always ready to play the listening ear but she would have no more idea about how to flush out whoever was trying to ruin her professional reputation than Sarah.

It was much too farfetched to believe that her persistent tormentor had been responsible for stealing her car and running down an innocent colleague just to set her up as a murderer, but she couldn't throw off the instinct that it was all connected in some way. Especially at two o'clock in the morning when sleep stubbornly refused to come. If someone was prepared to engineer an accident to do her serious harm then he obviously had no scruples but, she had to admit, it would have been far more logical to target her directly rather than Eunice. Whatever could she have done to drive him to this?

Lucy was still bristling when she came in the next morning and determined to broadcast what had happened to the whole college.

She saw it as her mission to rectify the injustice and was intent on a major hunt for the individual who'd dared to attempt to discredit her. Sarah eventually persuaded her that they should tell no one, at least for the time being.

'Our best response is to act as if the whole thing was so trivial that it created no problems at all. The more everything ticks over efficiently the better.'

'But it's not just what happened yesterday,' Lucy argued. 'If the attempt to falsify the report was made public, people would know that all the rumours are untrue.'

'What rumours are they?' Sarah asked lightly, although after the governors' comments, she could make a fair guess at what they might be.

'Well,' Lucy looked sheepish. 'Lots of people have commented that you've been under a lot of pressure just lately.'

'You mean they think I'm on the verge of a nervous breakdown?'

'Something like that,' she confessed reluctantly. 'I didn't think so for a moment. I've done my best to tell everyone it's all rubbish but you know how gossip spreads in this place,' she added hurriedly.

'I believe you,' Sarah said.

'I didn't want to tell you before because I thought it would only make things worse.'

Poor Lucy. Sarah hadn't appreciated until then just how difficult the last few weeks must have been for her. Torn between loyalty to her boss and her own suspicions, which, despite her strenuous denials, must at least have crossed her mind, she, more than anyone, would have known about all the trivial slip-ups that'd occurred.

'It's odds on that whoever planted that particular snippet of poisonous misinformation was tied up with the disk fiasco,' Sarah said.

'That's what I thought. I lay awake for ages last night trying to remember who mentioned it to me first. Several people have asked if you were all right but that doesn't mean anything,' she said regretfully. 'Still, from now on I'm going to keep an ear out.'

'I don't think it would be very sensible for you to ask around. It will seem very suspicious if you start questioning everyone.'

'It'll put the culprit on his guard you mean?'

'Possibly,' Sarah said warily although she was more worried of what might happen to Lucy. 'Let's wait and see what happens. Our friend is probably keen to know the governors' response to what happened yesterday so let them find out through that source. With any luck, when he realizes he's failed, he'll give up.'

'I still think they ought to be caught and punished,' said Lucy adamantly.

After promising not to ask any questions, Lucy went back to her room but Sarah doubted her secretary would be working at her usual efficient strength for some time.

Sir Richard made no reference to what had happened in the board-room when he came in for their regular monthly meeting a few days later. For once, he paid little attention to detail and let her do most of the talking. As a consequence, they got through all their business in half the usual time.

Once he'd returned his papers to his briefcase, Sir Richard sat at the table looking at her intently.

'Is there something the matter, Sir Richard?'

'I think you ought to know, when the Press revealed that your car was involved in the death of Ms Robinson, there were immediate calls for your suspension while the case was being conducted.'

The idea wasn't the shock that he might have anticipated it would be. It'd been one of the many thoughts that'd raced through her brain in the small hours in the immediate aftermath of those terrible events.

'Mine wasn't the only voice that pointed out how damaging such a move would be to the reputation of the college,' he continued slowly.

She was about to thank him when he leant forward and cut her short. 'You've created quite a stir in your short time as principal.'

'If you mean I've ruffled a few feathers, I'm afraid that goes with the job. Though obviously, I would never deliberately upset anyone, I can't let that stop me taking the decisions that are needed to keep the college moving forward.' Had that come across as sanctimoni-ously smug as it had sounded in her own ears?

'True, but I wonder if you realize just how many enemies you have.'

'Isn't that putting it a little strongly?'

'I am sure you realize that at the time of your appointment, several governors, myself included, were not convinced that you had the experience or the backbone to take the necessary hard action that the position demands. However, the way you tackled the unenviable task of rationalizing staff and streamlining procedures was impressive but we all know that, though necessary, that process doesn't make you many friends. Earlier in the year, complaints about how you'd antagonized people began to filter up to the governors. It didn't take a great deal of digging to demonstrate that the stories were, for want of a better word, one sided and that, despite the redundancies and redefined job descriptions and conditions of service, staff morale had never been higher.'

'That's good to know.'

He met her forced smile with a dark frown and shook his head. 'At the end of last week there was a request for an extraordinary general meeting of the governors to consider moves towards your dismissal?'

'On what grounds?' she demanded sharply. The place suddenly felt icy.

'That you are no longer capable of doing the job. At the beginning of term, rumours started circulating about your inability to cope and general inefficiency and someone made sure that all the governors got to hear about it.'

Sarah sat for a moment trying to take it all in. 'So when is this meeting? Presumably I will be given an opportunity to answer any accusations?' She kept all trace of emotion from her voice.

He smiled, eyes as well as lips, and gently shook his head. 'There had to be a preliminary hearing but it was decided that there was insufficient evidence to take the matter further.'

She resisted the temptation to rub the circulation back into her arms which, like the rest of her body, had gone suddenly numb and continued to look back into the pale grey eyes keeping her expression as blank as possible.

'Nonetheless, it would seem, from the attempts at the last Board Meeting, that someone is still trying to force the issue. Spreading malicious tittle-tattle is one thing but deliberate sabotage it quite another.'

She licked dry lips before she was able to speak. 'I do appreciate you telling me all this, Sir Richard.'

He got to his feet. At the door, he turned and gave her his parting shot. 'You have never been one to retreat from difficult situations but you should know what you're up against. And remember, you do have supporters in the college. Some,' he paused giving her another of his rare smiles, 'in unexpected quarters.'

Chapter 32

Sarah didn't need Elizabeth's strictures to put all thoughts of work and her various problems far from her mind at the weekend. Though it was far easier said than done, and many times Sarah found her mind wandering especially during the matinee. Despite her reservations, their shopping jaunt in Bath had been far more fun than Sarah had anticipated. It was late when they eventually got back to the flat. After a long session sitting in front of the fire consuming a whole bottle of wine between them, it wasn't until the early hours that they got to bed. When she eventually woke the next morning, Sarah had a pounding head and a throat lined with sandpaper. The sunny radiance with which Elizabeth flitted around her flat didn't help her hangover.

Sarah was sitting at the kitchen table, still in her dressing gown, when Elizabeth breezed in washed, dressed and looking ready for action.

'You still drinking tea? You do realize you've only got ten minutes before you leave for church, don't you?'

Sarah groaned and, instead of leaping up as she should have done, she poured herself another cup. 'What are you going to do with yourself while I'm at mass? I should only be gone an hour.'

Elizabeth wasn't religious but had tolerated Sarah's slavish adherence to an indoctrinated upbringing as Elizabeth called it, since their student days.

'I'll make a start on lunch. Damn! That reminds me I've got a rather scrummy pud in the deep freeze that I meant to bring. I don't suppose I could borrow your car and go and get it could I?'

Sarah's sporty convertible had once been her pride and joy. A symbol of her independence from Nathan. A statement that she was no betrayed saddo and had every intention of living life to the full. But she could never feel the same way about it after all that'd happened. When the police finally released it, she discovered that despite being used as a lethal weapon, the car showed surprisingly little damage. The garage was able to sort it out in a matter of days and Sarah was able to collect it in time for their jaunt to Bath.

Sarah was about to suggest that Elizabeth wait until she got back, when they could go over together, but she could see the gleam of hope sparkling in her friend's eyes as she looked up over the top of her teacup. Elizabeth had never made any secret about how much she coveted Sarah's acquisition and, after all Elizabeth had done for her in the last few weeks, it seemed mean to deny her some small reward.

Not wanting Elizabeth to think that she didn't trust her driving, Sarah didn't go down to see her off. Standing at her bedroom window, she waited for the car to circle round the front of the row of houses and come into view on the top road. Even for a wintry Sunday, the whole area looked deserted. The road was still wet from an earlier shower but the sun was doing its best to smile through the shapeless grey clouds.

Sarah's sleek silver Saab was the only sign of life out there. Instinctively she waved although there was no way, Elizabeth could see even if she had glanced up at that moment. No way she could have heard Sarah's scream of horror as she saw a dark figure leap out from the cover of the trees and throw something at the windscreen.

Sarah watched the car brake sharply and skid diagonally forwards. The slow motion picture of it mounting the curb and hitting that first tree would haunt her dreams for the rest of her life. The car flipped over, end on end, and went crashing down the steep escarpment smashing the trees in its path like matchsticks.

She'd almost reached the half landing before her brain kicked in and she raced back up to dial 999.

Even so, Sarah was one of the first there as she slid down the slope to the wreckage. The car had finally righted itself but the fabric of the soft top had been cruelly slashed and mangled. Shreds of fabric hung from a deep gouge over the driver's seat. Through the open door, she could see Elizabeth sprawled over the wheel, motionless, blood pouring from a great gash across her temple. Only the seat belt prevented the unconscious figure from falling out. Someone was kneeling alongside feeling for her pulse. Sarah must have been screaming like a banshee. Strong arms grabbed her and held her close trying to calm her down.

'She's still breathing.' The speaker, a man she vaguely recognized from the end house, looked up and tried to reassure her.

The ambulance arrived within minutes but much of the rest was a blur. Sarah insisted on going with Elizabeth to the hospital. She remembered one of the paramedics wrapping her in blanket and sitting with his arm around her, talking in a low monotonous voice for the whole of the journey.

They put Sarah in a quiet side room while they waited for the emergency team to see to Elizabeth. One of the hospital staff phoned through to Graham. At some point she must have given someone Nathan's number because she knew she'd not phoned him. She was still dazed and rambling when he arrived. He held her in his arms while she sobbed uncontrollably.

Sarah refused to leave the hospital, even to go back home to get dressed. A young man in a white coat, who looked no older than one of her second year students, came in. He told them Elizabeth had several broken bones, including a badly fractured right ankle and severe bruising but the thing that was giving most cause for concern was a serious head injury. She'd been taken down to theatre for immediate surgery and it would be some time before they had any more news.

The police arrived and asked her to give a statement. They didn't seem to give a great deal of credence to Sarah's account of the mysterious figure in black especially as he'd disappeared before anyone else had had a chance to see him. The officers listened attentively but she could tell by the expression on both their faces that they judged her so distraught that she'd imagined the whole incident. Later, she remembered saying over and over again that whoever had done this had intended to get rid of her and not Elizabeth. She didn't think even Nathan believed her story.

Elizabeth was out of theatre and Sarah was sitting by her bed in intensive care by the time Graham arrived late in the afternoon. All he'd been told was that the car had gone out of control on a wet slippery road and by then Sarah had more sense than to try and tell him of her suspicions. He stopped short of blaming her for letting Elizabeth take the convertible in the first place although that was obviously what he was thinking.

Though it hurt her to do so, she left the two of them alone. Nathan tried to persuade her to go back to his house. It took some convincing him that she would be all right on her own. Nevertheless, after he'd driven her to the flat, he insisted on coming up and making her a hot drink; she couldn't face the thought of food. By then she was very drowsy. One of the doctors had given her "something for the shock" and she wasn't really in a state to protest when Nathan put her to bed.

Chapter 33

Though the curtains were still drawn when she woke, Sarah could tell it was quite late. She lay there, still exhausted, for a few minutes before the memories hit her. She was about to pull herself out of bed and get to the phone when she heard a noise. Someone was moving about in her flat. Every muscle in her body stiffened and then she realized that it must be Nathan. He'd obviously stayed the night. She wasn't sure if she was relieved or annoyed.

She struggled out of bed but her dressing gown was missing from its customary hook on the back of the door.

Footsteps approached along the corridor and there was a gentle tap. He came in and handed her a mug of tea.

'I've phoned the hospital and they said Elizabeth spent a comfortable night and is holding her own.' Sarah was grateful that he hadn't wasted time asking her how she was. He knew how much she hated fuss at the best of times.

'What does that mean?'

He shook his head. 'That's all they'd tell me but it sounds encouraging.'

'What time is it?' she asked sinking back onto edge of the bed.

'Just after ten,' he said. 'I've phoned your secretary and told her you won't be in today. She asked me to say how sorry she was to hear about the accident and to tell you that you're not to worry about college. She'll see to everything until you can get back.' Nathan began opening drawers until he found one of her cardigans. 'At least I'll know what to get you for Christmas this year. You need a new dressing gown. Apart from all the mud, your old one's torn to shreds.'

'Shouldn't you be at work?'

'I've explained what happened and told them I'm taking the day off.' He stooped to drape the cardigan around her shoulders and she shied away from him.

'That won't be necessary,' she said more sharply than she'd intended. 'I appreciate I must sound very ungrateful after all you've done but I really don't need looking after.'

'But…'

'Nathan!' The warning in her voice was unmistakable.

'Is there anything else I can do before I go?' The hurt in his eyes very nearly caused her to relent.

She followed him to the top of the stairs and watched him descend. She knew she was being unfair. How many men after being chucked out would have been ready to put themselves out for her as he had done? But she wasn't ready to be cocooned. More than that, though logic said he could no longer be considered the most likely candidate for the role of her tormentor, she wasn't quite convinced about Nathan's motives. There was something that was making her very uneasy about having him here that was more than just her feelings of guilt.

Despite her long sleep, she still felt far from rested but there was a great deal that needed sorting out. However tempting the idea of crawling back under the duvet, it wasn't a luxury she could afford. Still, she could procrastinate a little longer and she ran herself a bath.

There was much to think about as she lay soaking in the too hot water heavily perfumed with the expensive aromatherapy oil that she kept only for special occasions. In the twenty four hours since the accident, concern for Elizabeth had kept her from trying to work out the "who" or "why" of what had happened. Despite her tentative efforts over the previous weeks, she'd come no closer to solving the identity of the individual who was hounding her. As it was evident that now he would stop at nothing to get rid of her, it was a task she could no longer ignore.

She still didn't want to face it and now there seemed so many practical problems demanding her immediate attention. The water had begun to get cold when she eventually pulled herself out but, even before she got dressed, she rang the hospital. It wasn't that she doubted Nathan, but she wanted to find out if Elizabeth was well enough for visitors. She was given the same non-committal message, word for word, and curtly told that only close family were being allowed to see her.

'Thank you for nothing,' she snapped at the phone as she banged down the receiver.

They couldn't stop her taking in some flowers and she might be able to see Graham and learn something more from him. It was then that she realized that she would have problems getting across to the hospital. At least it was the right side of town. The thought of having to approach the insurance company again, only a couple of days after the car's return, did nothing to improve her spirits. It was a task she would need to tackle soon but she'd no intention of facing it today.

It was then that she felt drawn to the window. She could hardly bring herself to look out. The wreckage of her car had been long since been winched up and towed away but the sad line of broken trees would remain a scour on the landscape for a long time to come. A daily reminder.

Another of the things she would have to make time for was to find out how the investigation was going. The police would no doubt be in the throes of conducting an accident enquiry but she was far from convinced they would act on anything she had said. Although a totally different department would handle it, it might be worth talking it all over with Matt assuming that she could pluck up the courage to speak to him.

Elizabeth remained unconscious for three days. Apparently, it was current practice to keep serious accident victims sedated to allow the body to recover from the trauma. Sarah went up to the hospital every day but she was still not allowed to see Elizabeth. She knew that Graham was constantly at her bedside so there was no point in ringing their home. Elizabeth's parents had come down from Chesterfield but she didn't see them either. The bland reports on Elizabeth's progress she got from the nurses, told her absolutely nothing and left Sarah feeling isolated. It was hard not to take all the blame for Elizabeth's perilous condition on her own shoulders. Sarah may not have caused the accident but it would never have happened if she had taken more active steps earlier to track down her persecutor.

Sarah was back in college by Tuesday afternoon but not a great deal of work got done. Between them, Lucy and George sorted out priorities, pushed the occasional bit of paper for her signature at her and generally made sure that things ticked over satisfactorily.

It took until Thursday lunchtime before she was able to get to speak to Matt. She rang several times but was told that Inspector Grant was either out or not available and no one could give her a time when she could ring back to be certain of catching him. After leaving several messages, even one on his home answerphone, it came as a surprise when she eventually heard his voice when she picked up the receiver.

'Hello, I understand you've been trying to get hold of me?' He sounded friendly enough. Perhaps she imagined the trace of guarded apprehension in his voice.

'I don't know if you've heard, but Elizabeth – the friend I've talked about – was involved in a serious accident last Sunday.'

'I'm sorry to hear that,' he said automatically.

'The thing is, she was driving my car and well, I know this sounds strange but I wondered if we could meet up and I could pick your police brain so to speak? Unofficially.' She didn't sound like a rational woman even to her own ears.

They had arranged to meet in the tearoom the next day. It was convenient neutral territory; quiet enough for them to talk but sufficiently public for Matt not to feel compromised. He couldn't make it until two o'clock which had the added advantage of the place being less crowded.

Sarah arrived early to secure a table in a quiet corner where they would stand less chance of being overheard and to give her time to compose herself. The panic of the immediate aftermath of Elizabeth's accident and the subsequent numbness had left her long ago. An increased sense of danger had made her more determined than ever to refuse to be intimidated and to unravel the conspiracy. The thing that made her apprehensive was having to face Matt.

There was a wariness in his eyes as he sat down opposite her. Putting on her best efficient-principal's manner, she thanked him for coming and recounted her story as unemotionally as possible. It was as though there had never been anything between them. He listened attentively but he didn't seem any more convinced by it than the other officers had done.

'At the moment, Elizabeth remembers nothing about the accident. Apparently that's quite common and it may be some time before everything comes back, if at all,' she explained.

'After your call, I had a word with the boys in Accident Investigation. They seem to think that Mrs Edington was probably dazzled by the low sun shining off the wet road as she came round the corner. She was driving an unfamiliar car. It was a sports car. Perhaps she was tempted to put it through its paces,' he said guardedly. If Sarah had any suspicions that her evidence had been dismissed, Matt had just confirmed them. It was all too evident that she could expect no help in discovering the identity of the attacker from official quarters.

'But what about the man who jumped out at the last moment? I didn't imagine him,' she said still keeping calm and reasonable.

'Someone suddenly coming up out from the trees might just be the distraction that made her break and caused the skid. From that distance it must have been difficult for you to see exactly what he was doing.' He wouldn't look her in the face as he spoke.

'I definitely saw him lift his arm and throw something directly at the car.'

'Unfortunately the windscreen was totally shattered as the vehicle plunged through the trees. There's no way of proving your story. And there were no other witnesses.'

'Isn't it suspicious that this man didn't come forward? Surely his evidence is crucial.'

They sat silently for a few moments, he looking out of the window, her staring fixedly at the clenched hands in her lap.

'Why would anyone want to hurt Mrs Edington?' Matt reasoned gently as though to a difficult child.

'It was my car.' She actually managed a smile. 'Perhaps someone wants to get rid of me.' She said it without a trace of emotion but he still looked at her as though she was a lunatic. 'It's not the first time someone has made an attempt to cause me serious injury.' As briefly as she could she told him about the wire across the stairs. 'I did tell Inspector Parson all about it.'

As soon as she'd said it, she knew it was a mistake. It was as though he physically shied away from her. She caught him taking a quick look round to make sure that no one who might recognize him had seen him talking to a suspect in a murder case.

He must have seen the look on her face. He ran his tongue over his bottom lip in concentration as he tried to find the right words. 'Is the stalker you talked about still following you?'

'Yes. He's been sticking to me like a limpet all week.' she said, instantly regretting the admission. 'But he wasn't the mystery man who caused the accident.'

Matt raised an eyebrow. There was no point in trying to explain and she could give no concrete details, only a feeling.

'Have you reported this stalker?'

She shook her head. As though to belie his earlier reaction, he put his hand across the table and laid it on top of hers. She did her best not to flinch from the patronizing gesture. It said more clearly than any words that he thought that at best she was overreacting or she was so distraught that she was imagining things. Why she hadn't gone to the police long ago? Even she had to admit, it didn't sound like the actions of an intelligent woman.

Arranging the meeting had been a mistake. She had no doubt that she was under serious threat. But she'd no idea why. There were several people who would have no regrets if she were to leave but to imagine that any one of them was prepared to cause her direct harm was a jump of gargantuan proportions. Even though she knew she'd insufficient evidence for the police to act on, she'd hoped that at least Matt would believe her. She thought he would be eager to suggest what she should do to protect herself against the escalating treats. It'd been foolish to expect him to help her work out a strategy to force her persecutor into the open.

It was with a heavy heart that she trudged back up the hill to the college but by the evening she'd stopped feeling sorry for herself and was just plain angry. It had to be faced, she was on her own but no one was going to almost kill her closest friend and get away with it. He had declared war and she was the only person who could fight the battle. It was up to her to smoke him out.

Chapter 34

Although Sarah had finally decided that her persecutor was most likely one of her colleagues, it was paradoxically at college that she felt safest – at least during the busy day. Added to which, the sheer volume of work occupied all her thoughts leaving little time for speculation.

Nevertheless, it was difficult not to regard everyone with whom she came in contact with suspicion. There was a great temptation to read all sorts of hidden meanings and motives into the most innocent of remarks. More than ever she was aware of David's tight-lipped bridling at her every remark, Frank's habitual petty provocation and George's evasive answers and determination to scuttle back to his own hole at the earliest opportunity whenever they came in contact.

News that one of her close friends had been seriously injured had quickly become common knowledge but, as the days past, she received fewer enquiries about Elizabeth's recovery. Whoever had caused the accident would have no idea that she'd seen him at the vital moment. Every time anyone made the conventional murmurs of sympathy, she waited for questions about how much Elizabeth remembered of the ghastly business. Unfortunately, the culprit was too clever to give himself away so easily.

It was very tempting to ask her colleagues where each of them had been on that fateful Sunday morning. But to do so would reveal that she knew that Elizabeth's appalling car crash was no accident and might well result in precipitating even more violent steps to silence her.

George's impatient pencil tapping was beginning to get on her nerves.

For once, it wasn't Frank Wagner who kept them waiting. He sat with a smug look on his face as though he'd got one over on Sarah by being early for once. The sympathy and support he'd shown on the night of Eunice's death had been short-lived but, in a strange way, she felt more comfortable with the predictable old Frank.

'Young Dave's still got a minute or two,' he said to no one in particular looking at his watch.

They drifted back into silence. Except for Frank, comfortably ensconced and showing a complete indifference to the preparatory shuffling of papers going on around him, everyone seemed much more on edge than usual. Even the normally outgoing Barry kept his head down. 'What have you been doing to yourself?' asked Dev, who was sitting beside her, trying to fill the hiatus. Sarah had been violently rubbing the back of her hand and the tiny red scratches now looked raised and angry.

'It was only the downstairs cat,' she said.

'That'll teach you not to pull its tail,' goaded Frank from the far side of the table. The others smiled politely at the poor joke.

'You ought to complain to the owners,' said Tom.

'The couple in the flat below are away for a few days and I've been put in charge of looking after it. I don't think it likes me very much. The silly animal's always running off. I've had to go out and look for it every morning so far this week to get it to come in for its breakfast.' At least the pointless chatter helped to cover the strained atmosphere.

'Cats aren't like dogs,' Dev said sympathetically. 'They don't come when they're called.'

Sarah glanced at her watch. They'd waited long enough. 'I make it two minutes past.' Before she could say anymore, the door opened and David hurried in.

'Sorry I'm late, everyone.' He seemed surprised to see Frank already there and, looking contrite, sidled into the empty place.

'You're just in time. George was about to start reading the minutes of the last meeting.'

Throughout the various reports, she was able to sit back and study her senior staff. The mood was heavy and sombre and she didn't think she was the only one to feel the tension. George kept his head down busy scribbling away. David, looking more than ever like a scared rabbit well out of his depth, gabbled through his own report and spent the rest of the time trying to make himself as inconspicuous as possible. Tom sat back, arms folded, staring up at the ceiling trying to demonstrate a sublime indifference to all that was being said. When they moved on to the main topic on the agenda, extending their links with local business, Barry did much of the talking. He argued his case well, demonstrating his undoubted flair but, for once, his wit failed to raise the usual smiles. Frank, who as director of the Business Studies faculty, ought to have been more proactive in this area and knew it, began to glower at everyone and the usual sniping ensued. Only Dev, the habitual observer who missed nothing, seemed his normal self.

As she looked at each man in turn, Sarah realized how little she had in common with each of them. She'd never socialized with her colleagues and, though it was an exaggeration to say she actively disliked them, there wasn't one she would choose for a friend. Even worse, she couldn't find much respect for any of them. She knew her jaundiced view was only temporary and that suspicion was colouring her judgement. To dismiss them all as cardboard caricatures would be arrogantly foolish. She tried to see herself through their eyes. Those pictures were even more unflattering. For all that, it was very difficult to imagine that any one of these men could find sufficient cause to loathe her so much. Which of them would be prepared to work so hard to drive her over the edge, to think up ways to doctor documents to discredit her and, when all else failed, attempt to cause her actual physical harm? Surely not one of them had sufficient ruthlessness, resourcefulness or sheer imagination, even if she could dream up a sufficient motive?

'We all have links with local companies in our related areas, if only through work experience, and it's up to all of us to capitalize on those networks.' Barry's mildly hectoring tones brought an end to her musings.

'Some of us in this place like to spend our time working not swanning off having lunch with local bigwigs,' said Frank with a sneer.

'It's in our own interests to take a more high profile stance. We can't afford to be isolationist. All I'm suggesting is that we each compile a list of our faculty's existing links so that we can come up with an overall picture. We can then see where we need to concentrate our efforts to fill in the gaps,' Barry insisted.

'Does that mean you've still got a few spaces in your little black book? I'd have thought you'd have sussed out all the local talent long ago.'

'That's enough, Frank.' Sarah cut in. 'Good idea, Barry. I suggest you all raise it within your own faculties and bring the results to the next meeting in the New Year. Well, gentleman, unless anyone has anything else?' She looked around at the shaking heads, 'Thank you, everyone.'

She pulled her papers together and found Dev at her elbow wanting to bring her up to date on timetable changes for the new term. Throughout their short conversation, Sarah was aware of a continuation of the bickering that'd been going on between Frank and Barry. As the two were in the habit of trying to score points off each other, it wasn't until the door slammed violently that she turned to see what was going on.

'You know you shouldn't bate Barry like that. He's having a tough time at the moment.' David looked accusingly at Frank. 'Did you know his wife has left him?'

This was obviously as much a surprise to everyone else as it was to Sarah.

'Serves him right. Bloody philander.' Frank's habitual antagonism towards Barry was in no way mollified.

'That chatting up all the women is just an act. He dotes on Valerie. He can't see what a bitch she is. She's bled him dry, demanding the high life. When the money ran out she upped and left taking the kids with her.'

'Don't expect me to shed any tears for him.' Frank looked at his watch. 'Almost lunch time. Coming for a bite, Tom?' The two men walked to the door.

Thank goodness they were all gone. Pity she couldn't get rid of the smell of them as easily. All that body heat. It was still too warm. Even though she'd opened the window, the place still reeked of Frank's tobacco, the vague mixture of oil and Swarfega from Dev who'd obviously been working on the engines and the various hints of aftershave. Aftershave. That meant something. It jogged a half forgotten memory but she couldn't quite pull it back.

The faculty meeting had left Sarah feeling depressed and ill at ease. She was still trying to puzzle over what it was that had seemed so familiar when she walked into the living room to see the light flashing on the answerphone. She felt a surge of panic. Even though it'd been nearly a couple of months since the last menace call she doubted that she would ever be able to look at the thing without some degree of apprehension. Telling herself not to act the helpless maiden, she stabbed at the play button.

'It's Jenny...Um...I hate these answer things. I wanted to talk about Dad's birthday. As it's his sixtieth it would be nice to do something a bit special. It's not for a bit so there's no urgency. Perhaps the two of us could get together over Christmas and come up with something?'

Sarah caught sight of the silly grin on her face in the mirror and laughed out loud. It was the nearest thing she was going to get to an attempt at reconciliation from her sister. Her father's birthday wasn't until March but as a peace offering it could hardly be bettered.

Suddenly the world seemed a brighter place. Not only was the feud over, the prospect of a big family party was something to look forward to. The two of them would have great fun planning it together.

She picked up the phone and punched in Jenny's number.

The cat was nowhere around when she let herself in through the back door of the downstairs flat. Sarah called out its name but it still failed to appear. She took the half empty tin of Whiskas out of the fridge and went to wash up the dish before putting out fresh food. Then she realized that the silly animal had upset the saucer of milk all over the kitchen floor. She was already later than she'd intended and was none too pleased at having to stop and clear up the smelly mess.

Months ago she'd promised the Ericksons that she would look after their cat while they were off on holiday. After the accident, Margery had suggested putting Blackie into a cattery to save Sarah the trouble but when they'd done that in the past, the animal had pined and refused to eat. The elderly couple were good neighbours; they kept themselves to themselves and had always been friendly but never intrusive. Sarah was lucky to have them and, she reminded herself as she mopped the floor, this minor inconvenience was a small price to pay.

Blackie had left most of the food she'd put out the previous evening and she didn't like to think of the animal going hungry. She went outside and started calling again. A faint mewling came from somewhere at the side of the house and she turned the corner to see what it was up to. To her surprise, the door to the cellar was slightly ajar. It was full of old junk and discarded gardening tools that were long past their prime and contained nothing worth stealing. Arnold Erickson left the key in door so that she could use the place to store old bottles and glass jars until she had enough to warrant a trip to the bottle bank. She clambered down the cellar steps, pulled the door open a little further and peered into the dim depths.

'Blackie. Are you in there you silly puss?' Her voice echoed eerily but a faint pitiful cry came from the far corner.

'If you think I'm going to get myself filthy coming in there after you, you've got another think coming. Get yourself out here at once you stupid animal or I'll be late for work.'

Blackie's responding squawk of protest didn't suggest compliance.

'Here puss, puss, puss,' she tried again, in what she hoped were more persuasive tones.

As her eyes began to adjust to the minimal amount of light coming from the wide but shallow grill at ground level, she could see Blackie's dark shape perched on a pile of boxes stacked against the far wall. It was standing four paws together, back arched, tail held rigidly upright, green eyes staring accusingly straight at Sarah.

'Don't pretend you can't get down because I know better. If you got up there without help you can get yourself down.'

Why was she trying to hold a conversation with a dumb animal? She took a few more tentative steps. Blackie remained immobile giving the odd plaintive wail.

Sarah made her way, gingerly finding a place for her feet amongst the assorted obstacles and trying not to brush against the many years of accumulated dust and grime. She heard the door swing closed behind her and swore quietly under her breath. It was the next noise that made her insides turn to ice. A faint click. Someone had turned the key in the lock.

With a cry, she ran back crashing and stumbling in her haste. She rattled the latch then threw her weight against the door but only succeeded in bruising her shoulder. Sheer terror took hold. She screamed at the top of her voice and pounded with her fists on the rough wood until she could stand the pain no more.

Chapter 35

The panic didn't last for long. The situation demanded cold logic. With both flats empty and a set of garages between her and the nearest houses, nobody was likely to hear her cries for help. Unless her attacker planned on coming back later, she could be trapped down here until the Ericksons returned in three days time. No, that was ridiculous! She'd be missed at work and someone would come round to investigate when she failed to answer the phone. Perhaps not today, but certainly tomorrow. Surely she'd enough gumption to stick it out?

'Well Blackie, you and I might get a bit hungry but at least we've got each other.' She turned to look for the cat but it was no longer on its perch. 'Where've you got to puss?'

She looked around but there was no sign. It must have been frightened by all the noise she'd made. Trust the stupid animal to go into hiding. In her present predicament it would have been reassuring to be able to stroke the soft fur and feel the warmth of a fellow creature. They might even get to be friends sharing each other's company in adversity. For goodness sake! She shook her head at the banal thoughts passing through her mind.

Although she didn't suffer from actual claustrophobia, it was no secret that she didn't like being in confined spaces especially in the dark. It was why she was prepared to walk up several flights of stairs rather than take the lift and chose to live in a large, airy home with extensive views. At least she could console herself that the high cellar window, with its apt prison-like grill, provided some light even if the bars were too close for her to squeeze through.

But not too small for Blackie of course. The realization that the cat, the reason why she'd ventured into this hellhole in the first place, must have jumped through the narrow gap didn't improve her raw emotions. No doubt it was out there now, parading up and down, totally unconcerned about the plight it'd led Sarah into. Until today, she'd always thought of herself as a cat lover but Blackie was one animal whose nine lives were in dire jeopardy if ever she got out of this icebox.

She was already beginning to feel the cold penetrating her bones. As she'd not planned on staying outside, she'd not bothered with a coat when she'd left the house. She got up from her box and started stamping her feet and slapping her arms to keep warm. There was a good chance that she would die of hypothermia long before starvation and dehydration took their toll.

No point in sitting around waiting for it to happen.

In all the assorted junk there must be something she could use to hack at the lock. A screwdriver; a hammer? An axe would be good. All she had to do was make a large enough hole in the door to put a hand through and turn the key. After ten minutes of fruitless searching, it was evident that there were no such tools around. All she'd come up with was an ancient garden spade with a dodgy handle.

The slight curve on the bowl was just sufficient to stop her getting get the width of the blade between the door and the jamb. Repeated attempts to use the corner to chisel away at the lock resulted in nothing more than a few scratches in the wood, one severely bruised thumb and two very sore hands. The only consolation was that the effort had warmed her up.

Forcing herself to remain calm, Sarah began a slow, methodical search of the basement. Half an hour later, having moved piles of junk and searched every possible container, she was still no further forward. She sat down on a pile of old newspapers and tried to sort out her next move.

Hung on a couple of hooks on the wall opposite was a ladder. Although the bars of the grill at ground level some ten or so feet above her were too close together for her to squeeze her whole body through, it she could get up there, there might be something within reach which she could use. Perhaps she could send a signal of some kind. It was worth a try. Preposterous though the idea was, she had nothing to lose and doing something, anything, was better than sitting there imaging the worst.

In practice, manoeuvring the heavy ladder in the crowded, confined space proved a far more difficult feat than she'd anticipated. Several times she almost gave up the effort. When she managed to get it jammed at a ludicrous angle half way up the wall for the second time, it had taken all her strength and perseverance to shift it. Eventually she eased it up high enough to reach but the ladder was so long that the resultant angle was so shallow that she had to crawl rather than climb up to the opening.

At the top, her heart in her mouth praying that the thing would not slip, she had to let go the edge of the ladder and ease herself upright walking her hands up the wall. Her fingers gripped the sill and slowly she lifted her head. From her narrow range of view all she could see was the corner of the courtyard and a row of dustbins at right angles against the wall. There were no large stones or bricks suitable as a tool within reach.

She rested her forehead on the cool sill. Only when she raised her head again did she see that the bars were set in frame like a window and could be opened from inside. A fact she hadn't appreciated from below.

Carefully she undid the latch. If she pushed the whole thing up she might just be able to wriggle through. The ladder would have to be repositioned. There was no way she could scramble up from her present position.

Adjusting the ladder took some time and involved shifting a fair number of boxes to get it high enough and at a suitable angle. When she eventually squeezed her way out, she lay exhausted on the ground, relieved but totally devoid of energy.

'Sarah!'

The call was faint and she wasn't sure if she'd imagined it.

'Sarah.' Closer now and more urgent.

She struggled to her knees. Nathan came round the corner just as she got to her feet. Her ran to her and enveloped her in his arms.

She lashed out in wild fury and, like some crazed animal, pounded his chest with her fists. 'What the hell did you think you were doing locking me in? What bloody, stupid game were you playing at? How dare you terrify me like that?'

He grabbed her flailing arms and held her tightly to him, burying her face in the woollen sweater beneath the open trench coat.

'Shush, shush. It's all right. It's all right.'

Upstairs, back in the flat, they sat facing each another; she curled in the protective depths of the armchair, Nathan squatting awkwardly on the stool pulled up close.

'I saw your door was open so I knew you must be around somewhere.' His voice was low and reassuring.

The hysteria had gone and though she was prepared to believe that he'd not been her gaoler, she wasn't yet ready to trust him unconditionally.

'What on earth made you think that it was me who locked you in?' he asked with a pained, incredulous frown.

'You're the one whose been stalking me all these weeks,' she accused petulantly.

He stared at her for a moment then dropped his head, as though unable to look her in the eyes. 'I was worried about you. When you mentioned those threatening phone calls, I could see that you were more upset than you were prepared to admit. You're normally too self-composed to be affected by trifles. I only wanted to be sure that you were safe, especially after you'd been mugged. I did stop for a while after you nearly caught me in the pedestrian precinct that time. I was sure you'd recognized me. Then, when you said you were convinced that someone had deliberately caused Elizabeth's accident, I couldn't stop worrying. I've been desperately anxious about you.'

'The police thought I'd imagined him.'

'They don't know you like I do,' he said firmly choosing to forget that he too had been sceptical when he'd first heard her story.

It was difficult not to believe the earnest pleading in those eyes.

'How did you know they'd taken us to the hospital?' she fired at him suspiciously.

'After the accident? They phoned me.' He looked puzzled at her challenge.

'I know I was confused when they first took me in but I couldn't have given them your home number. I don't even know it.' He flinched at the harshness in her voice.

'You must have given them my name and I suppose they looked it up in the phone book. What are you suggesting? Sarah, you don't honestly believe it was me who tried to kill you do you? Good God, why should I, of all people, want to do such a thing?'

She shook her head. 'No. Not really.' She suddenly felt very weary. 'I kept going over everything in my mind right back to all that stuff that arrived through my letterbox.'

'I don't understand.'

'Whoever did that knows me pretty well. Brochures for holidays in China, Egypt, Mexico and other places I've always wanted to go. The books were my favourite authors. It was all the sort of things I might have sent for. You know my tastes better than anyone.'

'But why on earth should I want to persecute you like that? For God's sake woman, I love you!'

How could she explain that she thought he might be trying to drive her over the edge to get shot of her for good so he could be free to marry his new girlfriend? It seemed ridiculous now in the cold light of day but, lying awake in the dark at three o'clock in the morning, logic had gone out of the window. Catholicism may have ruled out divorce as an option for her but there was nothing to stop him taking such action if that was what he'd wanted. Far simpler and less troublesome.

'Is that why you sent me away after I'd brought you back from the hospital?'

Sarah shook her head dismissively. 'It was the aftershave.'

He looked at her. 'That doesn't make sense.'

'I recognized the smell. I knew there was something familiar about the man who grabbed my handbag but I couldn't work out what it was until that morning when you came into the bedroom and I smelt it again.'

'You don't think . . .'

She put a finger on his lips. 'It's a common enough brand and I've just realized you're not the only person I know who uses it.'

He took her hands in his. 'We've got to report all this to the police,' he said firmly.

'They didn't believe me before, why should they now?'

'This is different. And I can confirm you were locked in down there. You can't have imagined that!'

'Actually you can't. Think about it, Nathan. I'd already got out before you came round the corner. I could have engineered all that to make it look good. If senior officers didn't believe me about the wire across the stairs, including one whom I thought was a friend and who ought to have known that I'm not just an hysterical, delusional woman, how do you think I'm going to get anyone else to take me seriously?' she asked wearily.

'What wire?' he demanded in alarm.

As soon as he'd heard the story, he was on his feet. 'That settles it! We're going straight to the police station.'

'No!' she snapped. 'It won't solve anything to have more policemen tramping about all over the college asking questions. There's been enough of that for a lifetime.'

'The reputation of the bloody college is immaterial. Sarah, your life is in danger! You could have starved to death in that cellar before anyone found you. He's got to be stopped. And you know who it is, don't you?' His fierce indignation tailed off in a desperate plea.

'Possibly, but I could be wrong. A whiff of aftershave isn't enough to convince the police.'

The phone rang suddenly making them both jump.

'That will be my secretary,' she said. 'Wondering if I'm all right.'

Nathan handed her the receiver and she nodded as she heard Lucy's voice.

'I've had a bit of a problem but I'll be there in half an hour or so. Has anyone been asking for me this morning? Good. See you soon.' She put down the phone and smiled across at Nathan. 'It seems I haven't been missed so it's time for me to go and play sleuth.'

'I'm coming with you.'

'No. That wouldn't help at all.' She got to her feet and started for the door.

'Don't push me out, Sarah.' There was sharp edge to his voice that made her stop and look at him. This was no plea. It was an ultimatum. As they stared across at each other they both knew that if she rejected him again, she would lose him forever.

'I can't say I have the plan worked out in detail yet but there might just be a way to flush him out,' she said quietly. 'I need someone to stay here as backup. Someone I can trust.'

As she tried to explain the vague idea that she'd been formulating, it took on more shape. Although Nathan was far from enthusiastic about her strategy, it became more obvious that she would need someone she could rely on to be in the know.

Nathan's frown deepened but, before he could protest, she tried to forestall him. 'Give me an hour and if I haven't rung to say it's all going to plan, you can get on to the police. No. Better still, Sir Richard. You might have trouble persuading them but they'll listen to him. He has friends in high places.'

She looked up the telephone number and wrote it down for him then went to get herself cleaned up and changed. When she came back into the living room, he was still wearing a frown and his normally carefree, healthy countenance looked pale and drawn. She could tell how hard he was fighting every instinct to persuade her to abandon her plans.

'I'll ring you, I promise.'

'I'll be waiting. For God's sake take care. Don't do anything silly.' They walked into the hall and stood awkwardly at the top of the stairs.

'Won't they be expecting you at work or don't you have a job to go to?' she asked lightly in an attempt to break the tension.

'I've taken a few days' holiday,' he said looking rather guilty.

'To keep a watch on me?' She had to smile at his devotion.

He looked embarrassed and didn't answer.

'And what does Veronica think of that?' she chided.

He looked back at her with a puzzled expression on his face. 'What's my cleaning lady got to do with anything?'

'Absolutely nothing,' she agreed as a rush of warmth filled every fibre of her body. He looked more bewildered than ever as he watched her try, not very successfully, to swallow the hysterical laughter threatening to bubble over. 'Forget it. Right, I must go.'

As she turned on the middle landing, she stopped and looked up. Instinctively, she raced back, flung her arms around him and hugged him close. He kissed the top of her head. Then their lips sought each other hungrily.

For a woman who undoubtedly had someone out to get her at whatever cost, she felt surprisingly light hearted as she ran quickly down the stairs. At long last, she thought, something in her life was going right.

Chapter 36

George was busily tapping away at his PC when she walked in. His face registered surprise but not shock when he looked up.

'Good morning, Sarah. What can I do for you?'

'What time did you get in this morning?' she asked levelly as she sat in the chair in front of his desk. Best to appear casual.

'Usual time. Just after eight.' He looked puzzled at her question. 'Why is there a problem?'

'A personal one but it could affect the college as a whole.'

'Really? Can I help?' The offer sounded genuine.

'Were you aware that someone deliberately altered the faculty projection figures on the governors' report?'

'It hasn't happened again?' To do the man credit, he sounded angry.

'No. But I find it interesting that you've heard about that,' she paused. 'As far as I know, it's not public knowledge.'

'I wouldn't assume that if I were you,' he answered grimly. 'The governors weren't exactly sworn to secrecy and these things get around. Plus, Sir Richard has made it his business to let all senior staff know that he has no reservations whatsoever about your competence or the directions in which you're steering the college and that all the rumours and attempts to blacken your reputation have to stop.'

'Really?' It was a surprise to know that Sir Richard's support had extended to warning off the person who'd engineered her apparent lapses of efficiency.

'He has a great deal of respect for you. According to him, you're the only one with enough backbone to stand up to him. He admires that. Plus you've never been afraid to admit making mistakes. That's why he refused to believe all the tittle-tattle. If you'd been responsible for the cock-ups, he knew you would have had no qualms about owning up. Especially after being attacked in the street, no one would have criticized you for feeling under a strain.'

'Someone seems intent on increasing it,' she said grimly. 'And he's prepared to take more positive steps.'

George looked suitably stunned when he heard about the trap on the stairs.

'Someone could have been killed.'

'Possibly but it's not quite so certain a method as staging a car accident.'

George looked puzzled. 'Do you mean Eunice's hit-and-run? But I thought you meant the wire was intended for you?'

'I'm certain it was. I don't exactly know how, but I'm pretty certain those two things are connected and not just because they happened one after the other, but that isn't what I was referring to.' As briefly as possible, she told him about the stone throwing stranger responsible for putting Elizabeth in hospital.

'Good God.' He jerked back in his chair then sat shaking his head in disbelief. 'So what are the police doing about it?'

'Not a lot, by the looks of things. I'm not sure they believe me.'

'But you really think someone is trying to kill you?'

'I wouldn't say that exactly but they certainly want me out of the way.' She paused and held his gaze as she said, emphasizing every word, 'Somebody in this college.'

'Are you sure?'

'It has to be. Whoever it is knows all the routines and procedures and clearly has access. 'It has to be the same person who spread the rumours and doctored my disk.'

They held each others gaze for a long moment. George had the ability, as well as the opportunity, to have altered her report but spreading gossip was not his style. If he'd begun to act so out of character, she would have got to hear about it very quickly. 'It has to be someone who knew I'd given the disk to Lucy to print off or had the opportunity to read the details she put on the envelope.'

His eyes suddenly widened. 'You don't think it was me?' His voice rose to a screech.

'I'd hardly walk in here if you were still at the top of my list.'

His hands released their tight grip on the arms of his chair and he visibly relaxed.

'Does that mean you know who has been doing all this?'

'It has to be one of the senior staff. I have one or two suspicions but, as I haven't a shred of evidence, I'm not prepared to share them just yet.'

'So why tell me?'

'Things have reached a point where I can no longer sit back and let things happen. The police won't do anything and I've got to trust someone.'

George stared at her, his expression unreadable. Eventually he asked, 'Is this a test?'

'What do you mean?'

'I'd like to think the two of us have a good working relationship now but if we're talking about someone wanting you out of the way, logic says I'm the one with the strongest motive. I can't pretend I didn't want the principal's job when it came up and when you were appointed, I resented it for a long time. But things have changed. I may have been Sir Richard's choice before, but not any longer. Even if you were to leave, there's no way I could step into your shoes as he is well aware. I realized now that not only could I never do the job, I no longer want to. I'm happy doing what I do now and content in the knowledge that I do it well. If you were to go, it wouldn't be me that the governors would appoint. And I do know I don't want to work for anyone else as principal. We may never be friends but our working relationship is based on mutual respect. I may not always agree with your decisions but you've always listened to my point of view. I like my little niche. I don't want anyone upsetting it.'

'It's all right George. You don't have to convince me. I'm not here to accuse you. I need your help.'

'What do you want me to do?'

'I think the culprit's last little effort, trying to lock me in the basement, has not only failed but given me an opportunity to trap him.' George looked far from happy with the plan she outlined.

'You're certain it's one of the faculty heads?'

'It has to be. And just lately, I seem to have managed to upset every one of them.'

'That's not difficult,' he said with a snort, 'but it's hardly a motive. Which gives us five suspects unless you can rule anyone out. What about the night someone put the wire across the stairs? Who was still in the college?'

'Frank was on duty but even if the others had left earlier there was nothing to stop one of them coming back. He could have come in through the side door without being seen.'

'Frank has the computer skills to have doctored your disk but I'm not sure that Tom or David have,' he mused. 'Or the guts,' he added as an afterthought.

'And thinking about it, David wasn't in the room when I mentioned about my neighbours being away and having to go out and look for the cat every morning,' she reasoned.

George looked puzzled.

'That story might have given whoever it was the idea,' she said with shrug. 'Perhaps when he was lying in wait for me, he saw the cat and came up with the plan to open the cellar door and push the cat in knowing I'd eventually come to try and find it.'

He stared into space for a few moments. 'What about the person you saw throw something at the car?'

She shook her head. 'Too far away to tell anything. He was wearing an old duffel coat so it was impossible to judge his build and he'd the hood pulled up so I couldn't even see the colour of his hair. It all happened so quickly I can't even say how tall he was.'

'What about your friend, Mrs Edington? Can't she identify him?'

'So far, she doesn't remember anything about the accident at all. Even if she does eventually come up with something, I doubt she'll be able give the police a good description. I'm pretty certain he had a scarf wrapped round the lower part of his face.'

'Tom would like nothing better than to be offered early retirement so he doesn't have the motive the other faculty directors have.'

'Do they have a motive?' she asked in surprise.

'From the escalation of all this action, I'd say it's clear that who-ever it is, wants you out of the way before the faculty review.'

'Why's that relevant?'

'They could find themselves without a job at the end it. There's a real concern that the governors might favour scraping that layer in the hierarchy altogether. It would save a fortune and several other colleges have done just that in the last year or so since the FEFC have cut back the funding.'

'But that's not an option I've supported!' she said aghast. 'True Dev Sharma's faculty is now too small to be viable and it's obvious that we need to restructure but no one is going to get thrown out. It's odds on that Tom will be offered early retirement but he's made no secret that that's what he wants. I suppose, if the governors want to take more drastic steps, they might even offer that option to Frank but it's not my place to discuss that with him. Surely none of the directors could think that I'm trying to make any one of them redundant?'

'We all know they won't survive in their current positions.'

'But surely that's not enough to make anyone do all this?'

They sat in silence as Sarah thought through the implications. She didn't need to be reminded that finding another post at senior level when all colleges were being forced into the same rationaliza-tion process would be very difficult. To judge from the large number of references she'd been asked for, all three of the younger ones had made applications elsewhere. She'd assumed that the person who wanted her out of the way had been trying to get a clear path to her job but perhaps his motive was less ambitious. But how could anyone seriously believe she would deliberately attempt to use her position to influence the governors to force them out?

George's frown deepened at he took of his spectacles and started to clean. 'Are you sure there is nothing else you saw that might help to identify him?'

Sarah shook her head.

'No clues at all?'

'Well, I was much too far away to recognize his features but I'm pretty sure he wasn't wearing glasses.'

He looked up quickly. They exchanged sheepish grins. She could see the tension easing in his shoulders.

'Who knows you're here in the college at the moment,' George asked a long pause.

'Apart from you, only Lucy,' she said, a twinge of apprehension tightening down her spine. 'And Nathan.'

'I take it you came up the back stairs rather than through reception? You're positive no one saw you come in?' She nodded. 'In that case, if you're still adamant about not going to the police, we'd better start the ball rolling.'

Chapter 37

'Yes, Sir Richard, thank you.' George put down the phone and turned back to Sarah. 'He wasn't very happy and he insists on being in at the end. He's going to your flat straight away.'

It'd been George's idea to inform Sir Richard. Sarah would have preferred to wait and see if the plan worked but George, cautious as ever, insisted that if things went wrong, Sir Richard carried the most clout if hasty backup was needed. She watched him take a deep breath and wet his lips. He was as apprehensive as she was. Now the moment had come, she felt suddenly cold.

'Do you still want to do this?' He looked across at her, his hand on the receiver.

She nodded. Her voice would falter if she tried to speak.

He picked up the phone and dialled.

'Frank? It's George. Can you come over to my office straight away?' She couldn't hear the reply at the other end. 'I appreciate you've up to your eyes but we have a crisis,' he cut off the protests.

George continued to summon each of the senior staff. Sarah's senses felt numb and George's voice became a vague drone in the distance.

She was far from confidant about the plan but there seemed no better strategy. Picturing Elizabeth, a tiny, helpless figure imprisoned in the intensive care unit attended by silent, white-clad automatons, had stiffened Sarah's resolve. It was no longer a case of protecting herself against the escalating violence. Letting this maniac go undetected now endangered the lives of the people she loved. For nearly two weeks, she'd sifted evidence, scrutinized the actions of all possible suspects but got no further forward.

'I don't care if he is in the classroom.' George's bark roused her from her reverie. 'I want you to go in there now and take over. Tell Mr Ford that I need him in my office immediately.'

George got up and moved one of the chairs into the walk-in store cupboard in the corner of the room. 'If I leave the door slightly ajar, you'll be able to hear all that's said.'

There was just room for her to be able to sit between the rows of stacked shelves. She very nearly changed her mind when the door was pulled to. She wasn't sure how long she'd be able to stay silent in the dark windowless tomb but this wasn't the time to fall prey to petty phobias. She needed to listen to their responses – to judge their reactions for herself.

Dev and David arrived together. George had just put out the chairs in a circle in front of his desk. It would have been good to be able to see the expressions on each of their faces as they listened to what George had to tell them but she couldn't risk them catching her spying on them through the narrow crack.

'Is all this cloak and dagger stuff really necessary?' She could hear Frank's petulant demand as he threw open the door. 'Oh, I didn't realize we were all invited.'

Barry was the last to arrive. 'What on earth is all this about?' He sounded as truculent as Frank.

There was a shuffling of chairs as they got themselves settled.

'It looks as though we are going to have the police descend on us again,' George began. 'They're going to want statements from each of us, but it is obviously best for the college if we try to keep the whole thing as low key as possible. We don't want all sorts of ridiculous rumours spreading through the student body.'

'Why? What's happened?' They were all talking at once.

'You all know that Mrs Harcourt's friend was seriously injured, well it seems that it wasn't an accident.'

'What the hell are you talking about?' Tom sounded irritated.

'Someone was seen throwing something at the windscreen.'

'But what's that got to do with us?' Frank asked.

'She was driving Mrs Harcourt's car and so Sarah was probably the intended victim.'

'Are you saying that someone deliberately tried to kill her? That's bloody ridiculous. And why in God's name should the police suspect someone here at the college?' From the general outburst of protesting cries, it was evident that Tom wasn't alone in his assessment.

'I presume it must be the usual procedure to interview the people she works with.' George was doing an excellent job of implying that the police believed the story and were about to act upon it.

'Was this witness able to give a description?' It was David who asked the question but there was no trace of apprehension in his voice.

'I don't know the details.'

'Surely, Sarah's friend should be able to identify him?' Tom sounded rather bored by the whole thing.

'That may be why the police have taken so long to get round to us. Mrs Edington was unconscious for several days and up till now she has been too ill to give a proper statement. I understand her memory is coming back very slowly.'

'If they're looking for alibis, I'm in the clear,' said Tom with a laugh. He obviously didn't take the idea seriously. 'I was on the golf course from nine thirty until the middle of the afternoon and I've a partner to prove it.'

'And I was tucked up in bed with my wife reading the Sunday papers until lunch time,' David added in the same spirit.

'This is no joke, gentlemen!' George cut in firmly.

'Oh come on! This is obviously some ludicrous fantasy that Sarah has come up with. Surely the police aren't taking all this seriously are they? I know the old girl has been on a razor's edge for a long time, but what with all the strain of Eunice's death, the woman's finally gone round the twist to make such absurd accusations. Why on earth should anyone want to get rid of her?' A muted chorus of grunts of agreement indicated that most of the others shared Barry's assessment. It was hardly flattering to discover that all her colleagues appeared to judge her totally irrational if not deranged.

'It isn't the first accident that someone has tried to engineer. There was an incident here in college on the night Eunice was killed.' George's emotionless insistence cut across the disparaging quips.

'So what happened and why didn't we hear about it?' asked Dev.

'The police were informed but the fact that they weren't able to prove anything doesn't mean that they dismissed the evidence.'

'If they're looking for motives, you'd better watch out George. You're the next in line for the boss's job.' Frank was still refusing to take the matter seriously. 'What's your alibi then?'

'As it so happens, I was down in Dorset the whole weekend visiting my sister,' George snapped primly.

'So that leaves Frank, Dev and you, Barry? So what were you good people up to at the time of crime? Come on, spill the beans,' teased Tom determined to turn the whole thing into a farce.

'For goodness sake, stop trying to play bloody Poirot!' snapped Barry.

'Ooh! Who's going to get caught out sneaking off for one of his naughty weekends?'

'That's enough, Frank!' George snapped irritably. 'I've called you all in here to warn you what's going to happen. It's important that we keep all this to ourselves. With any luck, it will be plain-clothes officers they send but, even so, a pack of official looking men descending on the college yet again and asking questions is going to provoke a lot of comment. We can't afford to let wild rumours run riot so it's up to us to keep things in check. I know Mrs Harcourt is very worried about the college's reputation.'

'Then she shouldn't spread such bloody, stupid rumours,' growled Frank. 'And more fool the police for giving credence to her persecution fantasies.'

'So where is our Lady Principal?' asked Tom.

'She's seeing Sir Richard later on this morning. I get the impression she's discovered something that will identify whoever has been doing all this. It's obviously a very sensitive situation so she's arranged to meet him at his office before they both go off to the station. I thought she was coming in first but either she's working at home until then or has gone straight there.'

From the scraping of chairs, Sarah judged that the meeting had come to a close. There was a good deal of muttering which convinced her that, doubts about her sanity aside, the prospect of an invasion by more officials to conduct yet another interrogation brought her popularity to an all time low. She heard the sound of the door opening and closing a few times but from her hideaway in the cupboard, she couldn't tell how many had left the room. Eventually, the sound of George's footsteps coming towards her cupboard told her they'd all gone.

'Did you catch all of that?'

She eased herself out grateful to be back in the light. 'Most of it. So, the sooner I get back to the flat the better.'

'Do you think he'll turn up?'

'He's got to if he plans to stop me spilling the beans.'

'You do realize he has nothing to lose now?' A deep frown spread across George's face. 'I'll come with you.'

'No. Let's stick to the plan. I won't be alone. Nathan and Sir Richard will both be there.'

'I'll ring and let them know that you're on your way. For goodness sake take care.'

Chapter 38

She and Nathan sat crouched on the floor of the half landing. For what seemed the hundredth time, Sarah cautiously raised her head to the sill and peered out of the window. The outlook was strictly limited, confined to only a short distance of road, but there was nowhere else that gave them a better view of anyone approaching the house without revealing what they were up to.

'Nothing happening,' she muttered and sank back down.

'You're shivering. Shall I get you a jacket or something?'

'No. I'm not cold, just on tenterhooks.' Nervous, even frightened, might have been a better word. The waiting wasn't making it any better. She glanced again at her watch. They'd been squatting uncomfortably for nearly an hour. 'Perhaps the plan hasn't worked and he's not coming.'

Nathan smiled and put a comforting arm around her that she didn't repel. She let her head rest on his shoulder but she found it impossible to sit still for long.

'You don't think he left his car out of sight somewhere and walked up. Perhaps we've missed him.' She was up at the window again. 'You can't see much of the pavement from here.' Even she could hear the rising panic in her voice.

'Calm down. He has to come past the house to get round to the cellar. Even if we don't spot him we'll hear his footsteps.'

Nathan knelt up beside her and gently pulled her back down.

'Ought we to check outside?' She knew it would be foolish but she wanted to be doing something.

'If he sees us, he'll be off and all this will have been for nothing.'

Once more they settled back against the wall occasionally shifting to ease the growing discomfort. The minutes ticked painfully by.

'It should be me down there in the cellar not Sir Richard. I should never have let him talk me out of it,' she muttered.

'He was right. It was too dangerous,' Nathan said firmly.

'But what's the point? We need to catch whoever it is in the act of trying to harm me otherwise he'll just plead innocence. There'll be no evidence. You can't assume he'll own up to everything the moment he sees Sir Richard.' Her voice was beginning to rise above the whispers that they'd automatically adopted.

'We've been all through this! What if he has a gun? He might take pot shot at you before Sir Richard and I could get in to stop him and before he even realizes we're there. Then it would too late. We can't risk it.'

'But...'

'Listen!' Nathan held up a warning hand.

Their petty squabble was cut short by the sound of approaching footsteps outside. They stopped immediately below the window. Sarah and Nathan turned and looked at each other, wide eyed.

The strident chime of the doorbell cut the silence making Sarah jump. Nathan seized her hands. She made to eased herself to the window but Nathan shook his head and mouthed, 'He might look up.'

They waited till the footsteps went on then made their way down the final flight of stairs trying to avoid any clatter that might give away their presence.

They paused by the front door but all was silent. Nathan gently pulled it open and peered out. He beckoned her to follow and they both slid along the wall to its far end.

Nathan slowly eased his head around the corner. Turning back, he mouthed, 'He's going down the steps.'

'Can you see who it is?'

He shook his head. 'Wait here.'

Nathan sidled round the corner bent low in case the man should glance back. Ignoring the command, she followed, but their visitor was already out of sight.

She heard him knock and call softly, 'Saraah?'

At the sound of that breathy whisper, the blood suddenly drained to her shoes. Even here, with Nathan by her side, she couldn't move. Had she been trapped in that black hole, alone, defenceless, she might well have been driven over the edge of reason. Her enemy knew just how far to push. She had to steal herself not to turn and flee.

The click of key turning in the lock sounded unnaturally loud in the still air. There was a long pause before the door scraped open and they heard the shuffling as he manoeuvred around it to go inside.

Nathan slowly rose from his crouched position and in long, determined strides covered the twenty yards to the railing. Swallowing her terror, Sarah hurried in his wake. From the clumping inside, it was evident the man was having difficulty adjusting his eyes to the poor light.

As quickly as stealth would allow, Nathan went down the steps with Sarah close behind. They listened with held breath behind the half open door.

'Sarah?' Perhaps he already suspected that the figure crumpled in the far corner wasn't her.

'Hello, Barry. Fancy meeting you here.' There was a sudden beam of light. Sir Richard had switched on the torch.

After that, things moved quickly. Nathan wrenched open the door and from beneath his arm, Sarah could see a black silhouette caught in the glare, hands raised to shield his eyes from the blinding light. Then, as Sir Richard attempted to get to his feet, the figure moved, taking a savage backhand swipe at the half recumbent man. As Barry's arm connected with the old man's head, there was a sickening thud. Sir Richard fell backwards and the torch flew up tumbling in a ridiculously slow arc, end over end, to land beneath the window, uselessly illuminating the row of half empty paint tins lined up against the wall.

Nathan was already diving across the intervening space. Barry turned at the sudden commotion behind him. The two men collided and fought like demented small boys in the school playground who'd lost all control.

'Sir Richard,' she shouted urgently above the grunts and ferocious clamour. There was a low groan but there was no way she could get to him past the punching, kicking figures crashing and rolling around oblivious of all else.

'Are you all right, Sir Richard?' she screamed again at the top of her voice.

A pile of large cardboard boxes toppled towards her and she had to jump back to avoid them. It was darker than ever. She struggled to push them aside but that did little to improve the light and the torch lay useless on the far side of the cellar.

Sarah could hear the old man coughing and she could just make out that he was pulling himself up into a sitting position. At least he was conscious. She turned her attention to the fight. There was nothing she could do to help. In all the flailing limbs, she'd no idea who was who. The fierce turmoil soon became less frenzied as the two men began to tire. A vicious right hook landed on a jaw sending its recipient sprawling across a pile of old newspapers. The upright figure stood fists raised but the other lay slumped, exhausted.

'Nathan?'

She saw Nathan drop his guard and half turn wearily towards her, sagging like a toy that'd lost half of its stuffing.

Suddenly, Barry sprang forward cannoning into the unsuspecting Nathan. The head butt caught him full in the stomach lifting him from his feet. Sarah screamed as the rag doll body went flying. Barry was blundering towards the door.

In a fit of fury, she threw herself at him. Her hand caught his sleeve and she wrapped herself around his arm clutching it to her chest. The more he tried to push her off the tighter she clung. There was no way she could overpower him but she would hang on for as long as possible. As she was dragged towards the door, trying to avoid the frantic blows reigning down on the back of her head, she collapsed to the ground, a dead weight. The hammer fist continued to pound across her shoulders and she felt her strength weakening. Her face was buried in the coarse tweed of his sleeve and in desperation she sank her teeth through the wodge of cloth.

Behind her, someone was struggling towards them. The laboured breathing sounded close. Whether it was Sir Richard or Nathan, she had no idea, but it gave her the strength to maintain her limpet hold.

'That's enough, Barry. Give it up. There's no where for you to go.'

Sir Richard's calm authoritative voice cut through the frenzy. For a long drawn out moment everything was still. Sarah felt the fury and tension throughout Barry's body collapse. His head drooped. The struggle over. He was a defeated man.

The figure behind Sarah moved forward and clamped an arm round Barry's neck. Turning her head, she could see Nathan still on the ground, but leaning up on one arm, trying to get his breath back.

'Nathan?' He raised a hand to wave away her concern. She wanted to go to him but she had to cling onto Barry's arm. Sir Richard was in no state to hold him back if the maniacal hysteria broke out again.

Chapter 39

Sarah thought that they must have looked a strange procession. Nathan frog-marching Barry with his arm yanked high up his back, Sir Richard following with her bringing up the rear. Marching like battle weary soldiers, which they could justifiably claim to be. At the front of the house, she fell out of line and came round to unlock the door. The great staircase nearly got the better of them all and, when they reached the living room, only Nathan remained on his feet towering above the now totally deflated Barry, slumped in an armchair.

'Have you got anything to tie him up with?' He asked without looking at her.

'No need,' she said too weary to look for something suitable. 'I've put the deadlock on. He can't get out without a key unless he's prepared to jump out of an upstairs window.'

Nathan, a picture of exhaustion himself, remained standing over Barry for several minutes although one look at the crumpled figure indicated he wasn't capable of crawling let alone running away.

'Why, Barry?' Sarah asked softly, breaking the long silence. Strangely, she felt no anger only the hurt of betrayal.

'I didn't set out to. It just happened. Valerie had been on at me for months. Said if I didn't get promotion soon she was leaving me. My world fell apart when I got that letter from The Jeremiah Peterhouse College. That job should have been mine. I had ten times the experience the other chap had. When we heard I hadn't got it, she said she wasn't stopping with a loser.' The feeble voice sounded near to tears.

'What the hell has that got to do with Sarah?' Nathan had no sympathy.

'I pleaded with her but she was adamant.' It was as though Nathan hadn't spoken. Barry was in a world of his own. 'She told me to leave her to think, to get out of the house. I went for a run; I didn't know what else to do. When I got to the underpass there you were, in front of me. You were the one who'd been holding me back. It was all your fault! You must have given me a bad reference.' His voice rose to a crescendo.

'You saw a copy of everything I sent off,' Sarah said calmly. 'You never raised any objection at the time. As I remember it, you were more than happy with what I'd written.'

'But it couldn't have been the one you sent. I had to check. I knew the disk would be in your bag. All I had to do was race past you and grab it. In the dark, with the hood pulled up, you'd never recognize me. Bags get snatched all the time. It should have been so easy. But you wouldn't let go and you turned towards me. I had to lash out before you could identify me. When you crashed into the wall and passed out I panicked.'

'You didn't stop at that though, did you? You tried to drive me into some kind of breakdown.'

'I though if you were out of the way for a bit, I might have a chance to show what I could do.'

'And when the phone calls and all those mail order offers failed, you tried to make me look incompetent.'

'Charles Shorecross implied that most of the governors would be pleased to see you go and that I could rely on his support if it ever came to having to appoint an acting principal.'

'You listened to the wrong man,' snorted Sir Richard.

'I was getting desperate,' Barry's voice broke into a wail. 'Valerie kept going on and on about how I'd never amount to anything and that all my promises were worthless. Then one day she took the kids and went to her mother's.'

'So you set about trying to kill my wife!' The venom in Nathan's voice made Barry recoil.

'No,' he cried. 'It wasn't like that. I thought she might just break a leg on the stairs and I never meant for the car to crash down the slope like that. I just needed Sarah out of the college for a while.'

'And you never meant her to starve to death in the cellar, I suppose?' Nathan spat at him, fists clenched in fury.

'No. I wouldn't have left you there, Sarah. You've got to believe me.' He turned pathetic, pleading eyes towards her. 'I knew you were claustrophobic. I thought a few hours would be just enough to …' He hung his head.

There was a long silence and, for a moment, looking at the pitiful figure, she almost began to feel sorry for him.

'Oh you are good, Barry! You nearly had me believing your pathetic little tale of woe. But what about Eunice?'

Nathan and Sir Richard turned to look at her with puzzled frowns.

'You deliberately ran her down.'

Barry hid his face in his hands.

'Did she see you planting that trip wire? Is that why you had to shut her up? It must have been difficult to come up with an explanation for trying to pull that little stunt. I'm not surprised she wasn't convinced. Did she threaten to tell everyone what you were up to? I'm surprised you didn't wring her neck there on the stairs but then it would have been a bit difficult to explain a dead body slumped in the corridor.'

She could hear the sharp intake of breath as the others took in what she was saying.

'It wasn't like that,' Barry tried to stem her stream of venom. 'She was standing at the bottom of the fire escape. Asked me what I was doing back in college. I spun her some story but she gave me that suspicious look of hers and flounced off. After she'd gone it struck me, when it came out that you'd fallen down the stairs she'd remember and I'd have some difficult explaining to do. I thought I'd better go after her. I only meant to follow her.'

'In my car!'

'By the time I got to the entrance, she was already out of sight. My car was in the top car park but when saw yours I remembered I still had your keys in my pocket. It seemed the obvious thing to do. She'd got all the way to Broad Street before I caught up. I slowed right down and she kept looking back and suddenly she started to run. That's what made me do it. I didn't plan anything. It just happened. I put my foot on the accelerator and went. I had to stop her!' He was like a small child passing the blame, expecting them to understand.

It was Sir Richard who broke the silence. 'How come you had Sarah's keys?' Even in the charged atmosphere of that dramatic scene, she noted that for the first time ever he'd called her by her Christian name.

'They were in my handbag when you stole it. It worked out rather well for you when I became the chief suspect for her murder, didn't it?'

His eyes narrowed and he gripped the arms of the chair poised like a wild animal ready to spring at her. 'Why haven't they arrested you like they should have done?' he spat. Nathan and Sir Richard were instantly on their feet ready to hold him back. 'You deserved to suffer. It's all your fault!'

'That's enough!' Sir Richard's voice was icily cold. 'Isn't it time you took responsibility for your own failure?'

Barry stared across at him, a look of shocked surprise on his face, then put his head in his hands and began to sob.

'For God's sake, pull yourself together man.' Sir Richard's plea barely registered on Barry's glazed, self absorbed features.

As suddenly as it had started the noise stopped. The bloodshot eyes blinked rapidly as Barry slowly rocked himself backwards and forwards.

Nathan caught Sir Richard's eye, and shook his head. Barry had lost all reason.

The sound of the police siren brought any further conversation to a halt and they all listened as it grew to a crescendo. Someone would have to go down and let them in.

Coming Autumn 2005

Another Physcholgical Suspense by

Judith Cranswick

Watcher in the Shadows

Sylvie doesn't know she has a secret watcher intent on ensuring
her innocence until the day he will claim her as his own.
Sylvie's carefree world turns into a nightmare when terrible
accidents start to befall her male friends. Is she jinxed or is someone
out to harm them? She must find the killer before he does anything
to the new man in her life.

For more details see

www.judithcranswick.co.uk